T0146733

"A Maggie Robinson book is like the best kind of chocolate: delicious and totally addictive!"
—Vanessa Kelly, USA Today bestselling author

Return to the scandalous secrets of the English countryside's renowned getaway for R&R—restoration and romance—in this delightful series from Maggie Robinson!

After two months of treatment at Puddling-on-the-Wold, Mary Nicola Mayfield has shown no improvement, and her condition seems impervious to rehab. But Nicola is not the typical guest of Gloucestershire's destination village for the wealthy and wayward. The trauma of surviving a horrific train wreck has rendered her mute; her injuries have healed, but try as she might, she cannot utter a sound. With her family and fiancé at their wits' end, Nicola knows Puddling is the resort—the last resort—that holds any hope for her recovery.

Lord Jack Ryder—baron, businessman and, some say, mad genius—has gone from the heights of success to hit rock bottom, after a faulty girder from his iron foundry caused a dreadful bridge collapse. Nothing has assuaged his guilt over the passenger train that crashed or the lives that were destroyed.

The stringent regimen at Puddling is not doing much for his deep depression—until he meets his mysteriously silent neighbor. Their fiery affair breaks all the rules, but will the unspoken truth be too hot to handle?

Books by Maggie Robinson

Cotswold Confidential Series
Schooling the Viscount
Seducing Mr. Sykes
Redeeming Lord Ryder

The London List Series
Lord Gray's List
Captain Durant's Countess
Lady Anne's Lover

The Courtesan Court Series
Mistress by Mistake
"Not Quite a Courtesan" in *Lords of Passion*
Mistress by Midnight
Mistress by Marriage
Master of Sin

Novellas
"To Match a Thief" in *Improper Gentleman*

Redeeming Lord Ryder

Maggie Robinson

LYRICAL PRESS
Kensington Publishing Corp.
www.kensingtonbooks.com

LYRICAL PRESS BOOKS are published by

Kensington Publishing Corp.
119 West 40th Street
New York, NY 10018

All Kensington titles, imprints, and distributed lines are available at special quantity discounts for bulk purchases for sales promotion, premiums, fund-raising, educational, or institutional use.

Special book excerpts or customized printings can also be created to fit specific needs. For details, write or phone the office of the Kensington Sales Manager: Kensington Publishing Corp., 119 West 40th Street, New York, NY 10018. Attn. Sales Department. Phone: 1-800-221-2647.

Lyrical Press and Lyrical Press logo Reg. U.S. Pat. & TM Off.

First Electronic Edition: November 2017
eISBN-13: 978-1-5161-0002-6
eISBN-10: 1-5161-0002-6

First Print Edition: November 2017
ISBN-13: 978-1-5161-0005-7
ISBN-10: 1-5161-0005-0

Printed in the United States of America

To all who need some Christmas magic.

Prologue

March 6, 1882

She wasn't dead. That was surely a good thing, wasn't it? But Nicola couldn't seem to move from the corner where she'd been tossed.

This wasn't supposed to happen in First Class.

The railway carriage loomed above her, compartment doors flung open. A few other passengers in the car, which had been mercifully mostly empty, were hollering for help or crying, clinging to their seats, their belongings tumbled about down the aisle. A shoe, quite a pretty one with a silver buckle, had hit Nicola's shoulder and woken her up not long ago. A bearded man with a bloody cheek lay inert just a yard away from her. Was *he* dead? She hoped not. They had been coming back from the dining car and he'd been a gentleman, steadying her arm when the tremors first stuck.

There had been an enormous rumble, she remembered, and then the sensation of flying through the air. The railway bridge had given way, and in Nicola's estimation, they must now be on the roadway below the underbridge. Help would come soon. A derailed train was far too big to miss, even if they were in the middle of nowhere.

Nicola had been to visit her sister Francesca in London. Frannie had just had another baby, a beautiful little boy. It was unfortunate that he had been named Albert after his papa, but his middle name was Nicholas, and Nicola had been immensely flattered. She was his godmother, so nothing bad must happen to her. She had a duty to see to little Bertie's immortal soul, and so she would, if she could ever stand up.

Her head hurt dreadfully. She shut her eyes, hoping to stop the nausea and dizziness.

It didn't work.

If only the wailing would stop. It wouldn't help anything, losing self-control like that. One didn't complain if one could help it. The roar of the bridge collapse was sufficient to alert anyone in the vicinity. Shrieking like a banshee was unnecessary. Gilding the lily, so to speak.

Nicola opened her mouth to request that the screaming woman be quiet. And nothing happened.

Well, not precisely true. There was a noise, a kind of rasp. Nicola tried again. Another odd sound, like an animal in a trap. She felt a prickle of anxiety. There was nothing obstructing her mouth to account for the odd, squashed noise. Was her throat damaged in the accident? Once she'd had a dreadful cold and had sounded like a man for a week. She and Frannie had laughed over it.

What had she wanted to say to the woman, anyway? She forgot.

It didn't really matter. Help would come soon. She closed her eyes and slept, even if she was upside down.

And dreamed that she was the screaming woman herself.

Chapter 1

From the journal of Mary Nicola Mayfield
December 13, 1882
I have been in Puddling now for two months to the day, and nothing is changed.

Nicola sat back and wiped her pen nib. What more was there to say?

Aye. That was the rub. She couldn't say *anything*. Still.

The scar at her hairline was barely noticeable now—her fringe performed its duty admirably. Yes, her collar bone ached when it rained, but that was a minor inconvenience. But she could not speak, no matter how many times she opened her mouth.

The accident had been more than nine months ago. Nicola had recuperated at home with her parents for seven of those months, until they had all been at their wits' end. Her hand had cramped from writing her thoughts and wishes until her family couldn't bear to read them anymore.

Her mother cried constantly; her father was nearly as silent as Nicola was. When a cottage became available in the secret spa, Puddling-on-the-Wold, her parents jumped at the chance to send her there.

To get rid of her, really, in the prettiest place imaginable.

The village was known to work miracles on difficult relatives with difficult problems. Nicola wasn't the usual kind of Guest—she didn't imbibe too freely, gamble, break engagements in fruitless rebellion, disrobe in public, flunk out of school, or do any of the naughty things that drove parents to disown their disreputable children, or children to hide their cringe-worthy parents.

She just couldn't talk, and her parents were exasperated.

She knew they loved her—they'd spent a small fortune they didn't really have on specialists. Doctors had poked and prodded at her. Inserted vile tubes down her throat. She'd worried sometimes that her jaw would remain locked open as they gazed into the dark depths of her windpipe. Her tongue had endured sharp needles; her tonsils were removed as a precaution.

More surgery had been discussed; one doctor went so far as to want to shave her hair off so her brain could "breathe." Thank heavens her papa had drawn the line there. Nicola was fond of her hair. It was long and gold and her one true beauty.

The rest of her was unremarkable, except, of course, for her lack of speech. Had she different parents, she might be in an asylum now, locked up with people who couldn't make sense. Nicola's wits were perfectly intact, but she was miserably mute, and her parents were desperate to help her.

Not at home in Bath anymore, though, which was just as well. She'd drunk enough of the foul-tasting water there in hopes of a miracle cure. And Richard lived right next door. After he'd broken their engagement, it had only caused her mama to cry harder. Nicola had been suffocated under her parents' concern and despair for her. Even Richard had been ashamed, but as an ambitious young MP, how could he marry a girl who couldn't campaign for him?

No, not a girl. A woman. Nicola was twenty-six, long past her girlhood. She didn't even really mind that Richard had cried off. While she had liked him very much and shared his political goals, it had never been a heart-fluttering love match. Marriage to him had seemed a practical arrangement to both their families, and she did so want her own children. It was not enough to be a fond aunt to Frannie's little boys.

Nicola had waited years for Richard to establish himself. But evidently he couldn't wait a few months for her to speak again.

She picked up the pen. *I want to talk. Dr. Oakley seems to think that if I have a positive attitude, my speech will return.*

But how could she be positive? It was almost Christmas, and her parents were going to Scotland to stay with Aunt Augusta, her mother's widowed sister. Frannie, Albert, and the boys too. Nicola would be alone in her little cottage with only Mrs. Grace for company.

Her housekeeper had been extraordinarily kind, had coddled her from the moment she was picked up at the Stroud station. It was the first time Nicola had been on a train since the accident, and the Puddling Rehabilitation Foundation governors had suggested she get over her anxiety by making the trip from Bath by rail. Rather like getting back on the horse after a fall, she supposed.

But Nicola had been worse than anxious. Much to the other passengers' disgust, she'd vomited repeatedly, and by the time she'd arrived she was so weak she could barely stand up. She'd been put to bed for a week, only getting up to play the church organ for a local wedding when the vicar begged her to. Music was her one release, and her father had donated a small piano for Stonecrop Cottage. She played for hours, when she wasn't staring at the blank pages of her journal.

She was meant to write down her thoughts and worries. Dr. Oakley or the elderly vicar, Mr. Fitzmartin, would then discuss them with her during their daily visits. Sometimes she would pray, the only time she didn't feel self-conscious about being silent.

Nicola snapped the journal shut and tucked it into a pigeonhole in the little desk. She had no further thoughts today, nothing that she hadn't already written for the sixty-one days she'd been present in Puddling.

The parlor was a bit cramped now with the piano, but it was cheerful, with a bright fire burning in the hearth. Mrs. Grace had gone home a little early for the day, pleading a headache. She'd left Nicola a chicken pie in the ice box for her supper. Raspberry tarts too—she'd already cadged one as they were cooling. If she wasn't careful, Nicola would return to Bath several stone heavier.

If she returned. She didn't want to be a burden to her parents. Perhaps she could stay here. Not in this cottage, of course; it belonged to the Puddling Rehabilitation Foundation. But she'd come into money of her own—a settlement from the accident. Guilt money. Her papa had written to her when he sent the piano. As a prominent Bath solicitor, he had negotiated hard on her behalf. The amount was enough to purchase her own home and keep her in modest comfort for the rest of her life if she was careful.

And why wouldn't she be careful? Nicola had always been conservative. She'd never been frivolous; she only owned two ball gowns that were refurbished on a yearly basis with new lace or ribbons or both. Richard had admired her frugality, for he earned very little in his own law practice and did not stand to inherit a fortune like some members of the House of Commons. Her mama had not been so sanguine, but Nicola simply wasn't much interested in evening clothes.

She didn't need her ball gowns for Puddling. Life was purposefully quiet here, so Guests could recuperate. But now that the steep streets were coated with a dusting of snow and a slick of ice underneath, she could use a new pair of boots.

It was part of her prescribed routine to walk around the village for at least an hour a day, and the exercise was becoming a touch treacherous.

She would write to Mama and ask for some better footwear, something suitable for a clumsy mountain goat.

Nicola knew she was treated differently than some of the other Guests had been. Apparently it was forbidden to contact the "Outside World" by mail or telegram or anything else during the course of one's stay here. But letters flowed freely back and forth to Bath, not that she had very much to report. Nothing ever happened in Puddling. There were five intertwining streets, and Nicola knew every house and shop, all *five* of them, by now. Everyone had been so welcoming. She was often stopped and given biscuits or balls of yarn or books by the friendly villagers and their children. She wished she could say thank you, but had to make do with her most sincere smiles.

Oh, she was feeling sorry for herself, and that was pointless. She'd go out for a short second walk, not too far. The sun would set over the Cotswold Hills in about an hour, but fresh air would do her good. Bring roses to her cheeks, which the mirror told her were as pale as the moon. Then she'd put her pie in the oven. Eat. Wash her dishes. Get on her knees. Go to bed.

How boring it all was.

Which it was meant to be. Evidently the Puddling governors believed that a strict routine was the key to recovery. No excesses of any kind. Which suited Nicola, as she was not an excessive sort of person.

Although the cottage had a small generator—and all sorts of modern conveniences, for it was the newest and most luxurious of the Guest residences, which wasn't really saying much—she was a little afraid of it. She preferred the golden glow of lamp oil instead of the harsh, erratic electric light. She extinguished the lamp on the desk and banked the fire. Her fur-lined coat hung on a hook by the front door, and she slid her stockinged feet into her old shoes.

A brisk gust of wind almost knocked her down in the front garden. The koi she'd seen in the autumn were asleep under a skim of ice on their pond, and the bare branches were stark against the graying sky. Would she be here in the spring to see the garden awake? According to Mrs. Grace, most Guests were enrolled in the program for twenty-eight days. Nicola had been here over twice as long, and was no closer to a cure.

Would they let her stay indefinitely? She knew more cottages were being built for additional Guests, having passed the new construction on her walks. She didn't want to take up a valuable spot for someone who truly needed it.

She might be a lost cause. She wasn't sure the routine and all the kindness she'd been shown was helping her whatsoever.

Nicola closed the gate behind her and took the stone steps down to the cobbled lane. Adjusting her hood, she headed away from the heart of the village, toward the bottom of Honeywell Lane. The fitful gurgle of Puddling Stream was audible the closer she got, and frost-covered hills were before her. Sheep foraged for grass through the snow and bleated plaintively— country sights and sounds she didn't experience in busy Bath. It was all very comforting.

Until her foot hit a patch of ice and she slipped, tumbling ignominiously to her bottom.

The pain in her twisted ankle was excruciating, but even though her mouth was open, there was no noise.

Damn.

It was difficult to get purchase to raise herself. She must look comical, rolling about the street like an overfed seal, her gloves and knees sodden. Nicola didn't know whether to smile—since laughter was out of her reach— or cry at her predicament.

Her decision was halted by the rapid footfalls behind her. She turned to warn the runner to be careful, but of course, no words came out.

The gentleman was luckier than she had been. He remained upright and over her, a concerned look on his face.

His rather handsome face. Nicola felt herself go hot. No white moon face anymore, she'd wager. She was always betrayed by her blushes.

"Are you all right, miss?"

She nodded violently. A lie. Suddenly shy, she wanted him to go away and leave her alone to wallow in the slush.

"Let me help you up."

She shrugged and he pulled her up by both hands. The weight on her ankle was too much, and she buckled before the man caught her.

"You're *not* all right! Is it your ankle?"

Nicola nodded again.

"Cat got your tongue? Go ahead, be unladylike and scream. I won't mind a bit. And lean on me. I promise I won't hurt you."

Oh, it wasn't that she was afraid of him. It was always so mortifying to have to explain her condition to strangers. She had a little card in her pocket for just such occasions.

But if he was a normal resident of Puddling, he should know all about her, shouldn't he? The entire village was a sort of lovely, lush hospital, and everyone knew everything. There were explicit dossiers on each Guest. Nicola had been permitted to read her own and invited to embellish it with any suggestions she thought might be useful to her improvement.

"I'll help you home." There was no arguing with that statement; she needed the help.

"Where do you live?"

Nicola pointed the way back up Honeywell Lane.

"On this lane? Me too. Which cottage is yours? I'm in Tulip. A ridiculous name, don't you think?"

Nicola covered her mouth with one damp glove and shook her head very slowly.

His dark eyes narrowed. "Ah. You cannot talk. You're not deaf, are you? Well, I suppose if you are, you won't be hearing me ask the question." She couldn't help but smile.

"Oh, good. I can natter on, and you can't talk back. A silent woman. Every man's dream, I imagine. Not mine," he said hastily. "I respect women no end. I'm thinking of my late father, who used to lock himself in his study when my mother was on the warpath. Which was often. They fought like cats and dogs. I'm making a fool of myself telling you all the family secrets, aren't I? I'm Jack." He took her hand and shook it with almost excessive vigor. "You're a Guest too, aren't you? Come for the famous cure of whatever ails you?"

Oh, dear. Nicola nodded with reluctance. What was wrong with this fellow? He appeared prosperous, was very good-looking with his neatly trimmed dark beard and sympathetic brown eyes. Eyes that were somewhat shadowed. Was he a drunkard? A womanizer? An opium addict? He was much too old to have had his bad-tempered mother send him here for youthful misbehavior.

Nicola knew some troubled souls signed themselves into the Puddling Rehabilitation Program for rest and relaxation. He might be one of them.

Something about her reserved expression must have given her worries away.

"Don't be concerned. I won't ravish you. That's not my problem at all," he said with a touch of grimness. "Here, let's go back up the hill. Can you walk, or do you want me to carry you?"

She made walking motions with her fingers, but after a wobbly step or two found herself swept up and firmly ensconced in the man's arms.

"No wriggling or writhing, and certainly no punching. When we get to your cottage, I'll drop you onto something soft and comfortable and fetch the old doctor. What's his name? Oakley? I only got here yesterday. I'm not even sure why I came, to tell you the truth. Another one of my harebrained ideas. Tap my shoulder when we get to your house, all right?"

All Nicola could do was nod. The man was a force of nature.

Chapter 2

He'd been warned by friends that he'd be bored to tears here, but Lord Jonathan Haskell Ryder—Jack to his friends—was rarely bored anywhere. Curiosity was in his bones. He'd been the despair of his parents and teachers since he cut his leading strings, not willing to leave things be but to radically change them like some Victorian alchemist. As a child, he'd deconstructed anything with parts, and, much to everyone's surprise, put them all back together with only the occasional loose screw or spring leftover. There were fewer mistakes like that as he'd aged, and he was considered by most to be kind of a mad genius.

To be sure, Jack didn't think of himself in quite that way. But his mind had always seen the possibilities, whether they were mechanical or metaphysical. As a youth, he'd long outstripped the lecturers at university, and had gone on to considerable glory after he dropped out, founding foundries, inventing inventions, and wooing willing women.

The foundry, however, had been his undoing. It had been months since the depression had settled so deep in his curious bones a canny Welsh miner couldn't have found it with a pickaxe. His numbers didn't make sense anymore, he hadn't invented anything interesting in ages, and as for women—well, the least said the better.

But here he was on the second day of his Puddling Program with a lissome blonde in his arms. Things were looking up.

He'd better look down, for this road was a nightmare of ice and dirty snow. What had this young woman been thinking of to come outside with flimsy footwear that was not meant for the outdoors? They looked like dancing slippers, for heaven's sake.

Jack was pretty sure no dancing was on the menu in Puddling. He'd read over his ironically titled "Welcome Packet" and had felt most unwelcome, given the numerous rules and restrictions.

Foolish female and her foolish shoes. It's not as if she could even call out for help. Jack wondered if she'd always been mute. *His* parents would certainly have approved of him being struck dumb by lightning and robbed of speech forever, for he had rambled on in his childish enthusiasm until his father caned him regularly into quiet.

Fighting with his father was over, however. Now it was just his mama who wanted him to behave according to her exacting standards.

Settle down. Slow down. Marry a suitable girl, sire a passel of ordinary children, stop being...different.

Almost impossible for a man like Jack, whose mind skittered from one thing to another with frightening speed.

His mother had been unsupportive when he told her what he was doing for his victims, reminding him he was not directly responsible for the accident. But he knew he was. If he'd not been so involved in other projects, he might have kept a closer eye on everything. Because of his negligence, two people had died.

Died. No amount of money would bring them back to life. And he had money. Tons of it. From patents and factories and investments, not counting his inheritance. Everything Jack Ryder had touched turned to gold, causing him to rest a little on his laurels. He'd wanted to prove that he was not just a baron, but a businessman, and he had.

The gods laughed. Hubris. A word with which he was now totally familiar.

True, the casting defect wasn't his fault. Even if he'd been on the foundry floor, he might not have noticed the imperfection. The girders had passed through many hands and many inspections.

The result was the same.

Jack had divested himself of three-quarters of his holdings. Anything that could blow up, break, burn down, or cause possible harm to the general populace had been sold. He could now personally guarantee that such industrial carelessness would not continue on his watch. His money was now tied up in harmless, nonlethal endeavors.

It should have improved his spirits, but it did not. He'd sunk further and further—

There was an anxious tap on his shoulder. Ah. They had reached his passenger's home. He carried her up the steps from the street and shouldered his way through a gate. A long slippery stone path led to a cottage. The sign near the door read Stonecrop. Much better than Tulip.

More masculine-sounding. He knew next to nothing about plant life, could not have identified stonecrop if he were thrust headfirst in a bed of it, but that could be remedied by books.

If only he could get his hands on some. Tulip Cottage's bookshelves held only musty sermons and other "improving" tracts. He'd been forced to take apart a butter churn before he could fall asleep last night.

"Here we are," he said cheerfully. "Is the house locked?"

She shook her head.

He turned the knob and sudden warmth surrounded him in the hallway. To the left was a small conservatory, its glass door closed. Not much was growing within, save for a straggly fern. Maybe this young lady could do with some botany books as well. To the right, a parlor with a plush horsehair sofa. He deposited her on it and looked around the crowded little room. The appointments were superior to his cottage, newer. There was even a piano. Stonecrop didn't feel quite so much like a prison as his pared-down abode.

"Shall I make you some tea before I fetch the doctor?"

More headshaking.

"You *do* want me to fetch him, don't you?"

The blonde bit her lip.

"That's it. I'm going." He gave the fire a few sharp pokes before he left so the cottage would stay warm. "Don't move. Not an inch."

The blonde scowled at him. And then stuck out her tongue.

Jack laughed. "I know I'm bossy. But it's for your own good. I'll be right back."

He remembered where the doctor lived, for he'd been given a map of the village yesterday in his packet. Once he read something, it tended to stick in his head. He usually could quote whole paragraphs of the most useless books and monographs without too much effort, one of the skills that had so frightened his teachers.

Jack could still see the newspaper headlines from last March all too clearly, even if his name had not been mentioned.

After making one wrong turn—he guessed he *was* a little worn out, for how could one get lost when there were only five streets, rambling though they were, to choose from?—he rapped on the door of the surgery. The brass plate read Charles Oakley, M.D. The man himself answered after the second knock.

"Lord Ryder, isn't it? What can I do for you?"

"Nothing for me, sir. I found a young woman on the street. Wait, that sounds odd, doesn't it? Anyway, she slipped and fell, and I picked her up and carried her home. She's wrenched her ankle, and I think you should give it a look. I don't know her name, but she lives at Stonecrop Cottage."

"Is Mrs. Grace there now?"

Jack felt a stab of disappointment. So his lovely, silent blonde was married. Where was her husband? Had he throttled her so hard she couldn't speak? People came to Puddling for a whole host of reasons, and Jack was naturally curious about hers.

"Yes."

"Well, she's in good hands then. Thank you for your help."

He wasn't prepared to leave his chivalrous stance just yet. "I'll walk that way with you. My cottage is down the lane from Stonecrop. But of course, you know that."

Oakley got into his coat and clapped a hat on his wispy white hair. He picked up the medical bag that sat on a bench in the front hall.

"Aye. Settling in, are you? I'll come over tomorrow to give you an examination. Should have come this afternoon, but the day got away from me. Three cases of purulent sore throat, one broken finger, and twins born over in Sheepscombe to boot. I haven't even had my lunch yet, but it will be dinnertime before I get anything in my stomach." He locked up his house and they were on their way.

"I don't want to hold you from your important obligations. An examination's not necessary. I'm perfectly well," Jack lied.

"So you say. But I can see you haven't been sleeping. You were cagey when you applied to come here at the last minute, but anyone can tell it's not for the clean air and good plain food."

Jack tried to open his eyes wider to look more awake, but he had a feeling nothing would trick this old fellow. "I just needed a change. A quiet place to think."

"We can't help you if you won't help us."

"What do you mean?"

"We usually have an extensive file on each of our Guests. You're a bit of a mystery, Lord Ryder. We only allowed you to come since our Christmas season is slow. Most Guests want to be with their families at this time of year. Of course, after January, our applications triple. Familiarity breeds contempt, I reckon."

A mystery? That made Jack sound far more interesting than he was. He had not been precisely forthcoming when he'd filled out the endless paperwork, though. There had been no mention of the railway accident and his part in it, and he preferred to keep it that way. He was frankly tired of trying to explain what he felt every waking minute. Nighttime too.

"Quite a racket you all have going on here. Popular place, is it?" The doctor came to an abrupt stop. "Do you doubt our efficacy? There are scrapbooks touting our success stories." "But I don't expect I'll ever get to see them. That would be a breach of confidentiality, wouldn't it? Pesky ethics." Jack knew his law and had read every word of the contract he'd signed. Everything about Puddling and its famously successful Program was hushed up, and one virtually took a vow of silence to be here. Mrs. Grace fit right in naturally. "Come along. Mrs. Grace is in pain."

The doctor shot him an odd look but shuffled down the hill as fast as was safe for an elderly fellow.

Impatient, Jack went faster. He decided he'd go home in a minute, once Mrs. Grace was settled with the doctor. He entered the cottage without knocking and found his charge still on the sofa, bare feet stretched out, trying to smile. Her inappropriate shoes were laid neatly on the floor, her woolen stockings rolled into them.

"Dr. Oakley's just behind me. Does it hurt very badly?" He could see himself that her ankle was twice the size it should be. He should have packed it in ice before he left.

She rolled her eyes at him. They were blue, fringed with short thick lashes that were slightly darker than her hair.

"You think I'm making too much of this, don't you? Well, I'm not. I hate to see people in distress." Animals too. He was too softhearted by half. Growing up, he'd mended wings and paws, and as an adult, he'd refined medical instruments that might even be in Oakley's bag.

She fluttered her hand at him, motioning him away. Through the parlor windows, Jack could see the doctor coming up the path, puffy breaths of cold air preceding him.

"All right. I'm going. But if you need anything, just let me know."

A roll of the eyes again.

"You can write me a note. You have a housekeeper, yes? She can give it to mine." Somewhere in the Puddling literature, Jack had read communication was cut off with one's family while one stayed here. That was fine—he didn't want to talk to his mother for the next six or seven years or so. He loved her, but was tired of hearing her plans for him, which usually contradicted any of his own. But the powers that be couldn't object to Mrs. Grace getting in touch with him, could they? He was only a few doors down. If she *could* holler, he might even hear her if the wind was right.

Maybe she was a widow. A young one. Although she was not in mourning. She wore a simple yet à la mode blue gown trimmed with darker velvet piping. He could see now that she'd discarded her coat that her figure was slight. Unexceptional. She certainly had not been difficult to carry up a hill. Of course, Jack was fit. Prided himself on it. His father had turned to fat before he was forty.

Jack believed in an active mind and an active body. Of course, nothing much stopped his mind and hands from whirring along like a clockwork. No wonder he couldn't sleep, and it had only gotten worse this year. That old doctor had cottoned onto that in a trice.

Oakley huffed in and set his bag on a table. "Now, my dear, this young man tells me you had a spill. The right ankle, yes? Raise a finger if my manipulation pains you too much." He looked up at Jack. "Thank you for your assistance, but I think my patient needs some privacy."

Jack stared at Mrs. Grace's ankles. Really, what was the fuss about catching a glimpse of something so bony and unappealing? He'd much rather see—

"Of course. Do remember I'm right down the lane if you need anything. Good afternoon."

Jack ducked under the lintel and left the cozy cottage. Stonecrop was nicer than his. But he hadn't come to Puddling for the architecture or décor. In two hundred and twenty six steps, he'd opened his door and sought out his housekeeper, Mrs. Feather, in the kitchen. She stood over the stove, stirring something that did not smell entirely divine.

"What's for dinner?" Lunch had been less than divine too. And breakfast? The oatmeal had been so thick it could have been used as wallpaper paste.

"Soup, my lord."

"And?"

"Soup, my lord."

"Yes, I heard you the first time. What's the second course?"

She turned to him, holding the wooden spoon aloft as if he'd been naughty and she longed to smack him. Which she probably did after twenty-four hours' acquaintance. Jack sometimes had that effect on people.

"Perhaps you don't understand. Have you not read your Welcome Packet? The Puddling diet is a simple one, designed to cool your blood."

"My blood's already frozen—I've been outside for two hours wandering about your little burgh. Really, just soup? No bread or cheese?" he asked, utterly without hope.

"No, my lord. And fine, fresh well water, of course."

"Of course." Jack enjoyed his liquor as much as the next man. But he knew after a longer-than-brief period of overindulgence after the accident that he wouldn't find consolation in a bottle. "I don't suppose there's any dessert?" He could have sworn he caught the whiff of raspberries in Mrs. Grace's cottage.

Mrs. Feather blanched, as if he'd suggested that she serve him a platter of opium. "Oh, no, sir. That wouldn't do at all."

Jack would have a word with the doctor when he came tomorrow. Twenty-six more days of this sort of treatment would turn him into a skeleton. Raspberries were perfectly healthy, God-given bounty. Half the time they grew wild.

Surely fruit was good for one. Didn't all those poor sailors suffer when they had no access to nutritious food? Acid fruit cured scurvy. Jack was no physician, but remembered something dimly from his studies.

Perhaps he'd been ill-advised to come to Puddling. After all, it was his mother's suggestion. He'd never heard of the place before in all his thirty years, having trod the straight and narrow during his adolescence and young manhood. He'd been too busy with his self-imposed schooling to become wayward, a bit of a dull dog, if one wanted to know the truth. Puddling had the kind of program that society people seemed to know about but wouldn't admit to ever resorting to. His friends had been shocked he'd chosen to sign himself in.

But it had been months, and all the projects and holidays and books and feminine amusements he'd tried to occupy himself with had done nothing to soothe his soul. It was time for a change.

If he did not starve to death first.

Chapter 3

December 17, 1882

Dr. Oakley had visited Nicola every day since he'd wrapped her sprained ankle. He'd done such an expert job, she'd even been able to prepare her own dinner that first night with some gritting of her teeth as she hopped around the kitchen with the aid of a stick. The reheated chicken pie had been delicious, and much against her better judgment, Nicola had eaten three of the tarts.

Mrs. Grace had offered to sleep over in the ensuing evenings, but Nicola liked her solitude. She read romantic novels sent by her sister—very much out of character for her since Nicola did not believe in romance—and knitted baby clothes for the poor, the Puddling Service that had been decided for her dubious skills. Her stitches were becoming somewhat less lumpy, and she felt useful for the first time in a long while.

After her daily sessions with the Reverend Fitzmartin, she was never far from her piano, although she wasn't using the pedals at the moment. Playing allowed her to gaze out the windows at the snowy front garden. No handsome bearded gentleman marched up the path, however. Nicola was very tempted to write questions about Jack to Mrs. Grace, though she doubted she'd get any honest answers.

Guests' privacy was of the utmost importance—the Rules were clear. Should one meet another Guest in the village, only first names were to be exchanged. And if one encountered a recovered Guest in the "Outside World," one must never acknowledge the circumstances under which they'd met.

Nicola knew of one other Guest in Puddling besides Jack. She was known only as the Countess, a handsome young widow whose elegant mourning clothes were finer than anything Nicola had ever owned. She'd seen the woman in church, but had had no occasion to do anything but smile. And obviously, Nicola could not start a conversation.

She would like a friend, even if a countess was a touch exalted for a solicitor's daughter. But her current speechless situation made that all but impossible. How she missed her sister, Frannie. They wrote to each other several times a week, but letters were not enough.

Bertie had three teeth and was crawling around like a little crab. Babbling. More than Nicola could do.

Oh, she was sinking in spirits again. The weather wasn't helpful. The unrelieved arctic dampness and gray skies for the past two days had depressed her. There were several sturdy walking sticks by the front door in an umbrella stand, but she really wasn't up to going outdoors yet. She was housebound, and even the new sheet music her mother sent had no appeal.

She reached for the knitting basket and pulled out her needles and the beginnings of a blue cap. It was hard to believe any human being could start out so small, so dependent. But she knew it was true. She'd held Bertie when he was brand new, his tomato-red face scrunched, his lungs in fine fettle.

Once, she had wanted children of her own. But how could she teach them now? Read them bedtime stories? Tell them she loved them?

An inconvenient tear leaked out of eye, and she wiped it away, annoyed with herself. She knew she was lucky to be alive, with all her advantages. Two men had not been so fortunate in the accident. She still had her sight, her hearing. Once her ankle healed, she'd be mobile again. There were many, many unfortunate people in the world who were steeped in misery and poverty with no means of correction. She was selfish to be sad.

Yet sad she was.

Her desolation was interrupted by the clank of the brass door knocker. There was a bell as well—Puddling was prepared for everything. The doctor and vicar had been here already today, but perhaps one of them had left something behind.

"Coming!" Mrs. Grace called from the kitchen. Nicola was perfectly capable of hobbling up to open her own front door, but the housekeeper was a stickler for performing the household duties the correct way. Nicola continued to wind the yarn around a needle and waited.

"Good afternoon. I've come to see Mrs. Grace."

Nicola dropped a stitch. She knew that voice.

Jack.

"Yes? What is it?"

"Mrs. Grace...is she at home?"

"What sort of game are you playing, milord? Have you eyes in your head?"

"I beg your pardon." His tone was frosty now. "If my visit comes at an awkward time, would you please tell her I called?"

"I *am* busy in the kitchen, but I can spare a minute. What can I help you with?"

"As I stated, madam, I'm here to inquire about Mrs. Grace's health."

"I'm feeling fine."

"I don't c—that is, I'm very glad, but the young lady who injured her ankle the other day, Mrs. Grace, how is she?"

"Oh! You mean Miss Nicola. I'll see if she will receive you." She shut the door loudly on the poor man, leaving him on the doorstep, and poked her head into the parlor. "There is a gentleman to see you. Another Guest. I don't have to let him in if you don't want me to."

She'd called him *milord*. Was he truly a lord, or was Mrs. Grace just being deferential? Nicola put the cap back in the basket and stood up from the sofa, nervously smoothing her skirt. It seemed Jack was under the impression that *she* was Mrs. Grace, which was rather amusing. She motioned to the housekeeper to open the door, and mimicked drinking tea.

"Well, if you're sure, I suppose I can add another cup to the tea tray. I was just about to bring it out to you anyway. Are you certain you'll be able to manage the fellow? We, that is the Rehabilitation Foundation, really don't know anything about him. It's most irregular."

Nicola nodded, clasped her trembling hands in front of her, and waited.

She couldn't catch what Mrs. Grace muttered to Jack before she let him into the hallway. Some dire warning, no doubt. Mrs. Grace had dragonish tendencies. He entered unscathed, hatless and carrying a small parcel.

"I hope I'm not intruding," he said, shrugging out of his coat. Mrs. Grace sniffed with disapproval and hung it on a hook by the door. "I didn't see you in church this morning, and came to see how you were doing. Your ankle and whatnot. I see you're standing. Can you walk on it yet?"

Very carefully, Nicola pirouetted, then curtseyed.

Oh, how very foolish she was being. There was something about Jack that made her *want* to be foolish. She couldn't remember the last time she'd flirted with anyone. In the time she'd known Richard—more than half her life, really—there had been little cause for flirtation. Richard had been a serious boy then and was a serious man now.

Jack grinned. "Well done, you. But perhaps you'd like to sit down and not overdo."

Nicola wished her dress was not a sensible gray, had a bigger bustle, more ruffles, and that she hadn't pinned her hair up any which way this morning. But judging from the heat flaming on her cheeks, she probably didn't look white as snow anymore.

"I've brought you something to while away the time while you're recovering. I mean about your ankle, not whatever has brought you here to Puddling. But don't get too excited—the shops here are very limited, aren't they? And they keep us impoverished too. I had to turn over all my pocket money to the fiend who works in my cottage when I arrived. Mrs. Feather is as strict as a nun. Probably worse. Nuns have to be charitable and take pity on one—it's in their contract, I expect. You would not believe the lies I had to tell the woman so she'd advance me some of my allowance."

Nicola waggled a finger at him.

"Of course I should have lied! I wanted to give you a gift, shabby though it is. I feel rather responsible for you. It's not every day that I get to save a pretty young lady from a life on the streets." He handed her the brown-wrapped package and sat across from her in a chair she knew to be uncomfortable.

Oh! A life on the streets! He was so cheeky. She should be offended by his teasing, but she smiled anyhow.

He passed her a small pocket knife. "For the string. Don't stab me later."

Nicola sliced open the string and unfolded the paper. Inside was a pocket-sized blank notebook and a pack of colored drawing pencils.

"I didn't know if you were artistic. If you are not, you can use the book to talk to me."

Nicola raised an eyebrow.

"You know, I'll say something—probably stupid—and you can write down your reply. Whatever you say back will be much prettier if it's in red or blue or green."

Nicola mouthed the words "thank you," and selected a purple pencil. She flipped the book to its first page.

You are very kind. But I am a terrible artist. She squiggled something after the words. *Can you tell what this is?*

Jack took the book from her and squinted. "Huh. A dog? No, a bear. Maybe a cat without a tail."

See? I'm hopeless. It is a rabbit.

"You've got the ears all wrong, you know." He borrowed her purple pencil and sketched an exquisite little rabbit next to hers.

That is very good. My rabbit wants to hop away in embarrassment. If he had proper feet.

"Well, one more foot, at least. They usually have four. Thank you. I'm a bit of a draftsman. Normally I draw machinery to mathematical specifications instead of cute fluffy creatures."

So, he was employed somewhere. Nicola had a healthy respect for those who earned their own bread. As a solicitor's daughter, she had no right to be snobbish, and thought it ridiculous that the idle rich were so very idle and so unfairly rich. Richard was a Liberal MP with a true concern for the poor, and she had planned to support him in his progressive ideas.

Did she dare ask what Jack did and why was here?

No. She would keep everything casual. Discreet.

And it was none of her business.

Mrs. Grace entered bearing a well-stocked tea tray. Jack leaped up to help her, but she refused. "Please sit down, sir. You'll only make me spill something."

It was true that now he was in the parlor, quarters seemed even tighter. He was tall and broad and so very *present*. Nicola was used to blending into the background, but no one could ever miss Jack.

The housekeeper set the tray on the low table in front of the sofa. "All right, Miss Nicola? Or would you like me to stay and pour?"

Did Mrs. Grace think she needed chaperonage? Jack did not seem dangerous at all, despite the fact that he was tall, dark, quite handsome, and took up so much space in the room.

Nicola hoped he was not a homicidal maniac hiding out in Puddling from the law. Or a married man with half a dozen children. She stole a look at his left hand. He wasn't wearing a wedding ring, but then so many men didn't.

"Milk and no sugar, please," her mysterious visitor said before she had a chance to gesture.

Her mother had raised her to be the wife of an MP, perhaps even a future prime minister, for Richard was ambitious beyond belief. Nicola usually moved with grace and ease, except when she was falling down an icy hill or skating. Ice seemed to be her nemesis. Perhaps she was meant to live somewhere in the tropics. She poured the tea and arranged a small plate of sandwiches and biscuits for her guest as any properly trained young woman would do.

But she hadn't the first idea what should come next.

Chapter 4

Jack had always been a talker. A chatterbox, if one was being completely accurate. He had so many ideas, a second would tumble out before the first was finished, and it had required a lot of patience from his friends to wade through his words. But he found his mind was completely blank now.

Mrs. Grace—Miss Nicola, since he wasn't supposed to know her last name—was sipping her tea, her face a delightful shade of rose. One of his former companies manufactured oil paint—paint was flammable, so no more factory—and he'd never seen pigment that delicate in color. She reminded him of the portrait George Frederic Watts had done of the actress Ellen Terry, all gold and pink and ivory. What was its name?

Choosing. The actress had been in a garden, deciding between the worldly red camellias and the humble violets. Jack bet that Miss Nicola would pick the violets if she had a chance.

It wasn't because she was childlike, for she must be almost as old as he was, but there was a freshness, an innocence about her. Perhaps if she recovered her speech, that illusion might be broken. She could sound like a fishwife, or worse, his opinionated mother.

The fire rippled along merrily, but he got up to stab at it. He needed something to do besides swallowing tea and biting tiny sandwiches in silence, even though the food on offer was a thousand times better than the swill he'd been served since he arrived. He'd have to speak to Mrs. Feather and complain he was being mistreated, for all the good it would do.

Jack wasn't uncomfortable with the quiet; it was soothing. But he was a man of action, wasn't he? He did enough damage with the poker, causing sparks to land on the hearth rug. He stamped them out with his large feet, then sat back down.

Come on. How hard could it be to have a civilized conversation with an attractive young woman? It had been ages. Ah.

"Have you been here long?"

She raised two fingers.

"Weeks?"

She flashed both hands at him several times.

"Two whole months? I thought this was a twenty-eight-day program." He didn't intend to stay any longer himself. If he couldn't get out of his funk—well, it didn't bear thinking of.

Nicola shrugged. So she had not been cured in the allotted time.

"You came to restore ability to speak?"

She nodded.

"What happened?"

She picked up the notebook he'd given her. *An accident.*

"I'm so sorry. Where is, uh, *Mr.* Grace?" He pictured some ugly brute with his hands around her slender neck and his fists clenched.

I have no idea.

Jack was shocked. The cur. The bounder. Dumping his wife in this backwater just because she couldn't talk! If Miss Nicola was in *his* care…

"You mean your husband has abandoned you here in Puddling?" He couldn't contain the anger in his voice.

Her lips turned up as she wrote. She should not be used to such iniquity and smile over it.

Mrs. Grace is my housekeeper. I am not married.

Ah, that explained why the woman thought he was a lunatic at the door. He'd somehow got the wrong end of the stick. Jack laughed.

"I apologize. I misunderstood something the doctor said. So there is no Mr. Secret Surname lurking about?"

Her cheeks flamed as she shook her head.

"No fiancé either?"

A very firm shake. Jack was encouraged.

"This proves men are idiots." Nicola was not in the first blush of youth, but neither was she old maid material. How had she escaped marriage for so long?

Jack had had a few brushes with the institution himself over the years, mostly because he wasn't paying proper attention. He'd been so preoccupied with businesses he'd almost wound up a bridegroom once or twice. He hadn't truly listened to a couple of conversations when every cell of his body should have been on high alert. Women could be dangerous creatures, if charming.

And there was the heart of all his problems. His mother was right—he had to slow down. Take a step back. That's why he was in Puddling, wasn't it? What was he doing sitting in Stonecrop Cottage? Nothing good could come of it. He was supposed to be atoning for his failures, not flirting with a pretty young woman.

But when he was with her—well, for the very few minutes, for that's all it had been—he forgot his own problems and worried about hers. How agonizing it must be not to be able to communicate. Jack thought of all the orders he dispatched on a daily basis and wondered what it would be like if he took a vow of silence. His retainers would probably welcome that. His browbeaten secretary Ezra Clarke might even do a jig.

"Where do you live when you're not imprisoned in Puddling?"

Bath.

"You're a city girl! A small city, to be sure. I live in London myself. And I have a country house in—well, wait a moment. I'm not sure we're supposed to be trading personal information. I haven't been here a week and don't know the ropes yet." The talks he'd had with Oakley and Reverend Fitzmartin so far had dealt less with Puddling Rules than his depression. He hadn't told them the exact particulars, but they were aware of some of his difficulties.

It's all right. I won't tell anybody. There was a wicked gleam in her eye.

"So you won't get me in trouble?"

Are you the sort of man who gets in trouble easily?

"I am afraid so. I could tell you stories, but I don't want to alarm you."

Oh, go ahead. I am tougher than I look.

She didn't look tough at all, just a pink and gold and ivory girl. My God, he was becoming poetic. Jack reminded himself he was a rational man, at home with compasses and protractors and slide rules. Thrilled to balance columns of crabbed figures in ledgers. Happy in laboratories with noxious fumes, a safe distance from china tea cups and lemon-flavored biscuits and blue-eyed females. He cleared his throat.

"I'll save my misadventures for another day. I'm still trying to make a good impression. You don't mind if I come to visit again, do you?"

Nicola cast those blue eyes down and shook her head.

"That's a 'yes, I don't mind' shake, isn't it?"

She looked up at him, and his brain got fuzzier. He'd seen a lot of blue eyes in his time. Why were hers having such a peculiar effect on him?

You may come tomorrow and take me for a walk.

"Are you sure you're well enough?"

If I stumble, I expect you to hold me up.

"I believe I can do that." Jack pictured her in her fur-trimmed hooded coat, clutching his arm. They would walk slowly, and her red coat would brush against his trousers. The wool would be having fun while he thought dampening-and-not-at-all-ardent thoughts. Counted to one thousand and six. Recited the alphabet backwards.

Remembered what he was trying so hard to forget.

"What time will you be ready?"

I like to walk in the morning. Shall we say ten o'clock?

"All right." His breakfast was served promptly at eight. He was expected to be downstairs and dressed too. No robe and bedroom slippers allowed. It was all part of the routine whose soundness Jack was not entirely sold on. Where was the logic in it? What difference would it make if he ate at eight thirty? One would think Mrs. Feather would enjoy an extra half-hour's sleep.

Of course, he was not sleeping at all.

He'd even spoken to Oakley about laudanum. The doctor had flatly refused. A crutch, he'd said, one that Jack would soon regret using.

Jack was already full of too many regrets.

She motioned towards his cup and picked up the teapot. Did he want another cup of tea? Not really, but if he agreed, he could extend his visit. And if he was smart, he'd eat up all the treats that were on the tray. Who knew when he'd get another good meal?

And if he had another cup of tea, he could look into Nicola's blue eyes a little bit longer.

Chapter 5

December 18, 1882

Nicola's heart was racing. Just a little. No need to call for Dr. Oakley, however. She was only anticipating going for a Monday morning walk.

She'd need to go miles to work off her breakfast—porridge with double cream and honey, poached eggs on toast, bacon, sweet rolls, stewed apples, and a whole pot of tea. She could barely bend over to hook up the new boots her mama had sent so promptly. If food was the answer to her problem, she'd be reciting the Magna Carta by noon.

She hadn't quite worked out how she was to respond to Jack on their walk—she couldn't very well bring the notebook and purple pencil along and lurch all over the lanes as she wrote. Maybe there would be no need for conversation, just a quiet appreciation of nature and the quaint charm of Puddling. It had snowed in the night, and the winterberries outside the parlor windows resembled frosted rubies. Nicola would take a sturdy cane just to be sure, but clinging to Jack's arm would be much more fun.

What had come over her? She was not normally forward. She'd never longed to hang on to Richard's arm as they meandered around Bath during their long courtship. They had kept a proper distance, a polite gap that neither one of them was especially anxious to bridge.

On the whole, losing her voice might have saved her from a stultifying marriage. Nicola deserved *more*.

If she recovered—*when* she recovered—she would look about her for a congenial companion, but perhaps not a husband. Her parents would be horrified if she took a lover, so it might be best if she removed herself from their orbit. She had the means now, and was beginning to feel the motivation.

She was finally *waking up*. Goodness.

She took one last look in her mirror. Her cheeks were pink, her eyes were sparkling, and she hadn't even taken one step out of her cottage. She'd managed to coax her fringe to curl, and her wine-colored dress was the nicest she'd brought with her. Its black frogging gave her a jaunty military air, although she supposed soldiers weren't jaunty at all most of the time. The possibility of getting killed at any moment was bound to be a dampening prospect.

Nicola took the stairs with care, clutching the bannister. Her ankle still twinged, but it was securely wrapped beneath the new boot. She settled herself on the sofa to wait, trying not to watch out the window like a lonely puppy. It was five minutes past ten, and just because Jack wasn't prompt didn't mean he wasn't coming.

And then it was a quarter after. Half past. Feeling a little silly, she rose and went into the kitchen.

Mrs. Grace looked up from slicing carrots. "He's late."

Nicola nodded. She'd brought her new notebook with her, and the blue pencil.

I hate to ask, but could you go to his cottage to see what's keeping him?

The snow wasn't deep. If he wasn't coming, she'd go out by herself. She could walk up and down her own front path and be safe enough if it came to it.

The housekeeper wiped her hands on a towel and removed her apron. "I don't like an unreliable man."

Nicola was sure Jack wasn't unreliable. Mostly. She watched Mrs. Grace don her own boots and a heavy cloak.

"You can finish up the carrots if you like. Not too thin, mind. They're for tonight's stew."

Nicola smiled. Mrs. Grace's stew was one of her favorite dishes.

She sat at the pine table and mangled a carrot. Her kitchen abilities were on par with her knitting, but she enjoyed helping Mrs. Grace most days. Nicola was picking up domestic skills that would be useful once she had her own household.

The clock on the Welsh dresser ticked loudly, and another carrot was brutalized. What was keeping Mrs. Grace? A simple "Yes, I'm coming" or "No, I'm sorry" shouldn't take so long. She hoped Jack hadn't fallen ill. Or fallen, as she had. Or maybe Mrs. Grace had slipped? Nicola was worrying too much, something she did more now in the last nine months than before. Danger lurked around every corner. No one and nothing was safe.

Just stop, she admonished herself. Nothing was ever solved by worry. One ruined one's time needlessly imagining the worst. If the worst came, there was usually nothing one could do to forestall it anyway.

She heard the front door bang open and leaped to her feet.

"Nicola!"

It was Jack. She found him in the hallway, looking like a madman. His face was haggard, his eyes sunken, his hair was windblown, and he wasn't even wearing a winter overcoat over his rumpled clothes.

What happened? she mouthed.

"I'm so sorry. I was up most of the night working on something, but must have fallen asleep around dawn. Mrs. Feather didn't have the heart to wake me in my chair—who knew she was less evil than I thought? Anyway, your housekeeper and my housekeeper pinched me to see if I was still alive and here I am. What a way to start the day with those two witches hovering over me."

Don't be rude. You can't go for a walk like that, she wrote.

He looked down on himself in surprise. "No indeed. And I haven't had breakfast either. Quick, before *your* housekeeper gets back! What do you have to eat here? Mrs. Feather just feeds me gruel."

He started to open up the wrong kitchen cupboards. Nicola lay a hand on his sleeve to stay him and felt a pleasurable little zing. She guided him to the pantry, where half a pan of cinnamon rolls sat, covered by a dish cloth.

Jack ate them all. Without a plate or a napkin, he bolted them down as if he would never eat again, licking his fingers—ink-stained fingers—between bites. He gazed at the well-stocked shelves in amazement.

"You have real food here! Just as I thought. They're not trying to punish *you*. Maybe *I* should stop talking." He colored, realizing his thoughtlessness. "You know what I mean. Please don't take offense. I'm sure the Puddling people are trying their best with all of us. With the prices they charge I had hoped for better dinners, that's all. Are those peaches? May I have a spoon, please?"

Nicola opened a drawer and handed him a silver-plated spoon. He proceeded to wolf down the contents of the jar, and she was considering opening another for him when Mrs. Grace rushed into the kitchen.

"Miss Nicola! Are you all right? I couldn't stop that man."

"Do I have telltale crumbs in my beard?" Jack whispered, ducking behind the pantry door.

Nicola brushed away a flake of pastry without even thinking first. Heavens. His beard was very soft, like fur. It was neatly clipped and gave him an air of distinction despite the disreputable state of his clothing.

Flushing, she stepped out of the pantry to prove she was unmolested. Jack followed behind, earning a glare from Mrs. Grace when she spotted the empty glass jar in his hand.

"Have you broken the dietary rules, sir?"

"I'm afraid I have, Mrs. Grace. I've always been a bit of a rule-breaker." He'd told Nicola yesterday he courted trouble on a regular basis.

"Well, you're in Puddling now. The rules are made for a reason. I shall have to report this to the governors."

"Shall I be made to walk the plank? Face the lash? Return the peaches somehow? I don't think they would be in pristine condition."

Mrs. Grace raised a silver eyebrow, which would have terrified Nicola had the expression been directed at her. "Don't be impertinent. There are consequences for your actions."

"Don't I know it," Jack mumbled. His crooked smile had flattened. "Very well, Mrs. Grace, I shall endeavor to behave myself in the future. No more fruit for me."

"It's for your own good, you know. A moderate, wholesome meal plan is the first step to calming one's nerves."

Oh dear. Jack did not look like he agreed with her, but at least he wasn't arguing back. Was he of a nervous disposition? He seemed…busy, but not manic. Full of life.

"I'll be a good boy. Or try to. Nicola, may I borrow your notebook? I have something to show you."

She followed him into the parlor, leaving Mrs. Grace to deal with the carrots and her temper. Jack flopped down on the sofa and began to sketch, a frown of concentration on his face. He flipped through several pages, drawing on each one. She took the uncomfortable chair, observing the rapid strokes from his deft if dirty fingers.

"Come sit beside me. This is all because of you, you know. Remember how you fell the other day? Of course you do—you're still limping. I got to thinking about your shoes. They were next to useless in this weather. But what if one could make a shoe that could have traction built right in for any weather event? See there—it looks like a regular shoe. But with a thicker sole. When you slide this button, lines of steel teeth roll out. You could walk on ice or mud without slipping or getting stuck. Slide the button back, the teeth retract and you're ready to dance. What do you think?"

She grabbed the pencil. *What an interesting idea. They could be used for self-defense too.*

"What a bloodthirsty wench you are! I suppose you'd like to go around kicking people with knives on your feet. I'd better stay out of your way."

He was very much in her way right now, sitting so close, the scent of starch and his masculine cologne inescapable.

The aroma of peaches too. A kiss of forgotten summer. Nicola sighed without sound, then wrote in her book.

Is this what you do? Make shoes?

"Not yet. But I could buy a shoe factory and start." He sat back. "I wonder if there's military application—not that they'd go about kicking the enemy, but such footwear might come in handy in all sorts of locations. I'd have to make some prototypes, though. I wonder about the weight of the mechanism. Steel might not be practicable if one is marching for miles." He dashed off a few words in the margins.

She read upside down. *Wheels? Blades?* It was pretty clear to Nicola that she and Jack were not going for a walk today. She squelched her disappointment.

Do you want to keep the notebook?

"No, I've got a dozen drawings just like this at home. And I can't do anything about anything for the next several weeks—we're all sub rosa here. Incommunicado. While the cat's away, my secretary, Ezra Clarke, is probably sitting at my desk with his feet up, smoking one of my best cigars and hoping I never come home. A fine time to get an idea, buried here." He looked slightly glum.

I can contact him for you.

Jack raised both dark eyebrows. "What? They give you real food *and* leave to write letters?"

Nicola nodded and wrote: *My father is a solicitor. We write several times a week. I can enclose your letter in mine, and you can trust him to deliver it.*

"You are encouraging me to misbehave. Break the rules. What will Mrs. Grace say?" He was grinning now.

Nicola grinned back.

"Oh, you lovely girl!" Jack threw his arms around her and kissed her cheek. Nicola was so startled by the contact that she moved, causing Jack's lips to slide right over her cheek to her mouth. Their breaths mingled for a second, and then she felt him rear back.

As any gentleman should.

She leaned forward, grabbed his wrinkled jacket, and kissed him full on the mouth.

He wasn't going anywhere now.

After a bit, his hand was in her carefully arranged hair, fingertips tickling her scalp. His lips were firm, warm and dry, and pressed against hers with the barest pressure. Nicola knew of open-mouthed kissing. Should she initiate it? It was rather peculiar, and she hadn't much enjoyed it when she and Richard had experimented.

Jack decided for her. His tongue traced the seam of her lips, and she opened. He was extraordinarily gentle, as if he expected her to object in some way. Bite his tongue. Slap his face. She wasn't going to. Prickles of sensation raced up and down her spine as his tongue layered over hers. This was entirely different from anything she'd experienced before. It was less, but somehow *more*. The messy, clumsy, embarrassing wetness was absent; instead, there was controlled heat and purpose to every flick of Jack's tongue.

Goodness. Although Nicola supposed goodness didn't have much to do with it. Jack kissed in a reverent yet masterful fashion, and she felt every inch of her skin respond. Hair was lifting, tiny bursts of hot blood scurried to the surface. She must be terribly flushed, but after a quick peek, Nicola knew Jack couldn't see her. His eyes were closed, his long dark lashes still.

She shut her own eyes again and allowed herself to feel only. Her hands twisted about his loosened collar, pinning him in place. In turn, one set of his fingers stroked her cheek while the other stole pins from her hair. She was coming undone in more ways than one. It was all like a dream, warm, lush, and exotic. It wasn't winter. She wasn't stuck in an odd Cotswold village, but cocooned in the arms of a—

"Miss Nicola!"

Oops. Mrs. Grace's horrified tone reminded her that it was broad daylight, and she was on her sofa, her mouth being ravaged by a relative stranger. No, not ravaged. Nicola couldn't think of the precise word, her head was spinning so. Feeling was so much simpler than looking for words in her fuzzy head.

Jack leaped up. "Forgive me. It's not what you think, Mrs. Grace."

"Isn't it? I'll thank you to go to your cottage right this instant and let Miss Nicola alone. The governors certainly will be hearing about *this* as well as your other infractions." Oh, that eyebrow.

Heavens. Surely they couldn't object to a friendship between Guests? Didn't friends kiss on occasion? But perhaps not quite like Jack had kissed Nicola.

And would do again if she had any say about it.

Chapter 6

December 19, 1882

Jack was in the doghouse; no meaty bone for him. No meat, period. This morning, he'd been visited and lectured by Mr. Fitzmartin, Dr. Oakley, and the head of the board of governors, who'd just returned from his honeymoon abroad and seemed disinclined to waste too much time with a misbehaving Guest so he could get back to his new wife. The man—around his age, someone called Sykes—had blistered him with the consequences of his actions, checking his pocket watch all the while.

There was some mention of scandal, accountability, trust. High standards. Rules and responsibilities. Puddling's sterling reputation through the ages, eight decades of success, a duty to reform the unreformable.

Which meant Jack, he supposed.

Quiet and wholesome country living was essential for the rehabilitation of Guests, which apparently did not involve kisses of any kind. Certainly no open-mouthed kissing on the sofa of Stonecrop Cottage.

Blah blah blah.

Jack pretended to agree with everything the three men said so they would go away as quickly as possible. He'd nodded so resolutely his neck ached. He wasn't exactly under house arrest, but had been strongly admonished to leave poor Miss Nicola alone so she could recover without his dastardly interference.

Jack wondered if he could kiss her into speech. Like waking up Sleeping Beauty or Snow White or another fairy tale heroine. The plot details were unclear—neither his parents nor his nannies had been fanciful people, and his knowledge of children's stories and magic kisses was as limited as his botanical awareness.

He was more than willing to learn, though.

He had gone back to Tulip Cottage in a daze yesterday, all thoughts of shoes and feet quite forgotten. He hadn't even noticed the cold, since in his rush to apologize to Nicola for his absence he'd come out without an overcoat. While he was up the lane, Mrs. Feather had picked all his papers up from the floor and stacked them willy-nilly on a table, and he'd been too feeble to complain about the disordered order. There was a method to his disorganization, and he was very particular about it, but how was Mrs. Feather to know that? Jack had done nothing scientifically useful since he'd arrived, just stared off into corners and played solitaire with an elderly deck of cards. It was four days before he'd noticed the queen of clubs was missing.

It hadn't taken the village drums long to alert his housekeeper to his amatory transgressions. Lunch and supper had been especially atrocious. Cabbage soup. And cabbage soup. One couldn't call a small hard-boiled egg breakfast, could one? Not even salt and pepper were on the table to make the food more palatable. Those filched cinnamon buns and peaches from Nicola's pantry would have to tide his taste buds over indefinitely. If he concentrated, he could almost still taste them; they were delightfully mixed up with the taste of Nicola's lips.

Today was another gray day, not only because of the weather. The euphoria Jack had enjoyed from his fancy footwear and Nicola's kiss had worn off after the tripartite intervention. He was back to questioning himself and his usefulness to society. Reminded of his carelessness and his irresponsibility.

Was he ever going to get over his guilt? He'd made all the amends he could, distributed a considerable fortune, apologized in person to everyone except for the young woman from Bath—

Bath. Oh. God. No. Could it possibly be?

The injured young woman's parents had been evasive as to her injuries, had just said that she'd moved away. They would see that she received her share of the settlement. Her father had been aggressive negotiating the amount...*because he was a solicitor.*

Perhaps a coincidence? Surely Jack had suffered enough for his hubris. But maybe not. He'd not suffered as much as those two dead men and their families.

Jack only knew the victim as a Miss M. Mayfield. M wasn't N, unless there had been a transcription error. And last names were forbidden here in Puddling. Nicola might tell him hers, however, if he was persuasive enough.

If it *was* Mayfield, then what? He'd ruin any chance he had with her if she found out who he was and what he'd done. Or not done. He was the man responsible for her accident.

Perhaps he was borrowing trouble, a silly thing to do. There must be plenty of solicitors in Bath. Plenty of solicitors' daughters. It was extremely unlikely that he and Nicola had both come here for the exact same reason. The mathematical odds were in Jack's favor, and Jack was an excellent mathematician.

Jack bundled up to go for his solitary walk to think. Or, preferably, not think. He wrapped a plaid scarf around his throat but eschewed a hat. He would do what he always did, walk up Honeywell Lane, turn at New Street, go along on Market to Vicarage Lane, and St. Jude's. Make the circuit a dozen times to kill an hour. Do it again to kill two, perhaps lingering outside the bakery just to inhale the spice-scented air.

It was less than a week until Christmas, and the humble stone cottages were sporting wreaths on their front doors and greenery in their window boxes, all very festive and depressing him even further. The five shops had seasonal displays in their windows, but Jack had no money to buy presents, and no people to buy presents for. His mother would not be expecting anything—she was in the south of France with Miss Pemington, her paid companion, whom Jack had hired. In Jack's opinion, the unfortunate Miss Pemington was compensated nowhere near enough to put up with Lady Ryder's endless demands. He'd grown adept at blocking out his mother, who knew everything and meant *too* well, and was grateful that her inevitable letters would never reach him thanks to Puddling's rules.

Jack fastened his gloves and opened the door. A blast of bone crushingly cold air assailed him. He thought of all the people who didn't have fleece-lined deerskin gloves and warm wool scarves and bespoke overcoats from Davies and Son. Jack supported various charitable institutions, but he was only one man, and there were very many needy ones throughout the empire and beyond. How did people live in poverty and survive?

So many impoverished children, working like slaves at machinery. It was legal to employ a nine-year-old for sixty hours a week. He'd never done so in his factories, but others weren't as scrupulous. With Christmas coming, he'd have to write to Ezra to increase his donations.

Nicola said she would help him contact the fellow, but dare he try to see her again? He'd been pretty thoroughly warned off.

But not by her.

She'd looked as dazed as he felt when Mrs. Grace had thrown him out of Stonecrop Cottage. He had a feeling Nicola didn't just go around kissing strange men, and was flattered. He'd bet half his fortune his fellow Guest was chaste, not that it should matter. Jack prided himself on being a modern man. He was no virgin, hadn't been since his teens.

But society women were treated unfairly, kept in gilded cages and expected to be nothing but decorative and submissive. In his opinion, they had a right to their pleasure too. Their vote, as well. Most females were as stymied as his voiceless new friend in expressing their opinions, his mother excepted, of course. Nothing could shut her up for long, but he'd rather have her state her mind in the open, even when her words weren't especially welcome.

Goodness, but he was turning political here in Puddling, nearly radical. He headed up the lane, mindful of patches of ice. He kept his head down, deliberately not looking up through Nicola's gate as he passed.

Hearing an unfamiliar refrain of music over the wind, he paused to listen. She played her little piano beautifully, with passion. Loudly, too, since the cottage's windows must be shut against the winter air. It was as if all her pent-up words were notes, tumbling after each other. He closed his eyes and imagined her at the piano, her graceful fingers at the keys, her head bowed and lost in the exquisite sounds she produced.

Had her vocal chords been injured in the accident she wrote about? It had been just two words in her notebook: *an accident*. Not carriage accident or, God forbid, train accident. Not a fall from a parapet or off a horse. Jack knew nothing about medical conditions, had been healthy all his life. He could ask Dr. Oakley, but didn't expect an answer under the current circumstances. He'd been forbidden to see her, hadn't he?

But when had he ever abided by the rules?

He thought about turning around. Knocking on her door. Kissing her when Mrs. Grace wasn't looking. Jack had a feeling now Nicola would always be guarded, and it would be up to him to find an inventive way to get her alone again.

A problem to solve. Jack made his circuit, keeping a brisk pace. He nodded to the few rosy-cheeked Puddling people he saw on the street. They still glanced at him with suspicion, since he hadn't been truthful on his application to reside here. They didn't know enough about him. The doctor and vicar knew he felt responsible for two deaths, but not the exact details. Jack wanted to keep it that way.

His mother thought him a complete idiot for carrying this indelible burden, for selling off his businesses, making reparations. She advised Jack to console himself that it was God's will that the bridge collapsed and the locomotive wrecked, but surely God was not that cruel.

Ah. He was becoming philosophical as well as political. His train of thought might be shared later with old Mr. Fitzmartin, who was a calming sort of fellow. He'd know the ecclesiastical answers, wouldn't he? *Someone* had to have some answers.

The air on this corner was perfumed with bread, and Jack took a quick gulp, reminding himself he was pretty close to starving. He was hungrier here than he'd ever been in his life, and didn't think much of the Puddling dietary restrictions at all. Lucky Nicola was not bound to it, judging from the quantity and quality of her larder.

Jack was uncertain how the Puddling governors decided on the best treatment for their Guests. Crystal ball? Turn of a card? Magnifying glass? He might not have signed himself in if he'd been aware of the full particulars.

No, that wasn't true. He'd met Nicola—surely that was reason enough to be grateful and stay.

He wandered down another street, having lost count of how many laps he'd made in the Puddling pool. He was so focused on not losing his footing on the icy cobblestones that he nearly barreled straight into a woman wearing a becoming fur-lined scarlet coat. He'd had that woman and her coat in his arms not that long ago. Her eyes sparkled as she put a cane out to prevent him from knocking her over.

He knew he was smiling like a lunatic, and tried to adjust his mouth to something more modest and less toothy.

"Good morning! Are you on your daily constitutional?"

She nodded her assent and looped her arm around his.

"You'd be better off walking alone, you know. I'm in enough trouble with our jailers as it is. They believe me to be a vile seducer of young women. And no, I'm not," he said quickly after seeing her own smile waver. "I mean to start with, *you* kissed *me* as I recall. I couldn't do anything else but respond in kind—I'm not made of ice. But as a gentleman, I didn't tell on you during my inquisition. Not one word. I've taken all the blame, *and* the punishment."

Her mouth opened in a concerned "o."

"Yes, it's as dire as you can imagine. They are trying to kill me. Two bowls of cabbage soup yesterday, as if one bowl wasn't insulting enough. An egg this morning the size of my thumbnail. The silent treatment—no offense meant—from Mrs. Feather. I had three of the governors on my doorstep at the crack of dawn reminding me I'm here at their discretion and I might be drummed out of the village at any moment if I continue to disobey. See those curtains twitch at the cottage across the street? Our movements are being reported even as we speak. Perhaps you should let go of my arm."

Jack was absurdly gratified that she clung tighter. "Very well. But don't say I didn't warn you."

They continued down the lane, holding onto each other. Every now and again, Nicola would tug on his coat sleeve so they could pause to admire a boxwood wreath or thatched roof or a painted garden gate. As a Londoner, he was slowly growing to appreciate Puddling's bucolic charms. He hardly ever spent any time at Ashburn nowadays, his country place in Oxfordshire, the next county over. Somehow Jack felt it still belonged to his father, although the man had been dead for over six years. Lady Ryder had yet to move into the dower house, her reign of well-meaning terror unabated, which made Jack's visits infrequent.

He had few pleasant memories of growing up at Ashburn. He'd been sent away to school at a tender age, his tutors proving inadequate for the task of teaching him anything he didn't already know. Holidays found him at other boys' houses while his parents engaged in their marital warfare.

As an adult, Jack had been too busy overseeing his various business enterprises to loll about as lord of the manor. He had an excellent steward in place, the farms were producing, the tenants taken care of. He often traveled to Manchester and Sheffield and Birmingham and points abroad. He could close his eyes and draw a map of the train routes.

Now he was sequestered in this trainless village with too much time to think.

But why dwell on unpleasantness when he had a pretty young woman on his arm? It was restful to walk with her, and after a while, his own nervous chatter stopped. Jack shortened his stride to accommodate her slower steps. Her walking was much improved, the cane mostly for insurance as they ascended and descended the hilly lanes.

If they were discovered flouting the rules, he'd probably be thrown out of Puddling as the guilty party. Oh, well. The first thing he'd order when he got back home was beefsteak with a gallon of béarnaise sauce on the side.

"Will you still risk censure getting a message out for me?" he asked on their third march up St Jude's Lane. Nicola nodded, then pointed to the churchyard path.

The iron gate creaked open and they were amongst the snow-dusted regimented yews, long lines of them, each clipped into a pyramid. There were a number of tempting table-like tombstones, and Jack wondered if Puddling's children enjoyed climbing up on them as he would have when he was a boy.

Nicola disentangled her arm from his and sat on a bench, patting the vacant spot next to her. His arse almost froze when he complied.

"Do you think we have some privacy here among the dead? Old Fitzmartin might jump out of the church at any moment."

She reached into a pocket and drew out the small notebook he'd given her. *I saw you walk by.*

And had come out to find him. Jack's heart stuttered.

"I heard you playing. It was magnificent."

Her pink cheeks pinked further. *Thank you.*

"Are you a professional musician?"

Heavens no. I do play the church organ at home, though. And once here. Mrs. Fitzmartin has offered me the job on a more permanent basis, but I've declined.

She had very neat handwriting. Jack was grateful he didn't have to write back. Half the time he couldn't decipher his own. "Why?"

Too many eyes.

"One can't help looking at you. You are, um, beautiful."

He realized it was true, a quiet sort of beauty. Jack ordinarily had no trouble complimenting women, but he felt somewhat shy with Nicola. She gazed at him with such blue directness, he didn't want to disappoint her. He felt a responsibility to carry the banner for all males of the species.

Don't be silly. I'm writing to my parents the day after tomorrow. Will your letter be ready?

He'd almost forgotten his shoe scheme. And there was something else he'd thought of, a surprise. "I'll make sure of it. I don't dare to deliver it to your cottage, though. Mrs. Grace will burn it along with me." He had visions of being doused with lamp oil and turning into a Guy Fawkes effigy. "It's one thing that we've bumped into each other on the street. I don't think the powers that be want me to visit you ever again."

Bring it here. Wrap it in something waterproof. Put it under this bench with a rock or whatever's handy by eleven tomorrow morning. I'll take my walk after and "find" it, then mail it the next day. Are you really in bad trouble because of me?

"I'm afraid so. I'd do it again, though," Jack said honestly. "Kiss you, that is. Or you can kiss me. It makes no difference. The end result is delightful."

She didn't meet his eyes. *I don't know what came over me. It's most unlike me to be so brazen.*

"Be as brazen as you wish. It was, um, refreshing." Refreshing was not the correct word, but Jack didn't want to frighten her. She'd inflamed all his dormant desire. With Nicola's flushed cheeks and swollen lips firmly in mind, he'd taken matters into his own hand once Mrs. Feather left for the evening yesterday. He'd felt almost liberated. Normal. Not that his joy lasted the night—the dreams returned on schedule.

Do you want to kiss me again?

He most certainly did. Jack glanced about, noting the drifting snow between the trees and the gravestones and the Norman church. Not the most romantic of spots, but the dead told no tales.

Chapter 7

Nicola lost her grip on the notebook, and it fluttered to the bench. She tucked the pencil in her pocket. Clearly she should not have looked out the window to see the top of Jack's dark head bob over the gate. Should have locked herself in her cottage when she did catch sight of him. Put a blanket over her head. Tied herself to a piece of furniture. Not chase after him, wondering which way he'd turned on his perambulations, slipping and sliding all the way in her search. Not feel so…thrilled when she found him.

Not write anything about kissing when she meant just to arrange for his outgoing mail.

She'd been awake a good portion of the night thinking about their kiss. It had, to put it plainly, knocked her sideways. She had little to compare it to—Richard had not been a demonstrative fiancé. Why should he be, when their relationship had been practical and more or less businesslike? There had been no stars behind her eyelids, no tremors shooting off like fireworks, no tingling lips, no *want*.

Nicola had practiced kissing her bare arm as she lay in the dark, feeling ridiculous but determined. Her skin was a poor substitute for Jack's mouth. His neatly trimmed beard and mustache had had been as soft as mink fur, quite unlike Richard's coppery bristle. Richard was attractive, but Jack was…um, beautiful. See, she could be inarticulate too.

She didn't feel the cold at all, just a wild sense of anticipation. Jack was very close, his quick breaths visible in the air between them. The last time they'd kissed, it was she who initiated the lip-to-lip contact. Nicola knew she'd taken him by surprise; now she waited to see what he would do. She imagined he was a man of experience—no one of his looks and charm and age could be expected to be celibate.

He leaned in, cupping her cheek with a gloved hand. "You don't regret your offer?"

She shook her head. If she'd had access to the notebook, she would have written *get on with it.*

"I've never kissed a woman in a churchyard before with, uh, graves about. Are we risking thunderbolts?" His eyes danced with merriment.

What a way to go, she thought. They weren't being disrespectful—babies began with kisses, and death eventually, inevitably followed. It was all very circle-of-life, wasn't it?

His mouth loomed, and she closed her eyes. He exerted the barest contact, just a whisper of a kiss. She held herself still, letting him set the pace.

But soon she was squirming a little, swept away by Jack's skillful tongue. Nicola had the strongest urge to lie down on the bench, which would indeed risk thunderbolts, and frostbite to boot. If her parents divined what was happening to her here, they would remove her posthaste.

Or perhaps not. Though they loved her, she was a burden to them now. Maybe they'd like to be rid of her permanently. Have someone else worry about her.

But Jack, like Richard, deserved a more participatory partner. He was so full of life and devilry. No matter how marvelous his kiss was, he was no doubt taking pity on a shameless spinster who, against all caution, had invited him to take liberties.

Do you want to kiss me again? Really, what man in his right mind would refuse? She wasn't a complete antidote, and men were known for their hotter natures. They sometimes were not discriminating at all.

Nicola realized her random mental meanderings were spoiling the moment. Who knew when she'd get the opportunity to kiss anyone save for her wire-haired fox terrier, Tippy? She hoped he was being well looked after—she missed him. Who would watch him when they all went to Scotland? When she wrote to her parents...

Oh! No more thinking of dogs. No more thinking, period. Nicola threw herself into Jack's embrace with enthusiasm, allowing herself to nibble his lower lip as she'd nibbled the soft spot above her elbow. He groaned and returned the favor. The brush of his suede-covered fingertips on her cheek brought on her blushes. She was quite warm everywhere despite the temperature. The kiss deepened with tangled tongues, and Nicola felt something loosen within, like a hopeless wet knot that suddenly gave way.

Jack drew back suddenly, holding on to her shoulders with some force. "I say! You made a noise!"

Nicola covered her damp mouth. Had she? She opened her lips to speak, but the usual nothingness came out.

"It's all right. I'm sure you'll do it again. We'll keep kissing until you're chattering like a magpie. You know, I did wonder if I was Prince Charming enough to kiss you awake. At least I don't have to climb a tower like that Rebecca story? You're looking at me funny. Rihanna? Whoever—the girl with the long hair. I'm not up on my fairy tales. And I'm not that fond of heights. You *will* be fine, I promise."

When he said it, she almost believed it. She grabbed her book from the bench.

What did it sound like?

"Hm. Don't cosh me, but rather like a cow—a quiet sort of ladylike one, just a little moo. More of an oo than a moo, actually. You've not spoken at all since your accident?"

Nicola shook her head. A cow was better than a chicken, she supposed. She tried again as the doctors had taught her, brought in air, expelled it. Nothing.

"Don't force it. When you're ready, it will happen. That's what happens with some of my ideas, you know. I can think and think on a problem until I feel my head exploding, but when I least expect results, there they are. There is no physical damage to your vocal chords, I take it."

No. Everything internal was just as it should be, which was why it was so very frustrating that she'd lost her voice. There was no reason that made any sense.

One of the doctors had accused her of faking to get attention. Nicola had wanted to scream at him, but of course she couldn't. Why would anyone deprive themselves of being able to communicate? The attention she had received had been entirely negative until she came to Puddling, where people were friendly and didn't pepper her with questions she couldn't answer. Nicola felt bathed in kindness. Every effort was made to relax her and accept her just as she was.

As Jack had. Unless he was just a bored rake who was taking advantage of the situation they both found themselves in.

Why are you here?

Jack sat back on the bench and tugged up his collar against the chill. He was hatless, as usual. "What an excellent question. I guess I came to find some solace. Something bad, very bad, happened on my watch. And, no, I'm not in the military—at least I haven't caused a war. Yet. Everyone tells me I'm not directly to blame, but I feel to blame anyway. I was hoping to learn how to work through the guilt. Sleep soundly again. So far, that hasn't happened."

The skin under his eyes was dark, his voice a bit bleak. Nicola gave his hand a squeeze.

"Thank you. I do feel a bit better having met a friend. A kissing friend. Maybe you can kiss me happy and I can kiss you into talking."

We can try.

His lips quirked. "That will be fun, won't it? If I'm not run out of town first. My time is up on January 9th. Yours?"

Nicola's parents had spent a small fortune to enroll her in the Puddling Program, but now that she had money of her own, she could pay her way for a while.

I can stay as long as I like, I think.

"Won't your family miss you?"

They know I'm safe here.

Was she? The man next to her had potential to upset her constrained world. What did she know about him really, besides the fact that he was well barbered, rather gorgeous, and visibly well-to-do? She'd seen a heavy gold signet ring with an inscription in the onyx, and his clothes—when they weren't slept in—were impeccably tailored. He appeared to be some sort of inventive engineer, which was unusual for a man of his class. Nicola suspected he was not a mere mister. Mrs. Grace had let something slip at the doorway the first day Jack had come to call. She'd said "milord."

It was against the rules to inquire further. All Nicola knew was that she felt comfortable with him, and flattered by his concern and kisses, even if he might be a cad. She didn't think so, however. There was just something about him that made her feel comfortable for the first time since the accident. Maybe even in years.

And playful. Nicola had never been a playful sort of person. Earnest, yes. Serious. Interested in doing good works, as long as they didn't involve knitting. Once she was done with Puddling, she vowed never to pick up another knitting needle unless her life depended on skewering someone with it.

What about your family?

Jack made a face. "My mother is in France at the moment. It's somewhat of a relief not to have to force myself to be jolly for the season with her. It's difficult at any time of the year, in fact—the mater is not a warm and fuzzy creature at the best of times. She is unusually sharp-tongued, blunt, and far too honest for anyone's good. Right now, I am in her little black book. Punishment is always nigh. If she was home for Christmas, I'd get a lump of coal."

Why?

"I'm a disappointment to her, I suppose. In *trade*." He exaggerated the word as if it were excrement. "She has an idea that I've betrayed my upbringing, disrespected my parents, although wolves would have been more sympathetic." His mouth turned upward, but the smile was not real. "I'm sorry—it's rather pathetic for a man my age to whine about the shortcomings of his family. I take it you are close to yours."

Nicola nodded.

"Lucky you. Here, you look chilled to the bone. Shall I return you to your cottage?" He extended an elbow, and she took it. "I shall get the letters to our hiding spot first thing in the morning. Thank you very much for facilitating my rebellion."

Nicola stood, planting her cane in the slush. She'd like to spend more time with Jack, but they had probably garnered too much notice already. Her afternoon was bound to be boring.

And kissless.

Chapter 8

December 20, 1882

Taking advantage of Nicola's generosity, Jack penned several letters, wrapped them in a scrap of oilcloth he found in the dank cellar of Tulip Cottage, and tucked them under "their" bench well before the stated time. He did his usual ramble, hoping to "accidentally" bump into her, but did not.

He was still being taught his lesson, diet-wise. There had been more cabbage soup yesterday, and then some brown sludge for dinner which was more or less unidentifiable. Jack had never cared much for what he ate before, but was rapidly becoming a frustrated gourmand. Last night he'd even stooped to reading a cookbook he found in a kitchen drawer, something Mrs. Feather had obviously never consulted. The resulting saliva that dropped on its pages had been embarrassing, but he was alone. Mrs. Feather was on duty from half seven to half five, so Jack was spared from more than ten hours of disapproval a day.

He was used to it. Despite his words to Nicola, he still felt his mother's wrath quite keenly. He couldn't remember a time when he'd enjoyed unconditional maternal devotion. His parents' relationship had been unhappy, and he'd borne the brunt of their misery from an early age. Poor little rich boy? That had defined him once, but he'd worked hard to overcome his inauspicious beginnings.

The fact that he was unlike most children had not helped. Neither his father nor mother could claim to be intellectual, and their comprehension of scientific inquiry was nil. Jack's father had resented a son who was smarter than he was and had beaten him accordingly. His mother had been better, but Jack knew he still bewildered her.

But there was no point to feeling sorry for himself. In fact, his deprivations had made him stronger, and he rarely dwelled on the past when there was so much present to deal with. And to be fair, since his father's death, Jack's mother had cheered up considerably if one knew what to look for. She wasn't a bad woman, just a tad difficult.

An unhappy marriage was hell for all involved. Jack supposed that was why he'd been reluctant up until now to even consider getting leg-shackled. His previous brushes with "settling down" had been caused by his inattention to convention. Who knew it was forbidden to dance with a partner more than twice of an evening? But when one was explaining one's latest project to a feather-headed debutante, more time was needed, even if the poor girl looked bored to death.

Jack had never meant to break any hearts, and on the whole, thought he hadn't. The two young ladies involved had been more interested in his title and fortune anyway, and hadn't a clue who Jack really was or where his interests lay. They'd gone on to marry ambitiously, for which he was profoundly grateful.

Jack returned home to await his appointment with the ancient vicar. They met for half an hour daily, and so far hadn't accomplished much. There was the usual discussion of divine forgiveness and redemption, but right now Jack just wanted to forgive himself. It was all very well for the Fellow Upstairs to welcome Jack into the fold without reservations, but it had done nothing to abate the bad dreams or hear the imaginary screams of the passengers on their way to Bath. Jack's negligence had caused harm and horror, and now was being visited upon him tenfold. No life was without obstacles; he knew that. Challenges made one tougher in the end, but Jack couldn't see the way around this one.

Two men were dead.

He supposed soldiers could justify their actions to take lives—they were killing the enemy, standing between them and their country. Their honor. There was a higher purpose. Freedom. Protection and preservation of a way of life that was dear to them, although what was happening throughout the empire was at best confusing. Jack was not naïve enough to believe that everything his country imposed upon others was right or justified. One had only to look at the recent debacles on the African continent to have serious doubts.

The rap on the door did nothing to rouse him from his moroseness. Mrs. Feather announced the vicar as if Jack didn't have eyes in his head. He didn't bother to move from his chair in front of an indifferent fire, but gave the man a wobbly, welcoming smile.

"Good morning, my lord!" Reverend Fitzmartin radiated happiness—justifiably, since the man was so old it was a blessing he was still alive. He had his health, a loving wife, all of his marbles, and most of his teeth. Plenty to be thankful for right there. While his sermons were not scintillating (Jack had only sat through one since arriving, and Advent was inevitably a solemn affair), the vicar made good use of his classical education and sprinkled his wisdom throughout his words. He seemed convinced that Jack would be cured of his melancholy if he would simply turn to God.

If only it *were* simple. Jack had spent months on his knees in prayer when he wasn't running around the United Kingdom trying to make amends, and had only worn out the fabric of his trousers.

Mr. Fitzmartin raised a white wooly eyebrow, casting his cheerfulness aside for a stern inquisition. "Are we behaving ourselves today?"

"We? I don't know about you, Vicar, but I have nothing naughty to confess," Jack said, crossing his fingers behind his back.

"You were seen with the young lady yesterday. Did you not understand the purpose of the governors' visit? You cannot get away with much here. Plenty of folks have already reported your liaison."

"It was hardly a liaison! We met quite by chance. Our daily exercise. With only five streets to walk, it's inevitable one encounters other Guests on occasion, isn't it?" He'd seen the Countess and her dog three days ago. They'd nodded and passed each other by without a word—the Countess, not the dog, who had growled most unjustifiably. She was a very handsome woman, perfectly beautiful, really, but did not make Jack lose his breath in any way. Her hair wasn't golden. Her eyes were not that special color of blue.

She wasn't Nicola.

"You disappeared into the churchyard."

"I have an interest in ancient gravestones. St. Jude's has very fine examples, don't you agree?"

The vicar gave him a familiar look. Jack had seen it on the face of every nanny his parents had ever employed and any number of his schoolmasters. "I wasn't born yesterday, as you can tell. Miss Nicola has been entrusted into our care. She has enough worry in her life without being taken advantage of."

Jack felt his face grow hot. "I would never do such a thing!" And anyhow, *she* had kissed *him* the first time, and asked him to kiss her again. Not that he was going to peach on her; it wouldn't be gentlemanly, and Jack was a gentleman despite dabbling in trade, much to his mother's consternation.

But Lady Ryder liked her jaunts to the south of France, didn't she? And new clothes and jewels and feminine fripperies. Where did she think the money came from? Jack's father had left her a stingy widow's jointure, trying to annoy her even in death. As annoyance was a permanent state for her, she'd taken the financial slap with her usual grace, which was to say none. Jack had heard her utter words he hadn't imagined she even knew when the will was read.

"I should hope not. We discussed this thoroughly yesterday, did we not?"

"Indeed we did. I remember nearly every word."

"Good. You seem a bright boy. No point to me beating the dead horse then, is there?"

Jack grinned. "No, sir. Cart it away to the knacker's yard. Lecture me on something else, if you please."

Mrs. Feather entered with tea and biscuits, the biscuits being solely for Mr. Fitzmartin's delectation. Jack was pleased to see they were burned at the bottom. Served them all right. He had a passing thought for Nicola's cinnamon buns and firmly rejected it. He was made of stern stuff and could do without.

After brushing the blackened crumbs from his front, the vicar proceeded to pray and pontificate. Jack nodded at all the appropriate lulls and pretended to look interested. Unfortunately, his mind had wandered to the churchyard bench and what had occurred there. To Nicola's sofa.

Kisses. Just kisses. He'd probably kissed dozens of girls in his day, not that a gentleman kept track or compared notes with other gentlemen. An ogre did not stare back at him in the mirror every morning as he cleaned his teeth, so Jack had made plenty of hearts skip a beat. Until now, however, he'd kissed and run. But there was something about Nicola that made him want to stay put.

Not in Puddling, certainly. He was looking forward to the time he could summon his coachman and hear the clank of the village gates behind him. He'd go to his estate in Oxfordshire or townhouse in London and eat until he couldn't button his trousers, then figure out a way to court Nicola properly.

He'd never really tried to do such a thing. His previous relationships had been casual, with no thought of the future or domestic compatibility. With his parents' example before him, marriage had never been one of Jack's goals.

Until now.

He knew he was being premature. He knew next to nothing about Nicola, and, irony of ironies, she couldn't tell him. Blue eyes and golden hair and a mischievous sweetness were not enough, surely. What in hell was happening to him?

For nine months, he was worried he was losing his mind. It seemed he'd been right.

What he needed was an uninterrupted night's sleep. A good solid five or six hours of dreamlessness. If he couldn't sleep at night, why not the daytime? The vicar was wrapping himself in his muffler, done with his diligence for the day. Jack could send Mrs. Feather home, or out on an errand. He'd climb the stairs, hopefully not hit his head on the doorframe, draw the curtains, punch down the pillows—

"Did you hear me, my lord?"

Jack covered his yawn. "Yes, yes. Whatever. I'm sure you know best. I find myself rather tired, Vicar. I believe I'll head up to my bedroom for a nap. Could you inform Mrs. Feather on your way out? I don't want to be disturbed for the next several hours. In fact, if she's thrown my supper together already, she might go home." Jack hoped he wouldn't be tempted to throw his supper *out*.

Reverend Fitzmartin waggled an eyebrow. "Are you sure?"

"Perfectly. As I'm sure you've heard, I missed a night's sleep recently. One must try to catch up."

"Very well. Don't forget."

Forget what? Jack almost asked, but then the vicar would resume lecturing him. He'd refresh himself about the details tomorrow during their regular session.

Jack went upstairs. Revered Fitzmartin's sonorous tones and Mrs. Feather's replies were muted from below. Jack undressed, pleased to hear the cottage door squeal shut twice. He was alone, no one telling him how to live or what to eat. Now if only he could close his eyes, clear his mind, and sleep.

Chapter 9

December 21, 1882

Nicola visited the Stanchfields' store with her lumpy brown envelope. Mrs. Stanchfield did not seem to think anything was amiss with her thicker-than-usual missive as she affixed stamps to the packet in her secret back room. The shopkeeper chatted amiably through the doorway as she always did, knowing Nicola had nothing to say back.

But the day before yesterday, she'd made a noise! Not much of one, but it was a start. She hadn't told her parents in her letter, especially the circumstances, not wanting them to get their hopes up.

It had been hard enough trying to explain why she was enclosing Jack's letters, for surely her father would know that she was aiding and abetting a rebel. She'd made Jack's invention sound like it was a matter of national security, which was not really such a stretch. It would be very convenient to have multipurpose shoes and boots; Jack was kind of a mad genius. She wondered what else he'd invented. He seemed to be a man of many parts.

Some parts of him were more interesting than others.

He had very fine lips between his clipped moustache and beard, full and firm. She liked his ready smile and the mischievous spark in his dark eyes when he turned everything into a joke. His eyelashes were longer than hers, which was annoying, but then so many males of the various species out-prettied their female companions. His shiny hair was over-long and had a bit of curl to it, and his nose was appropriately aristocratic.

And those were only what were visible above his stiff collars. If his broad shoulders were any indication, the rest of him was museum-worthy. Nicola had made the requisite visits to the British Museum with Frannie and had seen what the Greeks and Romans bequeathed to the wider world and wondered how Jack compared.

Her thinking was going in a very naughty southerly direction. Knowing she was blushing, she bowed to Mrs. Stanchfield and hurried out of the shop. It was a gray day and the scent of snow was in the air again. Just a few days to Christmas, and it looked like it would be a white one.

Though the sidewalks were swept, the cobblestones glistened with ice, and Nicola was mindful of her mending ankle. Best she got on with her exercise—the weather did not look promising for tomorrow, and she might be housebound. Each day in Puddling was much like the next, and her little intrigue with Jack had been the bright spot of her time here.

She'd missed him in the churchyard yesterday, which was probably just as well. No point in setting tongues wagging even more than they were already. Nicola wondered what he was doing right this minute. Complaining over the quality of his lunch and his upcoming dinner? She had hoped he'd leave a note for her too under the bench, but the only things inside the folded oilcloth were sealed letters to his associates. She hadn't wanted to pry, but two were to London addresses, and one to Ashburn in Oxfordshire. He'd mentioned a country estate, and Nicola wondered if that was its name.

She was stepping gingerly on the pavement when a large square of slate skidded off a roof and landed right in front of her, shattering into a hundred pieces.

"Oh, God! Watch out!"

The warning came much too late. Her heart thudded at the near-miss. Looking up, she saw a worker on top of one of the new cottages under construction. Why, she might have been knocked in the head by his carelessness! Wouldn't she love to give him a dressing-down.

If only she could. He'd have to be scared by her scowl. She arranged her face into what she hoped was a menacing glare.

He clambered down the ladder, losing his checkered cap in the process. That too tumbled to the ground, with much less potential harm. There was something familiar—

"Forgive me, Nicola. I am absolutely useless at the task the Puddling Rehabilitation Foundation has given me."

Nicola could only gape in wonder. It was Jack, dressed as a shabby workman, soot smudging one chiseled cheek. She assumed his clothes were borrowed, since they did not fit to his usual standard. She'd come out without her notebook, so there was nothing she could do but nod and stare.

"It's for my Service. I'm sure they have you doing something too. One of the regular work crew fellows broke his arm—falling from the roof of this very cottage—and I've been drafted to take his place. Somehow they thought because I was reasonably intelligent and could draw, I was handy with a hammer. They are very much mistaken."

"Oi," came a voice from above. "Time's a wastin'. It will be dark before you know it."

"I nearly killed this young lady, Tom. The least I can do is walk her home."

"You'll only have to make up the time tomorrow," Tom shouted down around a mouthful of nails.

"I'll be more than happy to," he shouted back. Jack took her arm and winked. "Not. This is the best thing that's happened to me all day. Not the bit about almost killing you, though."

Nicola rolled her eyes. She did that a lot when she was with him.

"I wasn't paying attention to old Fitzmartin yesterday, and to my great surprise this morning, Tom and the other men turned up to roust me out of bed. It wasn't even daylight, and just look at what they gave me to wear."

A rough homespun shirt. Torn jacket and tight pants in two different plaids. Thick hobnail boots that looked like they were pinching. Still, nothing could cloak Jack's innate attractiveness.

"Apparently I signed myself up to help finish this cottage before the new year so more of us can be locked up here. It's ironic, isn't it? Like prisoners expanding the jail cells, or zoo animals building cages. And I've rediscovered I suffer from more than a touch of vertigo. No, don't pity me. The job needs to get done before it snows, but Tom's a hard worker. I have every confidence in him. Tomorrow we'll be laying tile inside. Much more my thing. Two feet on the ground. A bucket full of muck and a trowel. What could go wrong?"

Nicola had never given any consideration to construction. Her neighborhood in Bath consisted of lovely Georgian houses that needed no further embellishment. The ceilings were high, the long windows sparkled, the floors were waxed to a high finish. Her parents' home was graciousness itself. Her father was a very successful solicitor and lived accordingly, though finding a cure for her predicament had taxed his financial resources.

Living in Puddling was like visiting an ancient fairy village constructed for gnomes. Even the new cottages conformed to their smaller brethren, blending into the landscape with weathered golden stone and a space for a small front garden. She wondered what it would be like in the spring, and hoped she wouldn't be around to find out.

Where would she go? Where *should* she go? Obviously today she was bound for Stonecrop Cottage, Jack's bare hand firmly over hers. Some of his fingernails were dirty and broken, but he didn't seem to notice. He was cheerful, whistling as they walked down Honeywell Lane.

"Do you think we can persuade your Mrs. Grace to give me a cup of tea? I'm half-frozen," he said as they neared her gate.

If Mrs. Grace objected, she'd brew the tea herself. Jack had been on that roof for hours, poor man.

They entered the cottage to find a merry fire in the parlor and Mrs. Grace arranging the tray for Nicola's tea. The housekeeper sniffed a bit when Jack requested an extra cup, and gave both of them a penetrating look.

Oh dear. But Nicola was twenty-six years old, mature enough to choose her own company. She wasn't afraid of Jack, although perhaps she should be. He looked a little wild at the moment, wind-blown and flushed. He warmed his hands by the fire while Nicola dismissed Mrs. Grace to do whatever she had to do in the kitchen. There was some slamming of cupboard doors and what was surely a quiet curse.

"Witch, just as I said," Jack whispered. "I hope she's not stirring up a potion to kill me."

Nicola nodded in agreement, although generally Mrs. Grace was as pleasant as could be.

Except when it came to Jack.

"We've done nothing to be ashamed of. They can't keep us apart if we don't want them to."

Couldn't they? Nicola had been lightly and politely lectured by the vicar on keeping her distance from Jack. She was a sensible young woman, he'd said. No reason to deviate from her well-ordered, normal, middle-class life. She didn't want to be a disappointment to her family and arouse gossip, did she? And the young man was a troubled soul, not ready to be released.

Jack didn't seem troubled, just tired and shaking with cold. She passed him the delicate china cup, which looked incongruous in his work-roughened hand. He drank it in one swallow and held it out for more. He must have a cast-iron tongue.

This time, his sip was more constrained. "Where's your notebook?" he asked, after stuffing a piece of gingerbread in his mouth and seemingly swallowing it without chewing.

Nicola went to the desk and opened a drawer. The notebook Jack had given her lay under her Puddling journal, and she fished it out, along with a colored pencil. Green for the season this time.

"How are you spending Christmas?"

Nicola felt a twinge in the area of her heart. She would miss her nephews tearing open their gifts, eating Seville oranges, wearing their paper crowns. Bertie would probably try to eat that too.

But, as she remembered, Aunt Augusta's Edinburgh mansion was usually cold enough to hang meat indoors, even in the summer.

Right here. My family is not allowed to come in case my progress is disrupted. Puddling rules. Nicola paused. What progress? If she was making any, it was only because of Jack's kiss, and an "oo" wasn't much. *They will go to Scotland for Christmas,* she wrote.

"You know my mother's in France. We've been abandoned, haven't we? Two orphans in a snowstorm. Let's club together. Surely the Puddling powers that be cannot object to that. It's Christmas, after all."

What do you mean?

"Why can't we have Christmas lunch together? We can do it ourselves. Give the witches a day off."

I don't know.

"What's to know? We've been reheating our suppers since we got here, haven't we? We don't have round-the-clock minders, thank God. If we can get the witches to prepare something edible for us—and that's a big if, if we're talking about Mrs. Feather—we can have a jolly time."

Nicola bit a lip. When Jack was enthusiastic about something, it was difficult not to agree. He was infectious.

She had pushed Christmas out of her mind, not wanting to feel sorrier for herself than she did already. She'd made no special seasonal requests to Mrs. Grace, although Nicola knew there was at least one fruitcake in the pantry, redolent of brandy, wrapped in cheesecloth in a battered tin. Her nose had led her to the discovery, and she was reminded of her father's political friends after a spirited (in all senses of the word) after-dinner discussion.

Alcohol was tricky to obtain in Puddling, not that she yearned for a nightly sherry as she was used to sharing with her parents in Bath. From what she understood, so many of the Guests had overindulged in their previous life that all temptation was removed.

Nicola wondered if Jack's problems included drinking to excess. He didn't bear any of the usual signs, though. His eyes were clear, his straight nose unveined, and if there was a softness about his chin, it was ably hidden by his beard.

Christmas lunch without wine. It could be done. It *should* be done. She didn't want to spend the day alone.

I can ask.

Jack beamed. "Better you than me. I don't think the witches like me very much, particularly your Mrs. Grace. She sees me as a corrupting influence upon you."

Are you?

"Only if you want me to be."

Chapter 10

December 25, 1882

In the end, it had taken more than Nicola asking. Jack was visited all over again by the doctor, the vicar, and the Sykes fellow who headed up the board of governors. They had made him feel a little bit like a half-dead moth pinned into a cigar box, but he must have flapped his wings enough through the interrogation to prevail.

He was somehow able to convince them that his motives were pure. That he was just being gentlemanly, taking pity on Miss Nicola, who dreaded being alone for the holiday. That she needed cheering up by a friend—in fact, she'd made a noise in his presence. That tidbit made the doctor perk up and grill him as if he'd murdered someone.

Well, he guessed he sort of had. Two someones. But Jack wasn't going to dwell on that now, when a delicious private Christmas lunch was nearly in his grasp.

He'd expressed his concern for the welfare of the housekeepers too, who surely would rather spend the day with their own loved ones. The doctor had turned scarlet, so something must be going on there. Jack didn't care which witch the man preferred, as long as neither one of them hovered around Stonecrop Cottage.

After a day of fierce deliberation on the part of the governors, it had been resolved that the Guests' Christmas celebration would take place at Nicola's cottage after the Christmas morning church service. It was larger and the larder was far better stocked. Miracle of miracles, Jack's dietary restrictions were to be lifted for the day. Mrs. Feather's contribution was to be a pan of roast potatoes—even she couldn't ruin so simple a dish, and a ham would be prepared to be sliced. Various side dishes were to be easily reheated, and Jack had a devil of a time not thinking with his stomach when he really wanted to think with his heart.

He'd have the day alone with Nicola.

And so he'd sat through Fitzmartin's sermon—for the second day in a row, as Christmas fell on a Monday—sung carols with abandon, and tried to meet Nicola's eye across the aisle. She was swathed in a short fur cape and enormous holly-bedecked hat, which should have looked silly but didn't. She gave him a quick shy smile, then slipped away at the end of the service before he could follow. He'd endured a few more admonishments at the church door, then stopped at home for his surprise contribution to the festivities.

He hoped it wasn't dying.

He'd dug the little bush up from his own unprepossessing back garden yesterday, stuffed it into a bucket, and planned to put it back tomorrow. It wasn't even a fir tree, but it still had pointy green leaves, shriveled red berries, and a vague holiday air about it. Jack had decorated the branches himself with twists of paper and cast-off odds and ends from the building site. He'd bent some already-bent nails into circles that dangled as he carried it down the lane. Snippets of wire had been tied into rusty bows and formed a tipsy star for the top.

It was altogether the most ludicrous thing he'd ever set his hands to, a far cry from the splendor of his mother's trees at Ashburn with all the German blown-glass ornaments she'd collected. But hopefully Nicola would give him high marks for his effort.

Clutching the wretched thing against his chest, he rapped on her door.

And then nearly dropped his offering. The Countess greeted him in Nicola's doorway and Jack found he was unable to do anything but stare.

"I see you were not expecting me. Don't worry—I shan't stay all afternoon. But I was persuaded to do my civic duty by providing you both some chaperonage by that divine Mr. Sykes. *Such* blue eyes. He was very hard to say no to, I'm afraid. Masterful. Well, he'd have to be, considering who he's married to. What a trial she's bound to be—he'll need every scrap of endurance." She gave him a brilliant smile, as if Jack would know what the hell she was talking about.

"And one does have to eat, doesn't one? Especially as it's Christmas, and Christmas comes but once a year. One becomes accustomed to figgy pudding, etcetera. Lovely overindulgence. I confess I'm really looking forward to it. I *do* have a sweet tooth."

Mouth still open, Jack nodded, feeling crushed by the surprise of the definitely unexpected Countess. She touched his elbow and guided him into Nicola's parlor, where she was conspicuously absent. He set his hideous bush down in front of the hearth, rather hoping it would catch on fire. The Countess immediately picked it up—she was stronger than she looked—and placed it on top of the piano.

"Very...festive. Your friend is in the kitchen. I've been helping, but find I am quite useless. My family would tell you I have been raised to be entirely ornamental, which is a bore but true."

The Countess was much more than ornamental. She was a statuesque brunette, whose skin resembled double cream against the black lace of her gown, her eyes aquamarines, and her lips crushed strawberries. She was possibly the most magnificent woman Jack had ever seen up close, and he'd seen his fair share of magnificent women in his travels.

"Really, this is where you are supposed to tell me that although I'm lovely, you're sure I'd have some sort of domestic skill if only I were given half a chance. I know Nicola is mute, but do you suffer from the same affliction?"

"Uh, no."

She extended a slender ivory hand. Every other finger sported a jewel the size of a large marble. "I believe you're called Jack? You may address me as Countess. Such quaint Puddling rules. I suppose you know who I really am."

"Uh, no." He was being repetitive. She raised a perfect plucked brow but said nothing for a moment, evaluating him with those blue-green eyes.

Jack paid very little attention to the misadventures of society despite his mother's constant nagging. Probably the mysterious countess was notorious, but Jack had never seen her before checking himself into Puddling.

"How remarkable. Have you been locked away in an asylum this past year? My likeness has been in all the shops."

Jack's lips quirked. "Only here, my lady. But my business keeps me out of London much of the time."

"Oh, I believe I'm international. But no matter. What sort of business are you in? I was told you were a baron. No last name of course." She winked slowly, her long lashes sweeping against the pale cheek.

"Guilty. I've recently divested myself of some investments and manufacturing plants. Going for a simpler life."

She gave a world-weary sigh. "Simplicity is not very simple, is it? I'm hiding from my family here in search of it. I drive them mad, and vice versa. They know where I am, but cannot get past the gates, and all their letters are automatically returned. I find that very satisfying. Shall we go into the kitchen to see how we may be of assistance? I suppose I can carry platters to the sideboard, such as it is. I believe its origin is a potting bench.

Nicola has laid a table in the conservatory, but I warn you it's rather chilly in there despite the brazier."

Jack had given no thought to where they would eat. He wouldn't have objected to the small scrubbed pine table in the kitchen, but it would be a squeeze for three plus the Christmas bounty. He followed the Countess into the warm room to find Nicola flushed, a tatty apron tied around her dark-red frock. She smiled distractedly, then turned back to stir something on the range.

"Happy Christmas!" he said, trying to sound hearty. In truth, he didn't know how he felt. The Countess had not been part of his mental equation, and lunch was apt to be an awkward affair amongst three strangers, one of them totally silent. "What can I do?"

Nicola pointed to the kitchen table, which was overloaded with plates and serving dishes. Jack scooped up a basket full of rolls and a quivering aspic studded with peas and carrot slivers and brought them to the glass conservatory.

What with the heavy clouds, not much sunlight slanted through the glass roof. The room was frigid indeed—they'd better eat fast. The potting bench had been made over to be a buffet and was covered by what appeared to be a bedsheet. Jack made several trips while the Countess conserved her energy in the kitchen, chatting with Nicola.

A round table was set with much prettier china than Jack had at his cottage. A glass bowl of holly branches served as a centerpiece. He picked up a wine glass and sniffed—not a Moselle but water. But there was an abundance of food—scalloped oysters, ham with raisin sauce, rosemary-sprigged roast potatoes, the afore-mentioned aspic and rolls, green beans, Brussel sprouts, cranberry compote, rice croquettes, cheese, wafers, and a fruitcake which was soaked in so much brandy he imagined the neighbors across the lane could smell it.

Food. Real food. But it would taste better if it was shared between two rather than amongst three, not that he had anything against the Countess. Under other circumstances, she might be very amusing. It was obvious she was sophisticated and had a story to tell.

Nicola entered with the Countess, apron gone, her golden hair a bit flyaway. She pulled her notebook out of her pocket.

All I did was reheat things. Except for the raisin sauce. It is my mother's recipe. Please help yourselves.

"And a magnificent job you've done," Jack said with real appreciation. He hoped he wasn't drooling, piling his plate high with food once the ladies had their turn.

They settled themselves around the delicate bamboo table, and Jack was alarmed when the Countess clasped his wrist just as he was about to spoon a succulent oyster onto his tongue. "We should say grace. Will you do the honors, Jack?"

He was not at all certain God would pay attention to him, but he did the best he could, including a plea for the health and happiness of all the residents of Puddling, native and temporary. Nicola gave him a grateful smile and gave his hand a squeeze. He was being manhandled by both sides, and it was not unpleasant.

He let the Countess rattle on while he shoveled food into his mouth. Each morsel was a delight, even the raisin sauce, and he didn't like raisins much. He presumed the feast had been prepared by their three housekeepers, so evidently they did know how to cook on special occasions. Jack wondered if the Countess was also on short rations. Probably not. By her account, she had come here voluntarily, more to rest than reform.

But then, so had he. Why was he being punished?

And then Jack wanted to slap himself for being ungrateful. He had a roof over his head. Well-tailored clothes on his back. Adequate, if barely edible, sustenance. He was alive, where others were not so fortunate.

"Do you think everything happens for a reason?" he blurted.

The Countess put her fork down. "What an intriguing question. Usually one has imbibed several bottles of wine before such a discussion. And is, perhaps, a decade or so younger." Jack figured the Countess was about his age, and had never had a metaphysical doubt in her pampered life.

What would be the purpose of me losing my voice?

Usually, Nicola's handwriting was elegant, but she had written with a kind of quick fury.

"I don't know. Maybe you are in Puddling to meet, um, the Countess. A friend for life."

"Or someone else altogether," the Countess said, giving Jack an arch look. "Are you asking if there is fate, or some sort of divine plan?"

"I don't know what I'm asking. Just that horrible things happen, and I wonder why."

Are you saying my luncheon is horrible?

This is why Jack liked Nicola so much—she lightened his mood.

"As if I'd be so crass to criticize this ambrosia. Really, it's the best meal I've had since the peaches in your pantry."

"'Peaches in your pantry?' Is that a euphemism I haven't yet heard of?" the Countess inquired, her lips quirking.

Jack could see why she drove her family mad. "No, my lady. We are talking about jarred fruit. In syrup." He turned to his hostess. "I don't like to appear greedy, but might more be on offer this afternoon?"

Nicola smiled and picked up her notebook from the table. *You might be too full.*

"Never. I am like a squirrel storing up nuts for the winter. Or for the next fifteen days, anyhow. Mrs. Feather is determined to starve me."

"Will you be leaving us then?" the Countess asked.

"I think so." Even if nothing changed, he couldn't see himself signing up for another stint of self-denial. "How long have you been a Guest?"

A deep V appeared between the Countess's dark brows. "Hm. I arrived near the end of the July. Or perhaps August. One month is very like the next. I know I was here for the fire."

"What fire?"

"At this very cottage. There was a mishap in the kitchen, and lots of smoke damage. It's all been refurbished, much nicer than my little bolt-hole. And yours too, I expect, Jack."

"You've been here for *months*? How do you stand it?"

"I find it very restful. Soothing. And as I said earlier, I am out of the reach of my grasping family. Wellington and I are quite content. My dog, not the late duke. I find dogs preferable to people at this stage, present company excepted."

I have a dog too. I miss him.

"You should arrange to have him sent here," the Countess said. "Perhaps our dogs can become friends on our daily walks, as we will be."

The implication was that Nicola and the Countess were to be Guests indefinitely. Jack didn't like the sound of that.

"Maybe I should get a dog as well." His mother had not been fond of animals, so he'd grown up petless.

"Only if you have the time and affection."

Jack had plenty of time, and was an absolute reservoir of untapped emotion. Who knew? A dog might be the cure to all his ills.

Chapter 11

The Countess had excused herself with excessive charm before she could be drafted to help clean up. Nicola was not at all annoyed to be left alone with Jack to do the drudge work, and suspected the woman had an ulterior motive to absent herself besides reluctance to get her soft white bejeweled hands wet in soap suds.

Nicola had not missed the Countess's shrewd, speculative glances and teasing repartee throughout the afternoon. No doubt by leaving, she thought she was facilitating an affair between Nicola and Jack.

Nicola had never contemplated having an affair in her life. Her future had been planned out since she was in her teens—an eventual marriage to Richard, a family if they were so blessed, a useful role as her husband's helpmeet on the political trail.

All that was lost to her now, and apart from the children component, she couldn't really say she was too broken up over it.

She had been hurt at first, of course, watching Richard step back inch by inch as she was so slow to recover. It had come as no real surprise when he finally withdrew his offer of marriage. To be truthful, her mother had been more devastated than she was. Nicola had seen his impatience and, yes, indifference long before he had come to her with nervous excuses.

Did things happen for a reason? A train accident resulting in fatalities was a rather dire way to break an engagement and be saved from a conventional existence.

Richard was a boring man, if she was to be honest.

Nicola imagined life with Jack would never be boring. He was so full of ideas and energy. Why, look at him scrub the pots and pans, as if he was trying to rub the enamel and copper off.

She couldn't picture Richard washing dishes for any reason whatsoever. He would consider it all far beneath his dignity, even if he fashioned himself a champion of the working man. Lord knows, Richard had as much dignity as two or three men combined. Always aware of the impression he made, he was close to being humorless and smiled only when it was politically expedient. Nicola couldn't even remember what his teeth looked like.

She mustn't think uncharitably of her former fiancé—it was Christmas, a time for peace and forgiveness. Wonder. And the current man in her kitchen was creating a wonderful impression all by himself.

Jack's sleeves were rolled up, exposing a light dusting of dark hair. One would not think wet bare forearms would be so appealing, but one would be wrong. He had seen at once that the tight fitted sleeves of her best dress were unsuitable for this kitchen task and had plunged right in, chattering away. Complimenting her on the lunch. Ruminating over the exact nature of the Countess's dispute with her relations. Laughing over the undeniable over-soaking of the fruitcake—Nicola felt a little drunk from the two pieces she'd consumed.

Reminding her about the peaches. He must have a bottomless stomach. Nicola was so full she barely had the strength to dry the dishes and put them back in the Welsh dresser. She would send him home with a jar, her Christmas present to him.

"There! I think we're done! Here, hold still." His voice was cheerful, his hand warm from the hot water as he tucked a loose strand of hair behind her ear. She felt her cheeks flame from the contact.

"Thank you again. It was quite the loveliest Christmas I've ever had."

That couldn't be true. Yes, the luncheon was filling, but all the usual trappings of Christmas were missing. There had been no paper hats and crackers, no pile of gaily-wrapped presents, no carols, no fir tree strung with cranberries and popcorn.

She was about to write her shortcomings down when he propelled her out of the kitchen and into her snug little sitting room. And there, in a dented bucket on her piano, was the oddest thing she'd ever seen. A raggedy shrub sported bits of builders' wire and bent nails and loops of paper. Nicola looked at Jack in stupefaction.

"It's meant to be a Christmas tree. Not my best effort, I admit. My resources were limited to what I swept up at the end of the day at Primrose Cottage. And I need to put the bush back into my garden before it dies or they fine me for stealing it. But I thought—" He shrugged. "I know it's a poor substitute for the real thing."

Nicola was so overcome she was stock still, then felt the tears form. She had stopped crying months ago, mostly—it was a worthless endeavor that solved nothing, just stuffed up her nose and made her eyes red. But she couldn't stop the flow now and didn't want to.

Jack had cared enough to bring a bit of Christmas to her, ungainly as it was. She thought back to the presents she'd received this year—the lush fur stole her parents had sent, her older nephew's attempts to draw her terrier, Tippy, who had gone to Scotland with all of them, to her relief, and the shell-covered box Frannie had decorated herself. The tree beat them all.

She opened her mouth to say thank you, but of course no words came out. She would just have to kiss Jack instead.

It was certainly not a difficult task. He stood close, his face a mix of pride, concern, and embarrassment. He was reaching for her face to wipe the tears away, so she kissed his work-roughened palm first. His brown eyes widened as her lips brushed against the web of lines.

Perhaps one's fate was visible on one's hand as the Travelers claimed. Jack had questioned the reason behind life events earlier. Could they be predicted? Avoided? What would a palm-reader say? Was the train accident a sharp branch on Nicola's life line, a detour from a simple straight line that would have led to a normal life?

Such as a marriage to Richard. Her role as a political wife would have had neat boundaries. Expected duty and circumspection and virtue would fence her in, her own opinions unexpressed in the service to her husband's career. No thoughts of women's suffrage or questioning "this is the way we've always done it." Nicola would have come second to his ambition, if that.

That second-place Nicola would not be thinking of kissing a man's hand or imagining what he looked like without his shirt. But that Nicola had disappeared on the way to Bath on a gray March day.

She had no duty to anyone now but herself. She was free to make a mistake if she chose, and would live with the consequences.

Jack had teased her that it had been she who'd made all the advances between them. She would continue to do so. Even if she couldn't speak, the man couldn't miss her signals.

She stood up on tiptoe and cradled his face, his beard as smooth as her new fur stole. He gazed down, tiny wrinkles crinkling at the corner of his dark eyes.

"You like the tree that much, eh?"

She nodded, staring at his lips.

He focused on hers. "You are driving me mad."

I do hope so.

She didn't have to fish her notebook out of her pocket and write it to make her intentions plain. Drawing his face to hers, she licked the seam of his lips, sweeping from one upturned corner to the other. He groaned and opened, and she took control.

She couldn't stand forever on her toes—she was no ballerina. Jack seemed to understand, holding her steady as the kiss took flight. Their tongues glided together in the slowest of dances, circling and swooping as if they had forever.

They almost did. Mrs. Grace wasn't coming back until tomorrow morning, nor was Mrs. Feather returning to Jack's cottage. The nosy neighbors should be preoccupied with their own Christmas festivities. Who was to know that Jack was still here?

Earlier, he had walked the Countess down to the front gate and then to her cottage a few doors away. As it was late afternoon, it was already dark. Maybe no one saw him come back up Honeywell Lane, through the path to Stonecrop, ducking beneath the bare branches. Nicola's cottage was fairly private, set back high from the road by a long stone path through its neat front garden. They weren't in the glass conservatory any longer, and no one could see through the parlor's closed velvet drapes.

The couch was just a few steps behind her. A bed would be an even better place in which to explore the absence of Jack's shirt, though Nicola was not sure she could make it upstairs without stumbling. Her head was spinning, her breath catching, her heart erratic beneath the black-frogged bodice of her best dress. The kiss was a dream, a solemn promise of an unknown journey that she was entirely willing to take.

So it came as a shock when Jack's hands came to her shoulders to set her aside.

Don't stop.

He blinked down at her. "What?"

Had she made another noise? The blood was rushing so loudly in her ears, she couldn't tell.

Don't stop.

Nothing. She stamped her foot in frustration.

"Yes, you spoke! Or sort of spoke. I take it you wish to resume kissing?"

Nicola nodded.

He walked over to the misbegotten Christmas tree and twirled a metal circle. "I don't know if that's wise. We are unchaperoned. The Puddling governors were perfectly correct to invite the Countess to join us to prevent anything untoward. I'm not sure I can be a gentleman."

I don't want you to be a gentleman, you idiot. Perhaps her phrasing was undiplomatic, but it was heartfelt.

He gave her a rueful smile. "You don't know what you are saying. Writing, I mean."

I do too! I am an adult woman, not a child.

"You are not a child, that much is true. You are...so lovely, a man cannot think around you. But someone has to. There are consequences to our actions if we keep kissing. I don't want you to be sorry later."

I won't be sorry.

He shook his head as if she couldn't possibly know her own mind. "You don't know what tomorrow will bring."

Exactly. I could slip on the ice again, roll down Honeywell Lane, and drown in the stream.

"Good God. I hope not. And anyway, I hear the stream has frozen solid. First time in a century, according to Tom. Do you skate?"

Nicola stamped her foot again. *Do not avoid the subject.*

"I'm not sure what the subject is."

Take me to bed, Jack.

One could not be any plainer than that.

Chapter 12

Was she drunk from two pieces of fruitcake? Jack had had three himself, glutton that he was, and couldn't detect any substantial change in his brain. No unusual loss of judgment or flight of fancy.

He wasn't woozy from drink, just kisses. His lips tingled as if he'd been stung by generous and loving bees, a whole hive of them. Every hair on his body was standing alert, and another part of him had stirred in an embarrassingly obvious manner. His eyes functioned so he could read, although he could make no sense of Nicola's blunt and unexpected demand.

Take me to bed, Jack. Five single-syllable words. Easy enough to interpret, yet somehow Jack could not get his mind around them. She couldn't possibly mean it; she must be making one of her jokes.

He had intentions toward Nicola. Honorable ones. Ones that didn't include taking her to bed just yet. He had wanted to court her somehow, if he could figure out how to do it from the freedom of Ashburn. It was closer than London, and he might move unnoticed through the Cotswold countryside. Sneak into Puddling somehow. Even if he wasn't "cured," he couldn't stay in Puddling beyond the requisite twenty-eight days.

Could he?

It was true he was dwelling less and less upon the accident. Keeping busy building Primrose Cottage for the past several days had helped. He was so exhausted after working from dawn to past dusk in the bitter cold that he fell into bed and was sleeping for two or three uninterrupted hours at a stretch, a very welcome alteration to his routine.

The guilt was still there, of course, but not as sharp as it had been. He'd apologized and made generous monetary settlements to all the injured parties and survivors; perhaps that would have to be enough.

He couldn't change the past no matter how much he wanted to.

However, he had some say over the future, and he wasn't going to take advantage of Nicola. He needed to respect himself; it was hard enough to hold his thoughts together as it was. Jack was only beginning to come to terms with what had happened, but if he overstepped—

The nightmares might never cease, and he would earn every one of them. Nicola was vulnerable. Isolated with her disability. It was natural that she would look for affection—she was alone in this odd place, missing her family.

Trouble was, he *had* affection for her, and wanted it to be more. Wanted, to be honest, to have sexual congress with her as much as she appeared to want to with him. One simple kiss told him that, though there was nothing simple about kissing Nicola at all. He'd never experienced the like.

She was a proper young woman, and deserved more than a quick improper tumble. She deserved a better man than Jack. One who was not distracted and lost in panicked dreams half the time. One not crippled by guilt.

Damn it.

"We cannot, Nicola," he said gently.

That foot came down again, along with a flash of anger in her blue eyes. *Why not?*

"Look, I like you very much. More than like, I think. I am honored you like *me* enough to even contemplate such a…" What to call it? "Thing." It was the best he could do.

"Believe me, nothing would suit me more if we came to know each other better. You make me feel, oh, I don't know, more comfortable than I've been in months. I enjoy your company." He touched her lower lip. "I enjoy your kisses."

So what is your objection?

"I'm not a good bargain right at the moment. You must know that, or I wouldn't be here in Puddling."

What had he told her? That something bad had happened. Maybe he should be more explicit.

Jack took a deep breath and a step back. "I am responsible for a railway accident that resulted in the death of two men. Countless injuries as well. I—I haven't been able to sleep much since. I wasn't there, but saw the photographs, the train cars dangling from the bridge. The spilled suitcases. The…the carnage. I can't get the images out of my mind no matter how hard I've tried."

Her face turned as white as the sheet that had covered the potting bench. She dropped the red pencil and it rolled beneath the piano.

What could she write anyway that would make either of them feel better? The horror was written all over her face.

If she'd had any desire for him, it was thoroughly scotched now.

But honesty was the best policy. Or at least that's what the vicar and the doctor tried to drum into him every chance they got. Jack was to face the past head-on, assume ownership, make amends, move on.

It was the moving on part that he was having so much trouble with.

"A foundry I owned cast bridge girders that failed. The flaw in the material was never noticed during construction—I was much too busy doing other things to pay close attention, and the people I placed my trust in were in the end not so trustworthy. They were careless, cut corners, which I would have known if I had supervised the company more closely. It's taught me a hard lesson—one has limited resources in life. Only so much control. Only so much time. I've narrowed my focus, but can't help feeling it's too late sometimes."

Nicola's paleness was alarming. He really should go—he'd said too much already. Honesty might *not* be the best policy in this case, and he was only digging his hole deeper. But he kept rambling.

"So, you see why I can't begin a serious relationship until I sort myself out. I don't think I have the patience to remain in Puddling, but when I'm better—when I don't have this cloud hanging over me—I would very much like to pay my addresses to you. That is, court you. Get to know you better, even if nothing comes of it. I don't care if you don't ever speak another word. I mean, of course I do for your sake, but I like you just as you are."

He was making a terrible mess of this confession, had never felt less articulate in his life. It wasn't quite a marriage proposal—at least he hadn't been entirely ridiculous. Nicola's lips had lost all their color and he was very much afraid she was about to faint. He touched her elbow to guide her to the sofa, and she flinched.

Yes, he definitely should go. So much for courting.

"Never mind me—I don't expect you to understand. I hardly understand myself. Thank you for a lovely Christmas lunch. It's late. Dark. I'll just take my silly tree back, shall I? You don't want something so unsightly spoiling the looks of your parlor."

He'd wanted to make those clever Japanese shapes out of paper for it, but there hadn't been time, not to mention he'd pounded his thumb once too often hanging cupboards in Primrose Cottage and his dexterity was off. Jack wondered who the next poor victim would be to move in and enjoy the fresh scent of new wood and the dubious benefits of the Puddling Rehabilitation Foundation.

All he knew is that he would be leaving once arrangements could be made—perhaps tomorrow or the next day. He couldn't stay in the village and know that Nicola held him in disgust.

He'd never forget the look on her face.

His overcoat hung on a hook in the hall. Shrugging into it, he returned for the tree and found Nicola twisting an uneven metal bow.

"Don't! You'll cut your finger."

She shrugged, as if it didn't matter to her what happened, and continued to bend the wire.

Did she understand? She should be grateful, not offended, for his refusal of her ill-advised offer. She must know that, tempting as she was, he was still clinging to a thread of gentlemanly behavior. When she woke up tomorrow, she'd feel nothing but relief.

He was unreliable, and she needed more.

Jack bent over to pick up the red pencil. Nicola took it and dropped it into her pocket, making no effort to write anything in her notebook.

"Well, I'll be leaving then. Happy Christmas."

She met his gaze. No more tears; that was a good sign. She would soon forget about him, their strange winter interlude an amusing anecdote if she ever felt the need to discuss Puddling with anyone. Jack was sure that she would talk one day, and was sorry her words wouldn't be for him.

He clasped the bucket to his chest and was nearly poked in the eye by a branch. The blasted thing probably would die, being uprooted in the dead of winter. Just another victim of Jack's mad ideas. He really should know better by now.

He'd more or less said good-bye. Why was he still standing here?

"Please don't be angry with me."

Her eyes narrowed, and the pencil and notebook came out of her pocket. *I am not angry.*

"Good. I don't want you to think I'm rejecting *you*, just the situation. You are much better off without me."

You don't like yourself much.

"Why—" He halted before he could argue. He'd never given the idea of liking himself much thought before. One didn't go about thinking of one's good and bad points all the time, at least if one was sober. But it was true that since the accident he'd been much more self-critical, which was only natural, wasn't it?

"I don't *hate* myself," he said finally.

You said you feel guilty.

"Well, of course I do."

How could you have prevented the accident?

An excellent question, one he'd asked himself for nine months. He'd been unable to give an answer.

"I don't know."

Her brow was furrowed as she continued to write. *You can't control everything. You said so yourself. Some would say you can't control anything.* She underlined *anything* twice.

"Are we talking about fate again? For I must tell you, I am a rational man. Usually. Of course, we have control over certain circumstances. Free will. We make choices."

This conversation was becoming suspiciously serious. But if Nicola didn't like him at all, she wouldn't bother writing in her notebook, a look of concentration on her face, her pink tongue protruding a bit from between her lips.

The doctors say there is no physical reason for my silence. Am I just choosing not to talk?

"That doesn't make sense."

None of this makes sense. Some things just...don't.

No truer words were ever written.

Chapter 13

Nicola was surprised she was still standing upright and making "conversation" with Jack. After the shock she'd just received, she should be lying on the sofa with a bottle of smelling salts at the very least.

Heretofore, she'd never given much thought to coincidences. Or kismet, for that matter. But she was in Puddling because of the railway accident, and so, it seemed, was Jack.

She didn't dare tell him—she'd already been enough of a fool inviting him to her bed. He had refused her, as a gentleman of his caliber should. She could blame the liquor-soaked fruitcake for her unseemly offer, but knew in her heart she would have made advances toward him anyhow if she'd never touched a brandied bite. Kissing him had unlocked something within her that she really didn't want to shove back into a dark corner. Nicola felt alive, prickly with desire, ready to cast away twenty-six years of modesty.

However, he was not smitten enough to abandon his principles. Nicola should be grateful, but wasn't. The cloud, as he called it, prevented him from living his life.

Jack felt the accident was his fault, which was ridiculous. He didn't pour the iron into the forms personally. He didn't erect the girders. It's not as if he drove the train over the unsound bridge determined to kill all the passengers.

It was an *accident*. A mistake. People made them all the time. Governments too. The world was a dangerous place, and no one in it was perfect.

How could she help him see that?

She had not once held any one person responsible for the train wreck. How could she? A number of unfortunate events had collided, and she was simply one unlucky bystander. Nicola might have left London a day early or a day later. She didn't blame herself for making the choice she had. There was no point in trying to change history, wondering "what if." It wasn't as though she'd intended the present outcome.

Nor had Jack. He was torturing himself over something he'd ultimately had no control over.

She could write him a letter, if she managed to organize her thoughts. If she spoke, it would be even better. That might be months, or, God forbid, years from now.

Damn. This was so frustrating! She vowed to do all the breathing exercises before bed. To imagine she was at a dinner table asking for the potatoes to be passed. To shout out a warning to a child who chased a ball into the street. To order Tippy not to jump on the gentleman's trousers. Silly scenarios, all, but much of life was made up of the mundane.

Jack still stood in his coat, holding the disastrously decorated shrub. Nicola didn't want him to leave—she should be mortified or embarrassed, but somehow wasn't.

Don't go.

Jack lowered his eyes to the absurd tree. "I cannot...do as you asked. Though I'm very flattered."

Never mind about that. I was stupid to have suggested such a thing, and hope you will forgive me. I treasure our friendship too much to spoil it. I shall play for you and you can relax. She made a great show of striking out the five desperate words she had written, then tore the whole page out for good measure.

"Play?"

My piano. Put that plant down and sit.

Nicola knew she was being bossy, but she wasn't ready to face the evening alone. She crumpled those damning words and tossed the paper into the fire, then spread her skirts on the piano bench. After a few moments, Jack set the bucket back on top of the piano, took off his overcoat, and went to the sofa.

"I've heard you before, when I've been out walking. You have real talent."

Her music had been everything to her since the accident. It was the one thing that proved she was still the same person, not the silent diminished creature that drove people away from her.

She acknowledged his compliment with a shrug and a smile, then set her fingers to the keys. She played from memory, a song she'd learned as a little girl from her first piano teacher. It had a simple refrain, yet she'd added chords and varied the tempo to make it her own. She moved on to another, then another, familiar old favorites that had kept her company for years.

A quick look over her shoulder showed her that Jack's eyes were closed. Perhaps he was asleep, and that was fine. He'd said he had trouble sleeping, and often looked on the edge of exhaustion, so if she could soothe him in any way, she would. They were linked together in their unhappiness.

What would he do if he found out she was a victim of his firm's carelessness? He had an over-keen sense of justice. Would he try to "save" her in some way? He *was* a gentleman.

Would he go so far as to ask her to marry him, to somehow make up for his role in her failure to speak?

Nicola didn't want to be married out of pity or duty. She stumbled over the notes and forgot what came next. Her hands stilled on the keyboard, her brain reeling.

Jack thought she had finished and clapped politely. "That was beautiful. I could listen all evening."

It was black as pitch outside now, the moon covered by clouds. It had been the oddest Christmas Day of her life, yet she would hold it in her heart forever.

He rose from the sofa, looking comfortably rumpled. She had played for more than an hour, losing herself in the music. He had probably been bored to near death.

He leaned over her as she sat frozen on the piano bench. "We are still friends, aren't we?"

Nicola nodded.

"I had thought earlier—well, I wondered if I should leave Puddling, even before my time is up. I would hate to think you hold me in aversion because of what happened. With me refusing your generous offer. And the train accident too."

Idiot man. Did he think she went around inviting men to her bed because she disliked them? But she'd done that before he confessed why he was here. She'd been so stunned she had no idea how what her reaction had looked like or how he'd interpreted it. Nicola had felt faint at his news, had an ominous ringing in her ears, and had seen scattered black spots. She'd almost fallen down to the carpet. But he couldn't see all that inner turmoil.

She'd pricked her finger purposely on a sharp leaf to bring herself back to life, then coiled a bit of wire, arranging her face to be as smooth as an egg. He must not suspect what had caused the cessation of her speech, or his part in it.

Truly, he *had* no part. Her problem was hers alone. But would he see it that way?

She picked up her notebook. *Don't go*, she wrote again.

Don't leave Puddling, she added to clarify. He had to go home to Tulip Cottage at some point. Nicola was worn out from her foray into the kitchen and trying to keep up with the Countess's arch conversation, plus thinking so very hard through the music this past hour. She looked forward to going to bed, even if she would be alone in it.

"I don't know if it's doing me much good. I have two more weeks of it. You've been here over two months—I *cannot* stay that long. I'll go mad. Madder. More mad? I've lost my grammar here." He gave a rueful grin.

You are not mad.

"Thanks for the vote of confidence. And thank you for everything else today. I...hold you in the highest esteem, Nicola. Please remember that." He held his hand out to shake hers.

A handshake? A good-bye kiss would have been much better, but Jack was resisting temptation tonight. She slipped her hand into his and squeezed. She drew him back into the kitchen pantry for the jar of peaches.

His face lit. "You do know the way to a man's heart. I'll have to hide this from Mrs. Feather."

If he was going to get into trouble, she might as well make it worth it. Nicola held up a finger, then began to wrap up a few slices of ham, three leftover rolls, a thick wedge of cheese, and a slice of fruitcake. Tucking everything in a basket she hoped Mrs. Grace wouldn't notice was missing, she handed it off to Jack.

"You are an angel! Now I know what to have when I awaken at midnight. Which I probably will." He sighed.

Her fingers went involuntarily to his cheek. She stroked his beard, wishing she could comfort him somehow.

But he wouldn't let her. Wouldn't engage in an affair that would bring relief to them both. She felt a flare of heat every time she saw him, and his kisses...well, they promised pleasure that she was quite unversed in. Nicola should thank him for guarding the virtue she was so hasty to get rid of, but was still a bit resentful of his superior control.

She had two weeks to seduce him. Redeem him. There were four jars of peaches left on the pantry shelf, and they might come in handy. She would use every resource at her disposal.

Chapter 14

Her fingertips were on his face, soft pads of blissful solace. Jack wished he could invite her to touch him everywhere, but one of them had to be strong. Sensible.

The latter word rarely applied to him. He was frequently off on a wild goose chase, lost in a conundrum, so absorbed in his work an elephant might sit down to take tea with him and he would pass the sugar without noticing.

As she'd played, he'd closed his eyes and imagined himself in a different life, one that was uncomplicated by shadows or disaster. It was an altogether perfect if impossible daydream featuring a scantily clad Nicola and a bottle of French champagne. Perhaps two bottles, to be on the safe side. He moved them to a suite at an exclusive Parisian hotel for good measure, for the anonymity and amorous adventure. Things whispered in French were always more *jolie*, in Jack's experience.

There would be endless hours exploring each other's bodies. He already knew Nicola was finely made, her figure trim. Jack longed to see her golden hair unbound and brushing her bottom. Her blue eyes would widen in marvel as he admired every inch of her with his tongue.

Blast. He could be having an Anglicized version of all this right upstairs in her cottage, minus the champagne. She had invited him, and he'd refused like the honorable fool he was.

Now she knew his reasons for his quasi-celibacy, and her initial shock seemed to have subsided. Apparently, she didn't hate him for it—no one could miss the affection in her touch or the level gaze she gave him.

He captured her hand and kissed her knuckles, one by one. She shivered, and he brought her closer, putting the basket down on the kitchen table so he could hold her. She fit perfectly against him, as she always did. When she was this near, it was as if a calm, warm cloud descended and enfolded them both. He didn't really understand the effect she had on him, but he wasn't looking a gift horse in the mouth.

Not that Nicola was any sort of horse. Her face was delicate perfection, with a short straight nose, no trace of any equine tendencies. She did have a certain sturdiness, though. She was, for want of a better word, plucky. She had to be in order to cope with what she was going through. Nicola wasn't steeped in sadness or self-pity, as he was.

Ah, she was lovely. She'd tucked a sprig of holly in her chignon, and she smelled as fresh as new-fallen snow. He placed his lips on her forehead and wished—

For what, exactly? Time standing still might work. Jack could hold her up against him as long as he wanted and no one would interrupt them. No disapproving Mrs. Grace. No useless sessions with well-meaning vicars and doctors.

In his fantasy, Nicola's silence would simply be the result of total relaxation in his arms. Words were unnecessary when one felt whole like this, superfluous, really. What could a muttered sentence accomplish better than their arms and lips?

It was inevitable that he move from her smooth brow to her pert nose. He gave her a friendly nuzzle, then went lower still. Her lips lay open in wait. She was smiling slightly in anticipation, her eyes closed.

Jack was only kissing her good-bye, as a good friend. A very good friend. That earlier handshake was most inadequate. Anyone could shake hands—as a man in business he was forever pumping someone's paw. But kissing Nicola was special, even if he would limit himself to a kiss.

Limits had their obvious drawbacks. Kissing was fabulous, but Jack wanted so much more. Physical contact would be very welcome. The mythical Parisian hotel suite was becoming real in Jack's mind again, a private place for them to escape, to lie naked amongst satin pillows and fine linen sheets. Nicola's dress would vanish and her soft pale skin would tempt him utterly. He might be so swept away that for once his overactive brain would stop bothering him and he would simply treasure the moment.

Treasure her.

Back in Puddling reality, it was just a kiss. But a long one, designed to tease and torment. Who was in charge of the teasing and tormenting was debatable. Nicola was giving as good as she was getting, and Jack felt the hot flush of lust from his scalp to the base of his spine. She had smoothed herself against him, imprinting her luscious form on his, her fingertips still at his jaw holding him in place.

Jack had no intention of moving away from this delicious agony. How long could one kiss and still remain upright? He didn't think he had the wits to count the seconds, and he counted everything. His traitorous knees longed to collapse and take the rest of him to the stone floor. If they gave out, hopefully Nicola would follow and not hurt herself. He could cushion her fall and continue this bliss. It would be a sin to stop in a search for icepacks or plasters.

But a hard kitchen floor was not the ideal setting for seduction. Jack reminded himself he was not engaged in anything more than a kiss, anyhow; it was the bargain he'd made with his overburdened conscience. He was not going to take an innocent virgin to bed, no matter how tempting her offer. He would just kiss her and kiss her and kiss her.

A score of kisses rippled into each other like the patterns of a kaleidoscope, blossoming into something beyond Jack's comprehension. He was dazzled. Dizzy. Damn his knees and his principles.

Why couldn't he kiss her to give her the ultimate pleasure? Nicola would retain the virtue she was in such a hurry to dispose of, and no harm would be done. He wasn't worthy, but he could let her know how much he valued her friendship.

The basket would have to go before its contents were spilled. He half opened an eye and reached for it.

Nicola noticed his altered position. Unfortunately her hands came down on his shoulders as she drew away. Too far away. No more lovely lips. No more elegantly twisting tongue.

What are you doing? she wrote, panting a bit. *Surely you aren't still hungry.*

"Oh, but I am." Jack tucked the basket beneath the table, and in one swoop placed her on the clean pine surface. She looked alarmed, but he would remedy that shortly.

"I am flattered—honored—that you asked me to be your lover," Jack said, his voice rough. "You know now why that's impossible."

She lifted her eyes to the beamed ceiling and shrugged.

"Allow me to be a gentleman here, resisting your very considerable charms. But I have thought of an alternate activity that should suit you nicely." He gave her what he hoped was a reassuring smile. "You can trust me on this. I promise you will be happy."

She gave him a puzzled look, then nodded.

Was it best to plunge ahead without explanation? No. He would soothe her with well-chosen words. If he could think of some. The activity he had planned would sound odd—shocking—to an innocent, no matter how he couched the description of what was to come.

He pulled a kitchen chair in front of her and sat down. He was now at the perfect level. Maybe he should loosen his tie; he was feeling choked and hot already. For a second he contemplated carrying her upstairs to her bedroom, but he might not be depended upon to behave himself once he got there. It was best to be a little uncomfortable—her enjoyment was paramount.

Jack put his hands on Nicola's knees and looked up into her clear blue eyes. The fabric of her deep red dress was good quality, but it was a nuisance at present.

"Do not be embarrassed, or think what I'm about to do is in any way... strange or unpleasant between two people who care about each other." He put the idea of Nicola doing the same to him firmly out of his mind before he disgraced himself.

"I am going to do something to your body that you might not know about. Don't be afraid. This will not hurt."

The only one apt to be injured was Jack. He hoped Nicola wouldn't kick him in the head when she came.

Chapter 15

Nicola had never sat on top of a kitchen table before. In fact, until she'd come to Puddling, she'd never spent much time in any kitchen. She knew how to manage domestic staff, of course, following her exacting mother's instructions to the letter. Now that Nicola took care of her own evening meal—at least heating it up—she was becoming somewhat proficient in all a kitchen's nooks and crannies, even if she murdered carrots in the peeling. She'd been very proud putting out today's Christmas lunch.

She gazed down at Jack, whose hands had taken ownership of her knees. They were broad, capable-looking, with visible traces of the labor he'd exerted on the new cottage over the past few days.

The expression on his face was peculiar. He said he wasn't going to hurt her. Perhaps he was about to massage her limbs. She'd tried all that in a fancy hydrotherapy spa in Scotland in one of her ill-fated efforts to reclaim her voice. There had been a terrifying Swedish masseuse who had pummeled her into oblivion but still silence. Nicola almost picked up her notebook to write that there wouldn't be any point.

No. It might feel very pleasant having Jack touch her, much nicer than the scary woman who had been so rough. She sat still and waited.

Inch by inch, Jack lifted her skirt, bunching the fabric between his thumb and fingers. Nicola couldn't object—she'd wanted to strip naked earlier. She kept her legs still as the material pooled into her lap. Her petticoats had come along with it, so now her white silk stockings and their ribboned garters were exposed.

"You have beautiful legs."

They worked anyway, now that her ankle had more or less mended. She might even do a cancan, holding up her dress. But without speech, she couldn't joke. Her notebook was quite far away, and anyway, her hands were keeping her upright, making writing impossible.

He slid over the silk, making Nicola want to wiggle out of her shoes. She shut her eyes, focusing on his touch. Back and forth. Up and down. She was simultaneously relaxing and getting rather perturbed. An odd sensation pooled in her belly, and she had an urge to...*do something.*

He spread her knees, and she felt a jolt of concern. He was talking very quietly, almost whispering. She couldn't hear him over the sudden drumbeat in her ears, but could feel his bursts of breath against her bare skin.

She opened her eyes. The top of his head was still, his hair thick and dark, with plenty of natural curl. Nicola could touch it if only her hands would stop gripping the edge of the table. She was afraid if she let go, she'd tumble off in a puddle of sharp need and land on the stone floor. Something was just beyond her ken, but she wasn't at all sure what it was.

He moved forward and kissed her inner thigh, almost causing her to loosen her hold. *Oh my.* He held her flesh between his teeth gently for a few tortuous seconds, then moved up.

And up.

Nicola's mind went perfectly blank. Jack's hot mouth, his tongue, his fingers, were performing an act she had no name for, right at her very core. Oh, one could call it a kind of kiss, she supposed, but it was more. She should be appalled at the wicked sensation and the oh-so-vulnerable position.

That would require organized thought, a skill she was presently lacking.

His tongue was sweeping inside her with both force and delicacy, his hands parting her folds to make her open to his ministrations. She felt herself thrusting, blooming toward him, wanting that elusive thing she had sensed that was approaching all too slowly.

Jack knew what she needed and where to seek it. The stuttering ripples made their way into her blood, causing even her scalp to tingle. He tugged and teased her inner flesh with his lips, using his gentle fingers to stroke a path to her rising pleasure.

And then he kissed and pressed a place that resulted in her sharp cry. It was too much. Hot bursts shot through her body, one after another, like a dazzling meteor shower.

He stopped at once.

No! But the word was trapped on her useless tongue and came out as a ragged moan.

"Nicola, my darling! Did you hear yourself?"

She nodded, frantic. She'd heard, but that was not the sense she cared about at present. Now was not the time to begin a conversation. She grabbed his face, trying to make him return to his earlier task. She wanted more. Wanted more of whatever this was.

Wanted it *right now.*

"So, I can assume you like this, yes?" He gave her a rakish grin.

Shut up and finish. She was shaking too much to write it down, but surely he could read her mind. He had read her body so well.

"All right, all right. Greedy puss." He buried himself between her legs and continued his assault on her wits and womanhood. The meteor showers returned behind her eyelids, light and heat coursed through her limbs.

He was wrong—this *was* hurting. Her legs stiffened in exquisite pain, her spine arching. She was going to break apart and fall from a very high distance, too high for a spinster from Bath.

Just when she thought she couldn't bear anymore of his touches, she was tossed to heaven. Jack caught her as she came back to earth, leaping up from his chair to hold her in a fierce embrace. Tears streamed down her cheeks, but she wanted to laugh.

And did.

She was stunned to silence again by the sound.

Jack squeezed her tighter. "Listen to yourself, you beautiful girl. You've made the most glorious sound in the world."

But that single short moment of laughter was all she could manage. No further noises spilled out as she clung to her lover. She had a lover! That went a long way in making up for the fact she was still mute.

But not half so miserable as she used to be. Her body was alive—on fire!— and her mind might eventually follow to some semblance of coherence.

Jack took a handkerchief from his pocket and wiped her face with tenderness. "Are you all right?"

She rolled her eyes to the ceiling beam overhead. He must know the answer to that. She cuffed him on the shoulder.

"Yes, I know. It's sad. I want compliments. Confirmation. One cannot help it if one is a man. We are very sensitive beneath all our bluff and bluster and need constant assurances of our proficiency."

He'd been proficient all right. Nicola drew his face down for a kiss, then flushed at the memory of where those lips had been. She'd been so very ignorant, but Jack was an accomplished teacher of what she would have deemed to be impossible. Unthinkable.

Well, obviously someone had thought of it, but had never told her. This wanton activity certainly had not been included in all her mother's subtle discussions about courtship and the eventual marriage bed when she was engaged to Richard.

Where had Jack learned to do such a thing? She decided she never wanted to know, discovering a possessive, jealous streak that had heretofore been absent. As far as she was concerned, she never wanted him to kiss another woman like that ever.

Nicola hadn't the right to place such restrictions upon him. In a couple of weeks, he'd be gone from Puddling and out of her life. Her eyes filled again, and his handsome face blurred.

"What? No tears, sweetheart. I want to hear you laugh again. And kiss you."

There was such comfort in his voice. In his presence. Nicola felt safe in his arms, treasured, despite the fact he posed a very real danger to her heart.

She was falling in love with him. Hell, she'd already fallen.

And was making a great mess, weeping into his jacket. She'd known Jack all of twelve days. She'd known Richard over twelve *years* and he'd never made her cry, not even when he broke their engagement.

Jack wasn't making her cry—her own frustration and confusion was. Nicola needed to pull herself together, retain her senses. She was known for being level-headed.

And perhaps a little prim.

She didn't feel at all prim now. Looking up into Jack's concerned face, she kissed him with every pent-up emotion she had, every blocked word, every year of useless innocence. She tasted wickedness and want and hope.

The kiss lasted as long as she could make it do so. But eventually she realized she was sliding off the kitchen table to her doom. He caught her and settled her, his hands firm against her suddenly much-too-tight corset, stepping back, his lips reddened.

"I've got to go home. To Tulip, I mean. If I stay any longer, I'll forget why I shouldn't."

Nicola didn't want him to go, but knew he was right.

For now.

Chapter 16

December 26, 1882

Boxing Day. If Jack had been in either of his houses, he'd be doling out gifts to tradesmen and servants. His secretary, Ezra Clarke, was taking care of all that for him this year. He'd had the opportunity to think ahead and write a great many instructions when Nicola passed his secret missives on.

Where was Nicola's Christmas present? The real one he'd tasked Clarke to obtain, not the misshapen bush that had been forgotten after their amazing encounter on the kitchen table.

Ha. A kitchen table. Jack was losing his finesse. He'd been accused of many things by women, being a distractable sort of fellow, but inattention to a lady's pleasure and comfort had never been one of them until recently.

It had been a reckless thing to take her as he'd done, but he couldn't regret it. He'd heard Nicola laugh. The sound had been pure joy, better than the beautiful music that flowed from her elegant fingers.

She was altogether a remarkable woman, which is why he had to be careful. Take things slowly. He was as fractured as could be, still sleepless, still weighted down with misery, even after last night. Perhaps more so, for he'd taken advantage of Nicola's hospitality in the most brazen way. Jack might not feel regret, but some shame had woken up with him this morning.

Nothing more could come of their relationship, at least for the immediate future. He needed to shape himself up, get whole, although how he was going to do that remained to be seen after so damn many months of inertia. Jack was stuck in a deep groove, treading over familiar territory day after day and night after night. He was boring himself witless waiting for the hopeless tangle to give inside him.

His elusive cure surely wasn't accomplished after the nice old vicar's visit early this morning. True, Reverend Fitzmartin was a calming, sympathetic presence—one got the feeling he'd seen a lot in his many years serving the Lord all over Great Britain, and did not sit in towering judgment. He was a recent arrival to Puddling, but seemed well-versed in its philosophy and gentle perseverance.

Maybe that was part of Jack's problem. Everyone had been so forgiving—his mother, his solicitors, even the victims who had been so overcome after his generosity that they wept onto his shoulder and thanked him. Thanked him! For upending their lives and livelihoods. For putting them in peril. Even the families of the two dead men accepted their fate and were grateful for the remuneration.

No one seemed to understand. Jack needed to be…punished for his carelessness. Indifference. Maybe he should investigate to see if hair shirts were still available for purchase. Scourging implements.

Perhaps he should simply ask one of the cottage work crew to hit him on the head with a hammer and be done with it.

He pictured old Fitzmartin clubbing him with a Bible. Jack hoped the fellow couldn't divine what he and Nicola had been up to last night. He didn't care for himself, but her reputation would be compromised. As much as he would love to make her his wife…

Wait. What? He was contemplating marriage seriously for the first time in his life. In his bumbling fashion, he'd requested her permission to court her yesterday once Puddling was behind him. But—

Ah. The big *but*. A three-letter word that had more power than one much longer and more syllabic.

Jack shook his head free of cobwebs. He knew better than to dally with an innocent woman. Last night had been more than fun, but neither of them was ready for more. It would be the height of folly to believe all their problems would disappear with a wedding vow that Nicola couldn't even utter.

Marriage was for life, and he'd known her less than two weeks. Thirteen days, to be specific, and during some of those they'd had no contact whatsoever, even if she was never far from his mind.

His lost mind, apparently. Could he be getting worse the longer he stayed here?

If he left, he wouldn't see Nicola.

That seemed a dreadful fate. In fact, he should go see her right now. Apologize for last night. Not that he was sorry—he'd have to be careful choosing his words. She might assume he hadn't enjoyed himself. Hadn't treasured her gift to him.

He had treasured it sufficiently to be able to conjure up the scent and taste of her all through the night, which was a kind of scourging in itself. It was unlikely the opportunity would present itself to repeat such a performance. His senses had been so overwhelmed when he got home, he hadn't even made a foray into the basket she'd packed for him. Jack had hidden it in his room and hoped Mrs. Feather didn't find it in her usual cleaning frenzy.

Guests were monitored during the day, their every movement noted by prying Puddling eyes. The most innocent of activities were duly noted and reported to the doctor, the vicar, Mrs. Grace, or Mrs. Feather. It was too damned cold to reenact their "chance" meeting in the graveyard.

But the rules had been relaxed for Christmas dinner. Perhaps they could find a way around them again. People went to bed early in Puddling. The five lanes were pitch-black at night, no signs of lamps or candles flickering behind the curtains. It was exhausting work being vigilant against Guest transgressions all day, he supposed.

Jack himself had a ten o'clock curfew and was diligent about extinguishing the lights, even if he was wide awake. Which was most nights. He wished his mind had an "off" switch, but so far one had not been invented. Certainly, liquor and ladies and hashish had been utter failures to cool and quell his scattered thoughts before he checked into Puddling. He'd indulged in none of them in too hedonistic a manner; he'd never been one to abuse good sense. If he couldn't think clearly, he couldn't work. Those ice boots were the first good idea he'd had since the accident.

He checked his pocket watch. The crew had been given the day off from working on the new cottage, so the empty hours stretched before him. His soul had already been poked at and found somewhat wanting by Mr. Fitzmartin. Mrs. Feather had disappeared down the ladder into the earthen-floored cellar, and Jack couldn't imagine what the woman was doing. He'd explored the space himself when he first arrived, its shelves empty of canned goods, very few respectable spiders thriving in such Spartan surroundings.

Jack felt like those empty shelves. What did he have to offer Nicola besides a few moments of delightful dalliance? She deserved more, from someone who was not as hampered as he was.

Bah. The day was overcast, but some fresh air would be better than the close atmosphere of his little cottage. If he happened to stop in at Nicola's, what was the harm? He had to put that damned bush back in the ground if it wasn't dead already, and he wanted to, if not apologize, assure her that the evening had very special meaning for him.

He dressed for the outdoors, then shouted down the open trap door that he was going out. Mrs. Feather mumbled up something back, and he left to climb up the lane to Nicola's.

The sky was leaden, promising more snow. Jack wondered how his mother was faring in Menton. If the Riviera resort town was good enough for Queen Victoria and her entourage as a respite from winter, there was a chance his mother would find it adequate.

He tried to picture his black-clad mama relaxing amongst the palm trees and blue Mediterranean and failed. She took her widowhood nearly as seriously as the monarch, for entirely different reasons. Lady Ryder knew she looked her best in mourning clothes, the more expensive the better. At fifty, her skin was as white and unwrinkled as porcelain, her dark hair only slightly threaded with silver. She was a beautiful woman, even if her tongue was a touch too sharp.

Jack loved his mother…at a distance. He knew she meant well, even if her methods were not always on the up and up. It was a great relief to be in Puddling beyond her reach. No sanctioned communication, no visits, hence no lectures.

What would she think of Nicola? Jack wasn't ready to find out.

He ambled up the slope, mindful of the icy patches. He had half a mind to write to the Puddling governors complaining about his and Nicola's safety. The Countess and her dog too, presumably. Since they were meant to walk and walk and walk every day, it was a wonder none of them had broken a leg or worse.

Perhaps he should be thankful for the poor condition of the lanes. That was how he met Nicola, wasn't it? In a lovely heap on the cobblestones. Bring on the bad weather! Maybe he'd be trapped with her at Stonecrop Cottage in a sudden blizzard. In his delightful imaginary scenario, Mrs. Grace would have to have left for the day, else it would be no fun. There would be plenty of food and frolic on tap, and he could resume his unconventional courtship.

Jack smiled at his foolishness. The entire village would be drafted to dig them out of hibernation posthaste—there would be no opportunity for any more seduction.

He straightened his plaid scarf and rapped on the door, hoping he wouldn't be turned away.

He was greeted, if you could call it that, by Mrs. Grace. She gave him a look which could have frozen fire.

"You have taken Miss Nicola's peaches."

He had, and they were hidden in a trunk at the end of his bed underneath a faded quilted coverlet.

If that's what she meant. Perhaps the word peaches had a hidden meaning for her, just as the Countess suspected.

Jack wasn't going to admit to anything.

"I beg your pardon?"

"Don't play innocent with me, my lord. Miss Nicola told me she gave you some, as well as packed up a basket. I keep an eagle-eye on my pantry. It's one thing to celebrate Christmas, quite another to stray from the Puddling diet the day after."

"I ate them last night," Jack fibbed. "Ate everything. Down to the last crumb." All he needed was Mrs. Grace to get Mrs. Feather to search his belongings. He was looking forward to a ham sandwich later.

She waggled a finger at him. "No more infractions. You still have two weeks left, and you wouldn't want to be booted out."

Wouldn't he? All right, he wouldn't. The thought of not seeing Nicola sliced his heart in two.

Chapter 17

Jack was here! Nicola felt her skin heat with embarrassment.

And lust. She hadn't really counted on him to turn up today, giving her more time to process what had occurred last night.

She was a fallen woman.

Or at least a stumbling, tripping one, perhaps not flat on her back, but close to. She had been very tempted to write to Frannie last night, but by the time the letter reached Scotland, her sister might be on her way home.

And what could she say? Does Albert ever lift up your nightgown and kiss you *down there*?

Nicola really didn't want to know. The thought of dull if dependable Albert doing such a thing to Frannie—or anyone—golly, her cheeks became hotter by the second. She'd never be able to look at her brother-in-law the same way again. All the men of her acquaintance would have to be avoided for eternity until she could get her mind around it all.

She smoothed the layers of her skirt and tried to seem engaged in the tiny bootie she was massacring. Some poor infant's ankles would chafe at the lumps and bumps. She really was no knitter. She pulled at a thread and a row dissolved.

Just exactly what was she good at, besides her musical ability?

Getting slowly seduced, apparently.

"Mr. Jack, miss," Mrs. Grace said, with very little grace at all.

Nicola looked up from the wooly mess. Should she smile? She wasn't sure she could make her face work right—her lips felt nearly numb.

"Good morning, Miss Nicola."

He sounded ordinary, if formal. *His* heart was probably not pounding wildly in his chest, nor were his hands shaking. She put the needles down before she impaled herself and bloodied the misshapen bootie. His ridiculous tree sat where they had left it on the piano. She pointed to it and lifted an eyebrow.

"Yes, exactly. I've come for my bush, but I wouldn't say no to a cup of tea. With no sugar, of course, Mrs. Grace. I wouldn't want to get giddy and forget those important rules."

He was trying to charm the housekeeper, a hopeless task. But he was charming Nicola, and she couldn't quite see where it would all lead. She'd lain awake for hours contemplating the consequences of their actions. So far, she hadn't been struck dead for her depravity, which was a good sign, she supposed. Maybe the Almighty had taken the day off for His son's birth.

Her thoughts were becoming sacrilegious. What on earth was happening to her? She could blame Jack, but was afraid her own virtue was rapidly unravelling like the bootie in her lap.

"Do you have your little notebook?" Jack asked, his tone a touch less jaunty. She nodded.

"Are you all right? Have you anything you want to say to me? I am here to be flayed alive if you think it necessary." His voice was barely above a whisper now.

Nicola found her book under a tangled skein of yarn. *Don't be silly. I am fine. And you?* Her hands were almost steady.

A look of relief washed over his face. "I am well, thank you. No, um, regrets?"

For what?

"You *are* torturing me. I just wanted to tell you that this Christmas was...special. The best one of my life, if you want to know the truth. And I thank you from the bottom of my black heart for, um, for..."

Stop now. Mrs. Grace's hearing is excellent.

His hand covered hers. "You don't want to talk about it? I mean to make it right, Nicola."

And how would he do that?

She loosened her hand from his. *It wasn't wrong.*

There. She was as wicked as she dared to be. She didn't write that she hoped it would happen again. That somehow they'd get the chance before he left.

Yes, she was entirely unraveled, down to the hollow core in a ball of yarn.

The rattle of the tea tray brought her back to reality. She sipped and chewed and hung on Jack's every word. She wondered if he always talked so much between battling back his yawns, or whether her silence was the reason that he filled the void. She thought he'd had as sleepless a night as she had.

Nicola was getting to know a lot about him. Only child, unhappy parents. Too clever for his own good. Attended a slew of schools where his talents brought him more punishment than accolades. Didn't finish university because he bought his first company with his own capital, investing his pocket money since the age of twelve with the help of a sympathetic uncle. Jack had glossed over any romantic entanglements, for which she was grateful.

Being a woman, she'd achieved considerably less so far. Wasn't expected to invent anything more compelling than a dinner menu. The American poet William Ross Wallace might have posited that "the hand that rocks the cradle is the hand that rules the world," but Nicola wasn't convinced.

She didn't want to rule the world, just make some positive contribution. If she had no children, as so many women didn't, did that mean her life was meaningless? She cast her eye on the baby bootie in disgust, seeing every uneven stitch. No innocent infant should be forced to wear it.

"I'm glad you feel that way. I confess my conscience has bothered me more than a little. I—I value our friendship."

Nicola felt friendship wasn't the right term, but let it go. She nodded, wondering if her neck would ache at the end of the day for being agreeable. She was so tired of her limitations, and the more she pressed herself, the quieter she became. Jack seemed to be the key to her talking so far, but she couldn't burden him and make him stay.

"What are your plans for today? I'll be back to working on the new cottage tomorrow, but perhaps we can go for a walk together."

Yes. Let me change my clothes.

That meant woolen stockings and a woolen petticoat. She climbed the narrow stairs to her tidy bedroom. She was as tired of her wardrobe as her life—her mother had helped her pack for a month only. Somehow a month had turned to more, almost three now, and she was not much closer to a cure than when she arrived.

Nicola knew she could ask her mother to send additional items of clothing, but that seemed like an admission that she'd given up. She couldn't stay here forever, but where would she go?

Goodness, she was blue-deviled. Jack had made every effort to be cheerful over tea, to behave as if last night had not happened.

But it had, and Nicola didn't know what to do about it. She certainly wasn't sorry, but what lay ahead for her?

It didn't take her long to dress for the weather, and soon she was arm in arm with Jack, navigating the slippery streets. They had just passed the Stanchfields' store when Mrs. Stanchfield braved the elements to call after them, wearing only an apron over her neat navy dress.

"Miss Nicola, there is a package for you, just come from Stroud on the mail coach. A Christmas present, I'll wager. Better late than never."

Nicola had already received and opened gifts from her family—the Mayfields were a punctilious bunch.

"Aha!" Jack whispered, a grin splitting his face.

Hm. A mystery that Jack knew about. Nicola recollected the bulky forbidden letters she's included in her missive home. He'd been up to something.

Mrs. Stanchfield handed over the paper-wrapped parcel. It wasn't especially heavy or large, and felt like…books?

Jack didn't know her taste in reading. It was always iffy to buy people books. One never knew if one's friend had read them already or would never read them unless they were trapped alone on a desert island without absolutely anything else to do.

He snatched it away from her outside the shop and tucked it under his arm. "Something inside is mine. We're going to have such fun!" He came to an abrupt stop. "You do know how to spell, don't you?"

She gave him a glare. Of course, she knew how to spell! She'd had an excellent governess, and had attended a prestigious young ladies' seminary in Bath.

"Don't give me such a withering look. I've been known to mix up the orders of my i's and e's, and I'm perfectly bright. Accurate spelling isn't a guarantee of intelligence, nor does inaccurate spelling make one stupid. Why, I once went to school with a fellow who wrote his letters backwards, and he was much smarter than I was. He has a good secretary now who cleans up his mistakes and you'd never know how much time he'd spent in the headmaster's study getting his knuckles rapped with the thickest ruler money could buy. I say! I should start a school for pupils like him! Remind me to write that down somewhere when we get home."

As if one could start a school just like that. But perhaps Jack could. He evidently had the funds and the enthusiasm for almost anything.

Nicola wondered about the present, though Jack was insistent that they took their numerous daily turns around the five rambling lanes. They finally stopped in front of the new cottage—Primrose—and Jack pulled out a key from his pocket.

"See, they're trusting me, more fools they. Would you like to see Puddling's latest prison cell?"

Detached from its neighbors, it stood close to the road, with a tiny side garden. There was a bare wooden fence and gate, and a short path to the back door. Building debris had been tossed everywhere, and Nicola minded her steps.

"The front door's going to be yellow, of course. They'll paint if it ever gets warmer. Mine, Heaven help me, is red, and I understand in the spring there are red tulips everywhere, which thank God I'll never see. Great attention to detail, these Puddlingites. Isn't stonecrop green? You have a blue door. Someone made a mistake."

Not true. There had been creeping blue sedum—another word for stonecrop—with touches of pink all over the nooks and crannies of the garden when Nicola had arrived in October. They were buried by snow now, however.

They entered what was to be the cottage's kitchen, which boasted a large soapstone sink under a window, a row of cabinets, and nothing else. It wasn't hampered by the usual Puddling low ceilings and lintels, and felt colder inside than out. Shiny rust-red tiles ran the length of it, and paved the hallway to front door. An open trap door in the floor led to a substantial drop to a dirt cellar.

"They're sending me down there to make shelves tomorrow. Apparently they think I can wield a saw without cutting off an arm. I do hope they're right. Now, let's go into the parlor and sit in one of the window ledges and open up this package before we get discovered and thrown out."

It was true—they had very little time alone unless they were out walking. With the distinctive exception of last night, Nicola thought, her blushes rising. It was nice to know no housekeeper was hovering in an adjacent room, no villager ready to report them.

The empty parlor featured a large brick fireplace, absent a mantel, and a freshly sanded floor. The sharp odor of wood shaving was pleasing, and Nicola took a deep breath. Beneath each window was a seat large enough for two to examine whatever came to hand in comfort.

No, not comfort. Jack was very close to her, too close, his breath a warm cloud in the frigid cottage. Nicola could smell his cologne and admire his eyelashes. She was forgetting why she was there, until Jack thrust the package into her hands.

Chapter 18

Jack felt a palpable frisson of excitement. He loved learning new things. Even if he never met another mute or deaf person in his life to test his skills, he would share this with Nicola.

"The botany book is mine. I decided I needed the diversion. Unless you want to read it first. But this is for you. Us. Here!" He handed her the large stiff illustrated card.

"It's the British Manual Alphabet," Jack explained to Nicola, who puzzled over the sturdy cardboard between her gloved hands. "Fingerspelling. Writing in the air, as it were, instead of your notebook." He thumbed through the accompanying slender book his secretary had sent.

"According to this monograph, some form of sign language has been in use for hundreds and hundreds of years. Isn't this interesting? One used to have to point to a body part that began with the chosen letter, b for brow, etcetera. Where would one point for zed, I wonder? There are various alphabets listed in here, but we'll concentrate on British. The Americans use something altogether different. Just like them, always rebellious."

Nicola studied the card, which had illustrations of two hands in various positions. She pulled out her notebook from her coat pocket. *I feel slightly overwhelmed.*

"Don't worry. We won't have time to learn sign language and all its nuances, but I thought it might be amusing if we had a secret code. Something to thwart our minders whose ears are always pressed at the door."

Nicola rolled her lovely blue eyes.

"What, you don't think I can learn this? There's an American university dedicated solely to educating the deaf and mute. I assure you I am as good as any American student, even if I left Oxford early. To prove it, I'll take a vow of silence with you. Starting, um, tomorrow. We'll communicate solely with our hands." A very provocative thought flitted across his mind, and he shoved it away. This was serious business.

Jack hoped he was not biting off more than he could chew. It would be a hardship not speaking, but Nicola had been so afflicted for months. Could he learn all the hand signals by tomorrow evening? Much of the next day would be devoted to work here in this cottage. But he'd never needed much sleep—which was a good thing, since he got so little of it now what with his nightmares.

Nicola shook her head. *You overestimate me. I will need more time to study.*

Relief swept over him. He was usually a fast learner, though a day or two more would be welcome.

"All right. It's Tuesday. I'll be busy here every day until Friday from dawn to dusk. Shall we say Saturday to meet and test out our new skills? I'll come for afternoon tea." The next-to-last day of the month. Sunday night would be New Year's Eve, and Jack wondered how Nicola intended to ring in 1883.

It might be fun to be silent, relying upon fingers and facial expressions. Lips too—wasn't it tradition to share a New Year's kiss at midnight?

Jack was getting ahead of himself. If he truly wasn't going to speak when he saw her, he should make his plans now just so he could be clear.

"I am giving a New Year's Eve party," he said with sudden decision. "Will you come?"

Is the Countess going to be there?

"Not if I can help it. It will be a private celebration. Just you and me. Do you dare to venture out and join me?"

Nicola bit a lip. *What if someone sees me?*

Puddling's streets rolled up awfully early, but New Year's Eve might be different. Did the villagers entertain each other? Jack tried to imagine mousy Mrs. Feather dressed in faux diamonds blowing a horn and failed.

The parish hall was a possible party venue, but the ancient Fitzmartins probably went to bed when the sun set. Most of the cottages were all too small for any sort of expanded festivity, and the Sykes estate would likely be off limits due to the newlyweds' reluctance to share their space with anyone. He'd seen Tristan Sykes and his red-headed bride in the bake shop the day before Christmas, but they had been so wrapped up in each other that they hadn't noticed him. Jack hadn't been anxious to listen to another lecture anyway.

He was going to defy the governors every chance he got, no matter who tried to talk him out of it.

"We can practice. Do reconnaissance as it were. I'll sneak out tomorrow night and observe any activity. Barking dogs, sleepwalking grandmothers, any peculiar nocturnal doings, and report to you at midnight on the dot."

Nicola's expression told him she knew where his real interests lay.

"I swear I will not lay a finger on you until you ask me to." He was fairly certain she might, hopefully tomorrow evening.

What if you get caught?

"What can they do? Put me on a diet of bread and water? It's just about that already."

They can send you away.

She looked properly disturbed at that. Excellent.

"I have some experience sneaking around at night. I was an adolescent boy once, you know. I'll be careful. Then you can try on Thursday. By New Year's Eve, we'll both be experts."

Aren't we supposed to be asleep at that hour?

"I'm usually up." It suddenly occurred to him that Nicola probably wasn't. There were no shadows under *her* eyes. "But I wouldn't want to disturb you."

No, it's all right. Two nights won't kill me. I can sleep in as long as I wish.

Ha. Of course. While he was getting dragged out of bed before the cock crowed, Nicola was snuggled under the covers. How different her Puddling experience was from his. Better rest, better food—and he liked to think he was enhancing her stay in some way too.

If Jack had his druthers, he would see her for more than two evenings. Why hadn't the idea come to him earlier? They could have had more unfettered time together if they had been meeting in secret.

But it wasn't until last night—until the taste and touch and scent of her imprinted itself on his mind—that it seemed so necessary to see her.

Not to take her virginity, however. That would best be left to within the bonds of matrimony. If he could straighten out, be *normal*—

Once again, he was getting ahead of himself. Surely he could give her pleasure, though, and derive his own from her artless responses.

"We are in agreement then. Tomorrow night I'll tiptoe to Stonecrop Cottage. Leave the door open for me."

Nicola blushed. Jack could watch that pink tint wash over her cheeks for hours. She was like the subject of a watercolor painting, muted with her fair hair and light eyes, yet unexpectedly compelling.

Enough. Would she notice he was getting aroused? He folded his own instruction card and slid it into his pocket. Then he rewrapped the monograph and hers in the brown paper, and put his botany book inside his coat so it couldn't be confiscated. It was, after all, contraband, although he would have preferred some Principe de Gales cigars and a pint of brandy.

"Don't let Mrs. Grace see this, or the jig will be up. Can you find a good hiding place?"

I think so. Until recently, Mrs. Grace left my things undisturbed. But lately—

She looked up at him with those trusting blue eyes, then returned to her notebook. *I think she suspects there is something between us.*

"She's right, I hope," Jack said, his voice a touch gravelly. "But you must throw her off the scent. Stick your tongue out when my name is mentioned and gag. Pretend you don't want her to let me in for tea. And hide your notebook too." He imagined Nicola tucking the little notebook into her corset near her heart and just about expired from desire.

A part of him wanted to declare himself, but he felt foolish. And unworthy. Despite his material advantages, he had little to offer a wife but his miasma of depression.

Funny, though, when he was with Nicola, his mood was instantly lifted. She acted like a tonic to him.

According to the vicar and the doctor, all change came from within. His demons were still there, waiting with their sharpened talons to be wrestled. No matter how sweet and sincere Nicola was, Jack couldn't depend upon her for his cure.

He had fourteen days left—he was at the precise halfway mark. It was inconceivable to him that he'd known Nicola a mere two weeks. Less, really, for he'd met her on his second day. His feelings were too intense for so short a time, but he couldn't help how he felt.

Maybe it was another sure sign that he was unbalanced.

Blast it. He'd never been one to dwell over mistakes—in his experience, they always led to greater opportunity.

None had resulted in death before, however.

He felt a tapping on his arm. *What is wrong?*

How long had he been sitting here in the cold, lost in thought? Wasting his precious time alone with Nicola? What the devil was wrong with him, and would it ever, ever go away?

"Sorry." He was going from euphoria to dismal reality.

What if she never regained her voice? What if he was stuck reliving the train tragedy at the least opportune times? Maybe he'd have been better off if he'd never come here and met her.

Chapter 19

December 27, 1882

Nicola yawned. Her book had ceased to hold her attention about an hour ago. All the words had clumped together, and she wondered if she needed spectacles. Her corset was killing her as well, forcing her to sit upright in her chair with no hope of relaxation. It had been tempting to greet Jack—if he did indeed come—in her dressing gown, but that way led to madness. She didn't trust herself, and wasn't sure she could trust Jack either. Not that she expected him to repeat the delights of Christmas night, but for all his swearing to be entirely honorable, she doubted she would let him be if she got the chance.

She had a secret seduction weapon: peaches.

The glass dish and its contents glistened in the low lamplight. She'd helped herself to one juicy slice and could see why Jack had consumed them so rapidly in the pantry that day. Mrs. Grace was an excellent cook, who had confided to Nicola that she usually did not get to show off her skills for the average Puddling Guest. Most Guests were forbidden to find any enjoyment of a sensual nature, which seemed very harsh.

The goal was moderation in all things. For Jack, that had resulted in a kind of anxious boredom. Nicola thought the nature of routine lent itself to Jack dwelling too much on the train accident. He needed stimulation, a goal to get lost in. He had too much time on his idle hands.

Well, she supposed his hands were not precisely idle at the moment, at least during daylight. Her walk had taken her by Primrose Cottage earlier. The sound of hammering and hollering had been almost deafening, and the aroma of varnish had been strong. None of the workmen were visible, so busy were they inside like a colony of ants completing the cottage. A new "victim," as Jack termed him, was due a week or two into the New Year.

Or the new Guest might be a lady, someone she might befriend. The Countess was lovely, but she and Nicola had little in common. The woman was so innately grand that she was a trifle fearful of her.

She was beautiful too. Nicola was not a jealous sort of person, and even wondered if that sort of regal beauty might be a curse. Despite her quick wit and attempts at frivolity, the Countess clearly wasn't happy.

Nicola stole a glance at the clock. Five minutes after twelve. Jack was late. Had he been caught? Or worse, tripped on the ice? She pictured him flat on his back in the dark, injured or unconscious. There was blood—

The image was so real it made her shiver. Nicola had never been fanciful, believed in dreams or second sight or premonitions, but her own blood ran cold.

If he didn't arrive in ten or so minutes, she was determined to put on her boots and go out looking for him. Perhaps he'd only fallen asleep in his chair as she would have done were she not encased in steel.

The creak of the front door gave her enormous relief.

"Nicola," he whispered.

Right here, she wanted to say. Instead, she rose and met him in the front hall. He was dressed in dark tweeds as if he were attending an elegant country shooting party. A black knit scarf concealed half his face. Nicola was grateful she was wearing her second-best dress, because he looked very fine.

He unwrapped the scarf and bowed with dramatic flourish. "Lor—uh, Jack at your service, milady, come to report."

She tugged him into the parlor by a sleeve. Sit, she mouthed.

Jack did as he was told, stretching his long legs out in front of the fire that Nicola had nursed throughout the evening. She'd drawn the curtains for their privacy.

"I say, this is very cozy after a wretched day in the salt mine. What a time I had—well, I don't want to bore you, but I shall never make a carpenter." His eyes lit. "Can those be peaches?"

She grinned and nodded.

"I'll only eat them if we share."

The fruit disappeared in no time, Nicola eating rather fewer spoonfuls than her guest. Jack ate with greedy enjoyment, his eyes half-closed, a beatific smile on his face. When he had scraped up all the available juices, he licked his lips and Nicola felt a certain twinge.

His kiss would taste of peaches. Did she dare rise up and sample?

No. No and a thousand times no. Every lesson her mother had ever taught her about dealing with men came rushing over. A lady did not make the first move, though she'd broken that rule more times than she cared to count already. Jack was a charming, tempting, very bad influence, and she had to hold herself aloof.

If she could.

"Thank you. You are a veritable goddess for feeding me. I'm so hungry I've stopped being hungry. Does that make sense? Of course, it doesn't. Now, for my evening adventure. Though I must warn you, it wasn't very exciting, which is all to the good for our purposes."

He loosened his necktie. Seeing him here at her hearth, casual and smiling, made her heart flutter. Oh, self-control was hopeless. Trying to focus, she pinched the skin at the base of her thumb. It wasn't painful enough to make her stop thinking of Jack's wicked kisses. She might have to resort to stabbing herself with a knitting needle.

"You know I'm a man of science, and measurements are of interest to me. There are two-hundred and twenty-six steps between our cottages, counting crossing the road. You might have to take a few more tomorrow night, as your stride will not match mine."

Of course not. Nicola was considerably shorter than Jack, although she was apt to be so nervous she might run instead of walk.

"You do know which cottage is mine, don't you?"

Nicola had never visited, but could read as well as anyone. All the cottages in Puddling had name plates. She nodded. Of course, looking for Tulip in the dark might prove difficult, so she'd simply have to do a dry run tomorrow and look for landmarks.

"There are seven houses on my side of the lane between us, ten houses on this side," he continued, "one of which appears to have a wakeful dog. Three doors down from here—the Countess's Wellington, if I'm not mistaken. In Lilac Cottage. I spied a black cat on a wall, who must have been quite cold to be left out on a night like this. It ignored me, as cats are wont to do, and we can blame it for the dog's barking if we must. I don't think the Countess will much care. She'll keep our secret if she discovers what we're up to—I think she'd be delighted to be a co-conspirator."

Yes. After Christmas lunch, the Countess might think of herself as a matchmaker. Nicola wondered how the woman spent her days when she wasn't out walking her dog. What was her Service? She couldn't picture those jewel-encrusted fingers winding yarn.

Jack let out a yawn, which he hastily covered. "Sorry. Where was I? All of the cottages were uniformly dark on both sides of the street. *No one was up looking out a curtained window, not a single sweet Puddling soul.*"

But now you have to get back home undetected, Nicola wrote in her notebook.

Jack's face fell. "You don't want me to leave already, do you? I have something to show you."

Would you like some tea?

Jack snorted. "What I'd really like is a snifter of brandy. Not that I drink to excess, mind, but the situation here in your cottage is ideal for unwinding and putting the world away. Respite. It's so cozy, and of course, the company is perfect. I feel like we've known each other forever."

Yes, Nicola knew what he meant, which was ridiculous, really. She didn't even know his true name, nor he hers. Despite him telling her about his boyhood, there was so much he had left out. She wasn't acquainted with his friends or his hobbies, or even what his favorite book might be. Apparently he was interested in botany, which was a difficult subject to study in the wintertime.

Their friendship—as he called it—was the oddest thing.

Yet. *Yet.* Nicola had never met a man she liked so well, who made her feel all things were possible.

She left him to fix the tea, having prepared the tray some hours ago. There were cherry jam tarts and slices of that drunken fruitcake on a plate, covered by a napkin. She'd have to be scrupulous in the cleaning up, so that Mrs. Grace wouldn't notice her kitchen had been tampered with. If necessary, Nicola would confess to having a midnight snack. A huge midnight snack.

The kettle burbled, and she poured the boiling water into the tea pot. Proud of her housewifery, she picked the tray up from the table—the infamous table—and carried it into the parlor.

And stopped. She hadn't been gone all that long, but Jack's bearded chin rested on his chest. His eyes were closed, and he was…snoring!

She set the tray down, rattling the china with deliberation. The noise failed to wake up her midnight visitor.

What should she do? Nicola knew the man suffered from insomnia and bad dreams—all probably related to the train accident. His face was often drawn, his eyes shadowed, and she'd watched him cover his yawns several times.

She herself couldn't remember much of anything from that day, not even in dreams, which was probably just as well. Just some snatches—a bad odor, the same feeling of hanging upside down from a tree limb as she'd done in her walled back garden as a girl, blood rushing to her head. Smoke and someone screaming endlessly.

Jack hadn't even been there. Yet he knew more than she did, or imagined the very worst far better than she would let herself.

She bit into a cherry tart, then poured herself a cup of tea. She wasn't going to watch Jack sleep, was she? That seemed almost rude. She wasn't a voyeur, had never peered in windows as she took her daily walks. But it seemed a shame to wake him when his rest came at such a premium.

What to do? She stifled her own yawn and finished her half of the food. What had Jack wanted to show her? Nicola wondered if he'd gotten a jump start on their secret hand signals. She'd looked the card over herself today, trying to think of memory tricks to help her recall the positions. The letter B looked like two bugs kissing, or possibly a butterfly or a bow. H was easy—two hands lay flat against each other. The finger shapes for C and X resembled the letters themselves, but oh, the rest. She wasn't sure she'd learn them all by teatime Saturday or teatime Saturday next year.

She would close her eyes for a little bit until Jack woke up. She had dutifully gone to bed every night at the assigned ten o'clock bedtime, no rebellion on her part, and her body craved routine. Just a catnap. She arranged herself on the sofa, resting her head on its arm and pulling the afghan over her legs, making sure her ankles were adequately covered.

But Jack had seen them and worse. She was in so much trouble.

Chapter 20

December 28, 1882

Yow, but his neck hurt. Jack opened one eye. It was gray and cold in the room, with near-dead embers in the fireplace. He had fallen asleep in his chair and had spent the whole night upright!

He had *slept*. A solid dreamless handful of hours. It was almost worth being stiff, his every muscle tight. He stretched, then rubbed the kink at his shoulder, twisting and turning to loosen things up.

Both eyes open now, he discovered Nicola curled up as innocently as a child on the sofa. Her hand was tucked under her chin, and her golden hair had come loose across her shoulder. Her breathing was regular, untroubled, and he hated to wake her. She resembled some sort of fairy princess, too much above his touch.

He stood up, somewhat unsteady. A tray lay upon the table, a linen napkin covering last night's post-midnight repast that he'd missed. Jack flipped up a corner. It was too dim to see well, but his nose told him brandy and cherries were on offer. He snaffled up the tart in one bite, then savored the fruitcake, licking his fingers of crumbs.

It was too much to hope for that the tea was still warm—it had been hours since Nicola left him relaxing by her fire. And relax he had. Jack was a little embarrassed that he'd gone to sleep. What a dull dog he was. And after all his hard work. He'd figured out a way to tell her something with his hands and wanted to demonstrate.

I like you.

It wasn't the most romantic of declarations. He wasn't ready to use the other L-word, although he believed it was becoming true. All he knew was that he was at peace when he was with her.

Would that change if she could speak? He remembered a pub he'd seen somewhere in Leicestershire. *The Silent Woman.* The swinging sign showed a headless female form, not the most sensitive of images with a queen on the throne for forty-five years.

Women were more than entitled to reveal what was on their minds. Of course, one did not always like to hear what that might be.

Time to leave before the world woke up. Jack pulled his watch out of his pocket. Good God! It was past seven in the morning! The world had been awake for hours. How was he to get out of Nicola's cottage without anyone noticing?

He was supposed to be at Primrose Cottage painting kitchen cupboards in fifteen minutes. He couldn't very well turn up in his best tweeds.

Frozen with indecision, the rattle of the kitchen door made his mind up for him. He dived behind the couch, praying that keen-eyed Mrs. Grace would not notice him.

But she *would* notice that second teacup and plate. He popped up again just long enough to snatch them from the tray and shoved them under the sofa fringe. He wished he could crawl right under with them, but his size was a distinct disadvantage. It was cramped enough against the wall.

"Nicola," he whispered, "wake up!" It was all the warning he dared.

He heard the springs in the sofa give, but no footfalls on the carpet. She had merely rolled around a bit, oblivious to their danger.

Sleeping Beauty.

A humming—a hymn, if Jack was not mistaken—and quiet clattering came from the kitchen as Mrs. Grace began to prepare Nicola's breakfast. Jack's stomach rumbled at the smell of eggs and bacon and toast, and wished he'd had time to eat the second slice of the fruitcake before hiding.

"Huh! Now where is that tray?" Mrs. Grace asked the empty kitchen. Jack heard doors opening and closing, and a fair amount of confused tsking and muttering.

Lucky Nicola probably got breakfast in bed, whereas Jack had to be fully dressed, hair and beard combed, teeth cleaned. If he ever got out of Puddling, he'd have breakfast in bed for a week. Maybe a month.

"This is very irregular. Oh, well. I'll just go upstairs and ask her to come down."

Jack talked to himself all the time too, so he found no fault with Mrs. Grace's musings. He strained to see around the corner of the couch. The housekeeper walked right by the parlor door and clumped up the stairs. When she got directly overhead, she gave an alarmed shriek that should have woken the dead. Still, Nicola didn't move.

"Miss Nicola! Miss Nicola's been kidnapped!"

Not the first thing Jack might have thought when he saw an undisturbed bed. He bolted from behind the couch and rushed into the kitchen, grabbing a piece of dry toast from the rack. One could wish for butter or jam, but he didn't have time.

A quick look out the kitchen window showed him it was snowing again, and his footprints would be obvious in the drift. He'd have to run around to the front of the house, go down the path to the street. Any number of people would see him.

Where could he hide? He'd missed his chance to the front door, but had been afraid Mrs. Grace would look straight down the stairs in her panic and catch him fleeing.

Trap door. Cellar. Maybe this cottage had one like his. He gave silent thanks for Mrs. Feather's industrious inspiration, and for the several hours he'd spent underground at Primrose Cottage making crooked shelves. To his delight, he saw an iron ring in the far corner, threw it open and didn't bother with trying to climb down the ladder. Pulling the door down behind him as quietly as he could, he jumped to the floor, jolting his left knee a little.

Despite all his recent walking, perhaps he was not as flexible as he thought.

A narrow window let in a shaft of frosty gray light, so Jack did not feel like Jonah inside the whale. Shelves very like the ones he'd just built, only straighter, lined one wall, but he was crushed to discover no gleaming jars of fruit or crocks of pickles for his breakfast, not that he wanted to eat marinated cucumbers at this hour. All that bounty was upstairs in the pantry.

It may as well have been up on the moon. This cellar was even cleaner and emptier than his own. How long could he lie low down here? And lying low was no exaggeration—he could barely stand upright.

If he didn't turn up at work soon, he'd be breaking the bonds of his Service. Would they think he'd run away? Did people ever fight their incarceration in Puddling? Jack had volunteered to give up his freedom— unwisely, said his stomach—but others were placed here under duress. Families had stashed their difficult relatives here since the beginning of the century.

The main road was closed off by a tall wooden gate, and if one did not know what to look for, would never suspect the wider world was just outside. On the other end of the village, Honeywell Lane petered out at the stream, which, because of its icy condition, would be crossable for the first time in years. The hills beckoned beyond, but when one was kept short of money and rations, how far could one get?

Mrs. Feather was probably looking under the bed for him right now, a pot of gruel on the range.

She wouldn't be surprised to find an unmussed bed in the morning—Jack frequently sat up in his plain little parlor, falling asleep in his armchair in the wee hours if he was lucky. He'd watched the fire ebb more nights than not since he'd arrived in Puddling, sometimes seeing the sun rise in the winter sky over the Cotswold Hills. Listening for the mourning doves, the farm carts rolling on Honeywell Lane, the flap of laundry on his neighbor's line.

He listened now, failing to detect any movement above his head. No floorboards squeaking, no thrills of joy that the mistress was simply sleeping on the sofa. In a minute or two, Mrs. Grace would discover Nicola in the parlor, and he would be stuck here for the rest of the day, waiting to hear good-byes and the kitchen door latch at the end of Mrs. Grace's shift unless he could miraculously transport himself out of the cottage.

He was in trouble for sure.

No food. No warmth. No logical plan of escape. He was much too large to boost himself up and squeeze out the single window. It was clear he had not been thinking strategically when he plunged into the cellar. The panic of discovery had overwhelmed him. Not that he cared what happened to *him*. No, it was Nicola's reputation that would suffer if a man was found in her house before breakfast. She might get thrown out of Puddling too, and Jack was relatively certain she didn't wish to leave yet.

Unless she had a better offer. Was he ready to ask her to marry him?

He sat on a ladder tread, trying to contemplate his fate. After a few minutes of his mind being as untouched as the snow on the path outside, there was activity in the kitchen above. He heard snatches of conversation, all one-sided, of course. Jack hoped Mrs. Grace in her confusion wouldn't notice the missing piece of toast.

Chapter 21

Nicola had been in a fog all day. She attributed it to her night on the couch and the blustery snow swirling outside. She had forced herself to put one leaden foot in front of the other, help Mrs. Grace with household chores, and begin a misshapen tiny pink sweater for some unlucky little girl.

Poor Jack must have left as soon as he awoke, only to find *her* asleep. What a vibrant pair they made. How could they possibly stay up for a New Year's Eve party, even if it was a party of two?

She'd already made up her mind not to attempt a surreptitious midnight visit to Jack tonight. The weather was atrocious, and she'd had difficulty heading into the wind and so abbreviated her daily walk earlier. It was a pity she couldn't contact him to tell him, but Mrs. Grace's suspicions would be aroused if she tried to get a message to him through the housekeepers.

The woman was already fretting about a missing tea cup, saucer and plate, and had muttered something about toast at breakfast as well. It seemed odd that Jack had taken the china with him when he left, though he'd managed to find the tart and fruitcake on the serving platter and presumably ate them, leaving a fruitcake slice behind to her surprise.

At around three o'clock, Nicola had encouraged Mrs. Grace to go home before it got much darker, and thus had to answer the urgent knock on her cottage door herself a few minutes later.

It was the head of the governors, Mr. Sykes, bundled up for the weather. His fierce eyebrows and eyelashes were dusted with snowflakes, and he wore a grim expression. Nicola immediately felt guilty. The man should be a judge—one look from him, and everyone would confess to crimes they'd never even committed.

In this case, though, Nicola *was* guilty. Good heavens, did Puddling know about Jack coming here last night? Was she to be interrogated and tossed out into the cold for breaking the Puddling Rehabilitation Rules? Nicola tried to arrange an innocent smile on her face. She was sort of innocent—nothing had happened that she wished would have happened anyhow.

"Forgive the intrusion, Miss Mayfield. May I come in? I need to ask you a few questions."

Heart knocking in her chest, Nicola nodded and stepped aside. She led him to the parlor, and he warmed himself before the fire for a few seconds, then turned. She pointed to the tea service Mrs. Grace had prepared before she left, but Mr. Sykes shook his head.

"I'm sure you're wondering why I'm here. We're making a house-to-house search looking for one of our Guests, and I wonder if you've seen him. You know him as Jack."

Nicola felt faint. Mr. Sykes noticed and grasped her elbow before she slid to the carpet.

"Sit down, please. I don't want to alarm you—I'm sure he's all right. Somewhere. It's just that he didn't turn up for work today and his cottage is empty. His bed wasn't slept in, though Mrs. Feather says that's not unusual. But she is in quite a state anyhow. I assured her he couldn't have got far on a day like this. Only a madman—well, he's not exactly that, is he? We've had madmen here before, and he doesn't fit the profile." Mr. Sykes paused, looking down at his largish feet as if they would tell him how to proceed without scaring her further.

"You have spent a little time with him, I think. Christmas lunch and whatnot. He didn't say anything to you that would—uh, that would lead you to believe that he's—that is to say—very unhappy here?"

Each stumbled word was worse than the other. Nicola was as alarmed as she'd ever been. It was obvious Mr. Sykes thought Jack might harm himself.

He wouldn't, would he? He'd seemed full of energy last night before he'd suddenly fallen asleep sitting up in her parlor. Wanted to show her something. Was pleased with himself. Nicola tried to recollect everything he'd said when he arrived.

A black cat. The Countess's barking dog. Two-hundred-something steps. He'd eaten the peaches with relish and wanted brandy. He wouldn't run off in a snowstorm for brandy, would he?

Nicola was uncertain. Should she tell Mr. Sykes that Jack had been here last night? Was he buried in a snowbank between her cottage and his, however many steps it was? He could have tripped and fallen—the steep streets were coated with ice despite ashes tossed upon them. Unsafe. She'd had an accident herself.

But someone would notice a body on the lane. If they were going from cottage to cottage, gardens would be inspected, although why would Jack be in one? Not digging up another bush, surely.

She shut her eyes, seeing that vision again of him lying inert. Helpless. Blood in the snow.

"What is it, Miss Mayfield? You—you almost spoke!" Mr. Sykes's eyebrows were lifted in surprise.

Nicola pulled her notebook—the notebook that Jack had given her—out of her pocket.

I do make noises sometimes. Not very often. Dr. Oakley is encouraged.

Of course, he wasn't aware of what she was doing when she made sounds. What Jack was doing to her. With her.

"That's excellent news. We pride ourselves in Puddling for restoring our Guests to good health. Which is why it's so vexing to think that Lo—uh, Jack has gone missing. No one intuited that he wanted to leave before his term was up. And he hasn't taken any of his belongings—Mrs. Feather was sure of that."

Oh. Worse and worse. Nicola bit her lip to prevent herself from crying. She needed to look concerned but not bereft. The continuation of their friendship depended upon it.

If it *was* to be continued. If Jack had truly disappeared—

This morning Mrs. Grace had thought Nicola had been kidnapped, a very silly idea. Who would do such a thing to an ordinary twenty-six-year-old woman? But Jack had scientific skills which would prove useful to any number of people or countries. His mind was *valuable.*

"He'll be all right, I promise. We'll do everything in our power to find him. You haven't seen him today then?"

She *had* seen him after midnight. Should she say so?

No. Nicola was quite convinced Jack would not want her to. She shook her head.

"All right. I'll be off. If you do happen to bump into him—although I do not advise you to go out in this storm—please tell him to report back to his cottage. Mrs. Feather will be spending the night there until he returns. She'll have hot food ready."

Which would be so awful he wouldn't want to eat, knowing Jack.

I will. Good luck.

Mr. Sykes left her sitting in the chair, desolate. The front door blew shut with a bang, causing Nicola's heart to stutter.

Where on earth could Jack be? Not in his cottage. Not at the worksite. Not striding around Puddling as if he owned the place.

Could his secretary have come to fetch him? No, someone would have had to open the gate to let him in to the village.

Perhaps he *had* left by himself. Climbed up a hill in the middle of the night, counting the steps to the next village, and was safe in London or Oxfordshire by now. Leaving her without saying good-bye. There had been no note, not that Jack would write one for Mrs. Grace to find.

But maybe he'd written something in her notebook! She flipped through the pages, almost smiling at their previous "conversations."

There was nothing in his hand except for his beautiful little rabbit and the sketches of those strange shoes.

The tears flowed now, and Nicola was too distraught to wipe them with the handkerchief tucked up her sleeve. She'd never felt so alone in her life.

"J-j-jack," she hiccupped. She was too upset to marvel that she'd said his name.

She should rise and light the lamps, but was stuck in the chair, her limbs useless. How had she come to care so much? The idea that Jack might be hurt or worse pierced straight through her.

A sharp thump in the kitchen broke her misery. It was probably the wind whistling down the chimney and knocking something off a shelf, but she pushed out of the chair to check.

Then slithered back down when she saw the man in the doorway.

Jack! This time no sound came out, but she'd never been so delighted to see anyone in her life. Nicola sprang up and rushed into Jack's arms.

"Now, now, what's this? I thought your company would never go. I was halfway up the ladder when I heard the knocker. Let me tell you I almost came up anyway. Another hour in that cellar of yours and I would have frozen my bal—um, my blood. May we stand by the fire? I'm stiff as a cadaver. Which I'm not, even though you are looking at me with a mixture of horror and fascination."

Nicola kissed him to shut him up, then remembered he was cold and dragged him to the fireplace.

"Ah, much better. Please resume kissing me—my lips are completely numb. Are they blue—mmf?"

The room was quiet save for the crackling fire. Nicola clung to Jack like a limpet, vowing never to speak to him again if he ever caused her such worry. That presumed she would talk one day, and right now she felt she was on the very edge. She had said his name, hadn't she? Not smoothly, to be sure. It was too soon to brag about it, until she was sure she could do it again.

However, talking was far less important than kissing.

She continued her onslaught, her tongue a perfect weapon of seduction. Jack was seducing her right back, meeting each thrust with one of his own, cradling her cheek, threading his fingers through her hair. Her scalp tingled, and other bits of skin followed. She felt herself swaying, but Jack would never let her fall. She trusted him.

But where had he been?

With great reluctance, she broke off the kiss, pleased to see a definitely dazed expression on the man's face.

Where were you all day?

"Didn't I just say? In your cellar. The whole damn day. I woke up when Mrs. Grace arrived and hid behind the couch for a bit. I'll give her credit—not a cobweb or dust bunny to be found back there, so I did not sneeze and reveal myself. When she headed upstairs to look for you, I ran into the kitchen, flung open the trap door and sequestered myself in the cellar. It was not my finest exit strategy, I admit. I *should* have gone straight out the kitchen door, but my footprints would have shown. And yes, I realized almost immediately that more snow would have covered them up, but by that time it was too late. And, anyway, I might have been seen closing your gate. Probably any number of your neighbors were looking out the window at the right time to catch me."

Nicola rolled her eyes, imagining Jack stuffed behind the sofa. The sofa that she had been sleeping on. It seemed she missed the whole show.

"I know you had roast chicken for lunch and it was all I could do not to emerge then. I was *drooling* at the aroma, Nicola, and there was nothing I could do about it. I didn't think to pack a picnic in my darkest tweed suit—I was just aiming for stealth last night. Thank God Mrs. Grace left early. But then that fellow turned up immediately after. Who was it? I couldn't hear."

Mr. Sykes.

"Oh, that busybody. What did he want?"

To find you! All of Puddling thinks you've run away! Or are dead!

Jack laughed. "Dead! Do I kiss like a dead man?"

Don't make a joke. What are you going to tell them? You have to go home!

"Not until I drink a cup of tea and eat all your biscuits. Do you think you can make me a chicken sandwich? I am famished."

Chapter 22

Jack prided himself on thinking on his feet, although he'd failed once today rather spectacularly, thus his sojourn in the cellar. Right now he was stumped again.

Where could he say he was all day? He'd never admit to being at Nicola's the entire time, even if she hadn't known he was right under her nose. That would bring the wrath of the governors down on them both, and who knew how they'd be punished?

He'd been so bored below he'd drawn in the dust, dozens of mechanical objects from memory and even a stag wearing a top hat between its antlers just for a change of pace—he'd scuffed up his illustrations to wipe away the evidence before he ventured up the ladder, which seemed a pity. Jack would have enjoyed showing Nicola his artistic and scientific talent.

He'd managed to nap for a short while too, quite an achievement on the stone floor with only his suit jacket and muffler to keep him warm. Jack's stomach had rumbled so loudly it woke him up. He was surprised Mrs. Grace hadn't heard it as she went about her chicken-roasting above.

The small cellar did not run the whole length of the cottage, but was directly under the kitchen and pantry ell. Knowing that all the food was directly above him, inaccessible, had driven Jack's hunger to new heights. Even two cups of tea, three roast chicken sandwiches, and eight biscuits prepared by Nicola and eaten in quick succession by him had not cleared his head.

Think, Jack. Apparently the whole village was out looking for him. From his vantage point in Nicola's spare bedroom, he could see lanterns bobbing below in the street in the gloomy dusk. The poor blighters would freeze to death as the frigid winter afternoon turned into frigid winter night, and he wasn't worth that.

He'd tidied himself up as best he could, washing his face and hands and brushing the dirt from his wrinkled clothes. He'd come out last night without his camelhair topcoat, as it was light-colored and would have been noticeable in the dark. Jack was reluctant to go outside, just when he'd finally gotten warm. The tea and kisses had been very helpful in that regard.

But he couldn't subject the well-meaning villagers to any more time spent searching for him, even if they were bleeding him dry for the cost of the program and starving him to boot. So, where could he have holed up since before dawn without anyone noticing?

St. Jude's bell struck four times, and Jack had his answer. He'd never question divine intervention again.

If he was lucky, he'd be able to hop over stone walls, trespass through a few gardens, and get to the church itself without using any of the lanes. Its doors were always open. If they had already checked there for him, he could claim he'd hidden in a cupboard in contemplative prayer and didn't wish to be disturbed.

Jack hoped God wouldn't strike him dead for his duplicity.

He went downstairs to a nervous Nicola, who was washing up all traces of his visit in the kitchen.

"I have a plan, not a very good one, but it's the best I can do. I'm going to church."

Nicola wiped her hands on a towel and took out her notebook.

What if they've already looked there?

He grinned. "They must have missed me. I fell asleep in some dark corner, didn't I? The sleep of the dead. Couldn't hear them when they called my name. Everyone knows I have trouble sleeping. When I finally do conk out, I might as well be deaf. I'll see if I can't curl up with the vestments for verisimilitude."

Be careful.

"Careful is my middle name. Actually, it's Haskell. Oops, not supposed to be telling you that sort of thing, am I?" But if Nicola was to be his wife one day, what was the harm?

Yes, he'd just about made his mind up to propose. No more pussy-footing with talk of courting, etcetera. Maybe he'd spring it on her the last day he was in Puddling. Every time he came home, he could be greeted with wild kisses from a beautiful young woman. Hell, a beautiful mature woman if he could keep her sweet as they both grew old.

Really, though, he should make an effort to know her slightly longer than two weeks before asking her to marry him formally, if only to assuage his mother. She would no doubt pepper him with questions when she returned from France, but with any luck, Jack would be wed by then.

He gave Nicola a fond kiss. She looked so adorably domestic, an apron tied about her slender waist, her hair coming undone from its strict pins, a charming rosy blush on her cheeks. He wanted to see this face upon waking every morning for the rest of his life.

That presumed he would sleep again. Well, he'd managed on a chair *and* on a stone cellar floor within the past twelve hours with no bad dreams. Nicola was curing him already.

"Wish me luck." Jack hoped he wouldn't snag his pants, or worse, private parts, on the triangular rocks that topped most of the garden walls he'd seen. The church couldn't be more than three or four house plots away—its spire was visible from Nicola's conservatory roof. Mummifying his face with his black scarf so that only his eyes were unobscured, he gave Nicola one last wool-covered kiss and crept out the kitchen door.

The wind cut through him immediately. All those poor souls out looking for him—Jack really did need to go to church and ask forgiveness. He sprinted over one wall, dashed through the snow-covered garden, then climbed the next two walls a bit more carefully as they were nearly as tall as he was. The church was in striking distance, its rooster-topped spire looming over him. He scurried between a shed and a patch of ice, then raced through the clipped yews in the churchyard to the main door.

It swung open in Jack's gloved hands, emitting an unearthly groan. The interior of the church was as dim as the advancing dusk outside, and just as cold, but it was thankfully empty. A few votives flickered to one side of the altar. Jack instinctively dropped to his knees, touching his head to the pew in front of him.

He prayed a rather straightforward entreaty, then, shivering, sat back on the hard bench. He hoped old Mr. Fitzmartin was snug in his house on Vicarage Lane. That was his next destination—he'd turn himself in and hope for the best.

Would the vicar know Jack was lying? Jack was out of practice, had never stretched the truth all that much growing up. Well, there was a first time for everything.

He was spared from disturbing the old man at his tea and perjuring himself. As soon as he screwed up his courage and exited the church to face the cold and consequences, he was faced with a trio of people coming up the path.

"Oi! There he is!"

It was Tom, the foreman from the work crew, and two men he didn't recognize. At least Jack wouldn't be fibbing *in* the church—being outside it was much better, wasn't it?

"Hello, Tom! I say, I'm so very sorry I wasn't at work today. I had trouble sleeping and let myself in to the church early this morning to, um, pray. Think. I guess I slept the whole day away."

"You've been in there all day? Didn't the bells wake you up?"

Jack shook his head. The village was very proud of its automated bells, though they still had human bell ringers who did things the old-fashioned way on occasion.

This was one of them.

"Stan, Joe, get up in the belfry and sound the all clear." Tom turned to him, his face dark with anger. "No point to anyone freezing their bollocks off any longer for the likes of you. Puddling has been turned upside down since the middle of the morning because of you. You're in trouble, Lord Ryder."

"I usually am," Jack said, feeling somewhat guilty. "It was an accident. I didn't mean to shirk my work." He was rhyming, but Tom was definitely not impressed.

"Oh, we got on for a bit without you, for you know you're rubbish at carpentry. Painting too. My own son, Tommy, could do better, and he's not ten years old yet. But we've been out searching for hours instead of finishing up at Primrose Cottage." Tom raised the lantern to peer in Jack's face. "So, let me get this straight. You're saying you were in the church all day?"

Jack blinked at the brightness. "Yes."

"*All* day."

"I just said so, didn't I? I resent the tone you're taking with me. I am a peer of the realm, and not used to my word being questioned." Jack sounded very much like his late papa, but there was no point to being a baron if you couldn't pull rank when necessary. Just imagine how a duke would handle this insubordination! Old Tom would willingly crawl into a crypt.

"You'll have to convince the governors. I'll take you over to the vicarage. Miss Churchill is there, and some of the others too frail to go out on a day like this to look for your sorry arse. Let's go."

Tom's attitude did not bode well for the future of Jack's Service. He saw himself getting hit "accidentally" with Tom's hammer. With the church bells ringing in his ears, he was led off to the slaughter.

Chapter 23

The church bells had pealed wildly some hours ago. Nicola remembered from her Welcome Packet that there was a system to alert the villagers in cases of emergency. A certain alarm for fire, for example, the bells rung in a particular order. She could only assume what she'd heard meant that Jack had been found and everyone could go home and defrost.

The lantern lights had disappeared from Honeywell Lane, but not the small cottage pie which had been intended for her supper. She had been too anxious to eat it. Instead, she'd drunk endless cups of tea, worrying over Jack's fate.

And her own. When she'd thought he was missing, possibly even—she couldn't say the word inside her head for shaking—she realized that she was in love with Jack Haskell Whoever. What she felt was not simple infatuation or lust. He meant too much to her.

And she couldn't tell him the truth.

For something to do before she put herself to bed, she studied the card with all the hand signals. She might as well have been looking at a foreign alphabet with those odd dots and squiggles over vowels. Nothing made much sense to her, and she despaired she'd ever learn enough to communicate with Jack without her trusty notebook and choice of colored pencil. She wondered if she should be "reading" the hands facing her or away, and tried both positions.

It was truly all Greek to her.

She was close to falling asleep on the couch again, and that would never do. Nicola needed a good night's rest—today had been a Russian Mountains ride, not that she'd ever experienced such a thing, or even gone to an amusement park. Normal train travel was frightening enough for her now.

How would she get back to Bath? Go to London to see Frannie and the boys? One more seemingly insurmountable obstacle to overcome.

Nicola locked the front door, after waiting longer than she should have to see if Jack would somehow find a way to come to her. She was halfway up the stairs when she changed her mind, going down to unfasten the bolt just in case he was foolish enough to break more rules. It was not as if thievery was rampant in Puddling—Nicola had never seen such well-fed, well-clothed, well-shod, prosperous people. She knew they all shared in the Foundation's profits. If she moved here full-time, would she as well? That wouldn't seem right somehow. Her presence would be evidence of Puddling's rare failure.

She undressed for bed, washed, and murmured her nightly prayers in her head. Her requests were simple and repetitious—health and safety for her family, especially her precious nephews, and the restoration of her voice. If push came to shove and she had to choose, she'd pick the first over the second.

Jack couldn't be expecting her tonight after the to-do today, could he? It *was* her turn, but she didn't know what she'd find. For all she knew, he was under house arrest. Maybe that Mr. Sykes with his grim countenance and fearsome eyebrows was stationed across the threshold of Tulip Cottage, armed with a blunderbuss. The image made her smile.

Mr. Sykes had looked entirely different on the day he'd married. Nicola had played the organ for the wedding, and a handsomer couple than Lady Sarah Marchmain and Mr. Tristan Sykes would be hard to find.

Weddings. Lilies and orange blossoms and veils and satin trains. Spoken vows—see, she'd never pass muster. Nicola wouldn't allow herself to think of any of them. She tucked the coverlet under her chin and shut her eyes. The counting of sheep, white and the occasional black ones, did not produce the sought-after results. She tried heartbeats, although they were so rapid she was unable to record them all.

Too much tea; that was it. She'd nearly drowned in the stuff this evening, anxiously awaiting word of Jack's circumstances. It had enervated instead of relaxed her, and now sleep was beyond reach, no matter how gritty her eyes were.

Nicola was not fond of warm milk but was desperate enough to drink a whole gallon of it. As she'd brushed and braided her hair earlier, she'd noted the shadows beneath her eyes. It wouldn't be helpful for her to alarm kindly old Dr. Oakley. She was supposed to be getting better here, not worse.

Of course, any time spent with Jack was well worth some bags under her eyes.

Down the stairs she went and into the warm kitchen. She lit a lamp, poured a generous splash of milk from the bottle in the ice chest into a pan and set it on the hob. Perhaps a sprinkle of cinnamon would make it go down easier, so she opened the pantry door where the spices were kept.

And caught Jack red-handed and shame-faced in the dark with a jar of peaches.

Nicola felt she might scream. Almost.

He put a hand out to her. "Sorry, sorry, I didn't mean to startle you. I didn't know if it was you or that dragon of a housekeeper come to spend the night to keep you company. Or protect you from my depredations. I was about to peek out the door and offer myself up to the gallows."

He would be the death of her, popping up when he was least expected.

"I came to see you as soon as the lecturing was done and the coast was clear, but you'd gone up to bed," Jack continued. "And I thought, as long as I'm in the cottage, why don't I have a little midnight snack? Though I must say I'm getting tired of your peaches. Familiarity must indeed breed contempt. But there was nothing edible for me to eat at home after my inquisition, despite assertions to the contrary. Mrs. Feather must have tried extra-hard to punish me. Beans. Faugh! Green. Broad. Yellow. And some speckled variety I've never seen before, as if variety made up for the lack of taste. They were all mixed up together in a gray broth with a bit of stringy meat. Don't ask me what kind of meat—I couldn't identify it if my life depended on it. Goat? Rhinoceros? I suppose anything is possible."

Nicola wished she could laugh; he really was amusing in his umbrage.

"Let me tell you, the Spanish Inquisition had nothing on the Puddling governors. I thought I'd never get away, and almost expected them to haul out a rack from the vicarage basement in their efforts to intimidate me. I'm very fond of my limbs just the way and where they are."

Nicola's notebook and pencil were upstairs. She made a rolling motion with her hand so he would tell her more.

"All right. Let me finish these first. Would you like any?" He held the glass jar out to her.

Nicola declined and tugged Jack to the kitchen table, where she could keep an eye on her milk. He sat down and finished off the last peach, drinking up the juice as if it were wine. So much for being too bored with peaches.

"So, here's my adventure. I left the church and bumped into a search party. Tom—from the roof at Primrose Cottage, do you remember him?—frogmarched me to the Fitzmartins and some other fellows yanked the church bell ropes for all they were worth to let the village know I'd been found. I expect you heard that—one would have to be deaf or dead not to.

My ears are still ringing, I think. Anyway, there was a little welcoming committee for me at the vicarage, some old ladies and then more people hustled in once they were notified of my capture.

"Your friend Mr. Sykes accused me of treason or sedition or some such. Apparently I upended all of Puddling with my thoughtlessness. The only one to speak in my favor was the vicar, who was pleased I sought sanctuary in his church.

"Don't give me that look. I did, didn't I? For at least ten minutes. And then I was frogmarched home again, told not to leave the premises until tomorrow morning upon pain of death and or dismemberment, and here I am, unrepentant and unredeemed." He gave her a boyish grin that she couldn't help being smitten by.

"I know I shouldn't have come," Jack continued. "But I thought you'd be worried. I was going to leave you a note on your pillow. You are worried, aren't you? You couldn't sleep." He pointed to the milk that was bubbling away.

Oops. Nicola got up and moved it from the heat.

"I'm glad you were concerned about me." The grin was gone now. "Very glad." He reached for her hand and pulled her down to his lap.

Nicola searched his face. His brown eyes were focused on her. Serious. There was a silent pledge there, something spoken words could not express. He valued her, yet was unsure of himself. He thought himself a bad bargain.

For all his good-natured bravado, she preferred this vulnerability.

What could she do but lift her lips to his? She tasted peaches and desire and Jack, a heady combination. The kiss was riveting, as per usual, sweeping her up in rapture. Her blood sang with the joy of it, and her previously erratic heart actually steadied.

She was safe in Jack's arms. Home. Where she needed to be.

Better yet to be in her bed upstairs.

Could she drag him there? He'd been resistant at Christmas, but that was before his brush with death and dismemberment.

Nicola drew away, regretting the loss of his lips immediately. She rose and took both his hands in hers, her meaning clear.

Jack shook his head. "I cannot, Nicola. I still have some honor left."

She was sure they could do *something* without infringing upon his ridiculous honor. He'd done it before, and this time she wanted to see *him*. She blew out the lamp.

"Sweetheart, I—oh, what's the use? I don't believe I can resist you altogether after being below you all day. I wondered what you were doing, what you were thinking when I was down in the cellar freezing my ar—

um, being cold. What you were dreaming when I woke to find you on the couch—I watched you for a short while this morning, you know, before your wretched housekeeper arrived and I hightailed it. I'd like to watch you all night long."

He was behind her now on the stairs, giving this very satisfactory speech. Nicola's nightgown and robe were as heavy and hot as fur, and it was difficult not to tear them off and toss them down the steps.

She was determined to learn something tonight—to be alive and aware of every precious moment. All right, fine, he wouldn't take her inconvenient virginity just yet. That didn't mean they still couldn't do some exploration.

Nicola was hesitant to put that idea in writing. So far her notebook was filled with innocent sentences, and those that were at all questionable had been torn out or marked over in multiple colors so no one could divine their original intent. One never knew with Mrs. Grace, although the notebook was usually never far from Nicola's pocket. She wasn't as restricted as the other Puddling Guests, didn't feel spied upon on a regular basis.

Mr. Sykes had given her a rather penetrating look this afternoon, though. She and Jack would have to be careful.

Nicola's room was just as she'd left it, a moderate fire in the grate, the bed turned down neatly despite her tossing and turning. A single candle burned, casting shadows on the wall.

She would like to light every lamp in the room, but that would arouse suspicion for sure if one of her neighbors was equally sleepless. She picked up her notebook.

What would your note have said?

"That I was safe. Safer than I am now," he muttered.

I won't bite.

"I should hope not. Although the occasional nip might be warranted every now and then. Christ, what am I saying? Really, Nicola, I should go. I took too much of a risk to come here. We've been lucky so far—"

Whatever else Jack had planned to say stopped when Nicola kissed him. Feeling feisty, she half tackled him and brought them both down on the bed. The springs squeaked like badly played violins, but Nicola didn't care. She'd never been so forward, so *physical*, in her life, and it felt marvelous.

"I warn you, I did some Greco-Roman wrestling at Oxford," Jack gasped. "You are not going to have your wicked way with me."

We'll just see about that.

Chapter 24

Who could imagine that a delicate, ladylike slip of a thing could knock him down like this? Jack had been completely unprepared for Nicola's amorous advances. He'd expected to cuddle a bit on the bed, kiss her senseless, perhaps bare a breast if he was very, very blessed.

He was rhyming again.

He'd drawn the line in his mind that he would not permit his body to cross. He was absolutely determined to leave without doing anything irrevocable.

Of course, some might see this current scenario as the path straight to Hell. Even if he and Nicola were fully dressed—she in a modest nightgown up to her chin and a thick woolen robe over it—there was no arguing that they were both discomposed on an unmade bed, flailing around like landed fish. Nicola was half on top of him, pulling at his collar as she continued to kiss him.

There was no question that being clothed was both unpleasant but necessary, and Jack vowed to himself he was not going to lose as much as a necktie. Kissing was fine. Anything else would be a breach of... something. He was not thinking too clearly at present to come up with an appropriate word.

He needed to calm down, especially in the one area that was threatening to ruin his resolve. With the agility he'd learned in his brief wrestling career, he executed a reversal, so that Nicola was no longer on top of him rubbing up against him so provocatively. He shoved a pillow between them, recalling days of yore when courting couples bundled. Proud of himself for not interrupting the kiss, he let himself relax on his side a fraction, still on guard against Nicola's next move.

He had not long to wait. One hand left his lapel and moved down his chest. It swelled involuntarily, being a typical manly chest, and regretted it was covered in so many layers. Jack told it to stubble itself and caught Nicola's small hand before it went farther south. Her fingers interlaced with his, and this simple act struck a chord deep within him. They were connected, even if they couldn't truly converse with each other yet.

He gave her lower lip one last lick and settled back. Her mouth was rosy and bee-stung, her eyes gazing at him with a directness he was not sure he could reciprocate. Nicola slid her fingers from his and put her fingertips through his beard. His cheek muscle jumped at the soft contact, and he knew he wanted that hand everywhere.

Which was why he should get up and go. Right this instant. Or perhaps five minutes from now. Before the church bells stuck the hour anyhow.

Tossing the pillow to the floor, she sat up on the bed, unbelted her robe and shrugged out of it. Her braided hair gleamed gold in the candlelight. Jack watched as she untwisted the strands and shook her hair free. His throat closed, preventing him from saying anything he might regret when he wasn't quite so dazzled.

Who was he kidding? Nicola would always dazzle him in her quiet, unassuming way. She was a beacon sent by God himself to guide his way out of the blackness. She'd probably think him crazier than usual if he uttered such a thing, so he kept his tongue still as his eyes feasted.

He told himself he was not disappointed that she didn't pull that virginal white nightgown over her head. Instead, she lifted an eyebrow and pointed to his jacket.

"You want me to remove my clothes?" Oh, it had not been enough for him to say the word coat—he'd thrown the lot in, right down to his stockings.

She nodded, her eyes bright.

"I—I shouldn't." The devil on his jacketed shoulder contradicted him, but Jack brushed him away.

She put her hands on her hips like a displeased schoolteacher.

He needed new rules, if only for his sanity. He and Nicola were far beyond Puddling Rules now.

"We need to come to an understanding. You may, um, look, but not touch. Is that clear?"

She nodded with no argument. Jack didn't trust her an inch.

"I mean it, Nicola. I have enough regret in my life without adding you to it. I won't forgive myself if I go too far with you. You are special to me. Precious. You may think my honor is a silly thing, especially when this world seems to be spinning out of control on every continent. I hear you thinking, 'What's the harm?' As much as I—well, that's reason enough. I want you too much. And I'm not ready to have you."

Not worthy.

He saw that his lame speech had gotten through. She nodded solemnly, placing a hand over her heart.

Jack knew instinctively she wouldn't lie. So there was nothing to stop him from taking off his jacket. He'd been in it over twenty-four hours already, and his time on the cellar floor had not done much to improve it.

Jack was sorry he had not bathed and changed before he came tonight, but he'd been compelled to walk the two hundred and twenty-six steps to Stonecrop Cottage as soon as possible. He may even have lengthened his stride and made it in fewer; he had forgotten to count in his hurry. Once again the village had been bathed in silent darkness—not even the Countess's dog barked this time as he dashed down the lane. The Puddlingites were sleeping the sleep of the righteous, secure now that their Guest had not defected and deprived them of a success story.

Jack didn't feel like a success, but he pushed his nightly melancholy as far out of his mind as he was able. He wasn't going to waste time when Nicola looked at him with such eager admiration.

He was somewhat ashamed to admit he'd been to a club once—or perhaps several times—where ladies undressed themselves before an audience of gentlemen. They'd done it through the smoke and music with a casual cheeky seduction which Jack was incapable of. His hands clumsy, he finally unknotted his tie, tossing it on the floor with his jacket. Each button of his fine linen shirt gave him difficulty before his undershirt was revealed; it was as if his fingers had turned into sausages.

He paused. Was this enough? His muscular biceps were exposed, and dark chest hair peeked over his vest. Jack would wager Nicola had never seen a man's naked arms before, not even her father's. A well-brought up young Bath miss wouldn't attend a boxing match or a haying party or a barn raising.

Her hands made that rolling motion again. More, she mouthed.

Blast.

He tore off his shirt and tried to smooth down his hair. She reached out to help but he batted her away. "Remember, I said no touching."

Nicola stuck out her tongue, then sat back among the pillows, rolling those naughty hands again. With a sigh, Jack rose from the bed and unbelted his trousers. He was going to keep his smalls on. He *was*. He unhooked his boots and kicked them off, making it easy to step out of his pants.

There he was, with his garters holding his socks up and his hands very firmly over the flap of his drawers. He doubted he looked like an Adonis in the near-dark, but he threw his shoulders back anyhow and tried to strike a pose.

That lasted all of three seconds. By God, he was embarrassed to be examined like this. It was one thing to disrobe in the natural course of things, being generally too busy to wonder what his partner was thinking. Preferably, she wouldn't be thinking *anything* if he'd done his job right. But Nicola's shrewd blue eyes were noting his every twitch. Her mind was definitely not in any sort of mushy state.

He cleared his throat, but it still sounded as if he had a mouthful of peastone. "This is all I'm prepared to surrender. You'll just have to imagine what my bare toes look like."

There was that tongue again. How he longed to catch it between his fingers and give it a good tweak.

Was he being selfish? After all, he'd seen and tasted Nicola's most private place. But he was protecting her.

Protecting himself.

He shifted from foot to foot. "I have to say I'm getting chilled. Are you finished?"

Nicola shook her head. Jack focused on the shadows on the ceiling, gooseflesh sweeping over him. He didn't need to look down to see that his nipples were hardened peaks, matching that other part of him that he was trying so hard to conceal.

She twirled a finger, and he obliged by turning around. It was far less uncomfortable in this position, where Nicola couldn't see his blushes or anything else rise. His male bottom was no great thing of beauty—at least he'd never thought so. A flat male bottom was so different from all the paintings of luscious odalisques through history. His behaved as it was supposed to, sitting down on sofas and horses and carriage seats. What more could one expect?

He straightened his shoulders and took apart a Foster pencil sharpener in his mind. No, its design was too simple. A Marion had more parts and could distract him longer. It functioned better than a knife, but improvements could be made. Beleaguered teachers across the British Isles would be grateful to pass out sharp-pointed instruments to their dull-witted students.

And what about the design of a school desk that was not bolted to the floor? Jack could never stand to be confined, though he could see why the squeal of moving chairs might get on one's nerves by the end of the day. Floor finishes would be scraped up too—

It was no use. Jack had never enjoyed the regimented classroom and was not enjoying it now.

He peered over his shoulder. Nicola's face was in shadow, and it was impossible to tell what she was thinking. He imagined he looked ridiculous in his black stockings and garters, his hairy legs on display. The male human body was an odd assortment of appendages and surfaces, really.

He needed to cover up and go home.

Chapter 25

Well. It was disappointing that Jack was wedded to the idea of keeping his drawers on, but Nicola could not quarrel with the rest of his performance. He stood tall and proud, his shoulders broad. His back was smooth, flecked with a few dark freckles that formed a triangle in the center of it.

His waist was not too spindly and not too thick—just right as per Goldilocks. His bottom was more concealed than Nicola would have liked, but she'd had the opportunity to admire it when he was in his too-small workman's trousers. The state of his thighs told her he took exercise beyond his daily walk when he was in his real life. His calves were rather nice too, what she could see of them covered by his stockings.

Altogether he was rather delicious and she wished he'd turn around again. She preferred his front, where there might be a tantalizing peek at his male endowments. Although Jack's hands were big, what he was trying to cover up was uncooperative.

He glanced over his shoulder, looking as if he wished she wasn't still there. She made that rotating motion again, and he reluctantly faced her. His chest—ah, his chest. A bit of curling hair and dark brown nipples. His lovely face, though he was a bit mulish standing before the fire.

All this nonsense about honor. What good was it when they would part in less than two weeks?

Honor be damned.

Honestly, she was losing her mind, but Nicola didn't care. Who knew when another such opportunity might arise? She had a splendid male specimen in her bedroom for her perusal, and he'd come of his own free will. At least he'd come to the pantry—she'd lured him up the stairs.

Her heart was beating swiftly again. She took a deep breath to steady herself and slid off the bed.

Jack jumped at her approach and backed away. "Oh, no! I insist upon no touching. I'll not be responsible—you must—you mustn't—"

More nonsense. She put a hand on his warm skin, tiptoed up, and kissed him. For a few seconds he was unyielding, his lips glued shut. And then... oh, glory. Nicola would never get tired of the way he commanded their contact, sweeping in and mastering her mouth with his. She followed his lead, since it was obvious he had much more experience than she ever would.

It didn't really bother her that Jack had had affairs before—it was the way of the world. A man's world. Annoying, but it only proved practice made perfect. Nicola felt sorry for all the women that Jack was not kissing. How miserable they must be.

He was holding her now, which was a very good thing as her knees had forgotten how to hinge. Nicola felt liquid all over, as though she was melting. Her hand remained over Jack's heart, and the reassuring rapid thump told her he was as far gone as she was.

She'd never suspected kissing could be like this. Even the hair on the top of her head felt alive, goose bumps skittering along her scalp. She could kiss Jack *forever.*

But she was here for more knowledge. She smoothed her way down his chest to the band of his drawers. Jack was so busy kissing he didn't notice she was trespassing. Or perhaps he'd changed his mind, too overcome to remember his own rules.

To her vast frustration, the string was tightly knotted and her shaking fingers were incapable of dexterity. The accompanying buttons were completely beyond her as well. But his rigid shaft, even if concealed by linen, craved contact. Nicola placed her hand where Jack had once covered himself up, and his cock—a word she'd never used or even much thought of before—leaped.

Jack groaned into her mouth but didn't withdraw or make any effort to stop her. Gingerly, she stroked over the fabric, wishing she could touch bare skin. There were gaps between the buttons; perhaps if she inserted a finger—

Suddenly she was shoved backwards. "By all that's holy, you must stop now," Jack said, his words ragged. "Do not make me ashamed, Nicola."

Why should he feel shame for something that must be normal between lovers? And he *was* her lover, if Christmas night was any indication. If it had been all right for him to touch her and kiss her so scandalously, why was she being forbidden to do the same?

Nicola bit a lip, wishing she could ask her question. Instead, she watched as Jack bent to pick up his clothing, muttering to himself. She reached out, but he backed away, falling into a chair with a pile of clothes in his lap.

He did not look at her as he spoke. "Believe me, it's not as if I don't want to. Want you. I have hopes once I get myself more settled—well, *if* I ever get myself settled—you mean a great deal to me. I've never felt quite this way before about anyone. But I want to come to you whole, Nicola. I'm no good to you otherwise."

Even more nonsense. Was there a limit to it? Nicola felt a rise of impatience. What if his bad dreams never disappeared and he never slept the entire night through? Did that mean he would deny himself companionship forever? It made no sense to her. She wasn't perfect herself. Just because she couldn't talk anymore, did she feel like damaged goods too, never to be rewarded with happiness?

Richard had thought so.

Damn Richard, and damn Jack. Nicola wanted to feel normal. Her life had been full of patient circumspection for *years*. She'd waited and waited for her long-postponed marriage to change her circumstances, and that would never happen now. Was she to simply embrace her spinster state, never knowing a man's touch?

It wasn't fair.

She was half tempted to pull her nightgown over her head and shock Jack into her kind of sense. Only his bleak expression stopped her. She might think his honor a silly construct, but it was obvious he did not.

She sat down on the bed with a sigh, an honest-to-goodness sound that had snuck out of her throat.

He'd done it again, prompted her to make noise. Not much of one, to be sure, but it was progress.

He gave her a lopsided smile. "You're almost speaking."

Nicola smiled back, though she didn't much feel like it. Ring the church bells in celebration.

Jack began dressing, and any hope she had that he'd change his mind evaporated. He was obeying society's strict laws after all. She should be grateful, she supposed, that he had enough caution for the both of them.

Dispensing with his tie and stuffing it in a pocket, he stood, his feet booted, ready to scurry back in the dark to Tulip Cottage.

Her notebook was somewhere on the bed. She flipped through the wrinkled covers until she found it, but no pencil. Jack reached into his pocket and handed her a stub.

"Always prepared, that's me," he said with forced cheerfulness.

Shall I come to you tomorrow?

"Deliver me from temptation. No, I'll come for *you* on New Year's Eve. I'll be a proper escort. Wear something dark and cover your hair. Well, you would—you're a lady, and all of you wear those outlandish hats, don't you? Lots of dead birds and fruit." He glanced at the little clock on her bedside. "It's the 29th already. I think a few days' break is merited after all the excitement, don't you?"

Nicola did not.

What did you want to show me the other night? Not his cock, unfortunately.

"I'm not sure I remember how to do it anymore. I crammed for the British Manual Alphabet. I was going to use hand signals to tell you…to tell you I liked you." She watched as Jack flashed fingers and palms, stopping and starting until she supposed he got it right. Her card was hidden in the Stonecrop Cottage Bible, and she had *not* crammed.

If Nicola was meant to be flattered, Jack had failed. *Liked* her? What a mealy-mouthed verb. One liked toast. Or a sunny day. Something quite unobjectionable.

Liked. Tasteless, like water instead of wine. She didn't want to be loved back, did she? That wouldn't work either. She and Jack were doomed from the start because of what had happened last March. She had been injured by what he perceived as his carelessness. No, there was no happy ending to be found.

Nicola didn't want an ending, but a beginning, and possibly a middle if they could get that far. How she was to convince Jack of that was tricky. Even her peaches were losing their appeal.

You are supposed to come for tea Saturday.

Jack frowned. "I'd forgotten. We were supposed to speak only with our hands, yes?"

Nicola would have to stay up all the nights to come studying.

"I'm not sure I can get away after all. My disappearance upset the completion schedule on Primrose Cottage—all the workers were dismissed so they could beat the bushes for me. I'll probably be tied up there spackling something Saturday. And even if they're not standing over me with a whip, it's better that we spend some time apart. To, um, think."

She swallowed her disappointment. He was serious about a separation. Would he renege on his invitation for New Year's?

Jack was getting cold feet, even if he was fully dressed now. Nicola didn't want to think. She wanted to kiss, and more. She'd been deprived of touching his male beauty, but seeing had been nearly as good.

There was nothing wrong with her eyes. She'd put them to good use New Year's Eve.

If the party was still on.

Chapter 26

December 30, 1882

Jack could not remember a time when he was so bone-tired. As foreman of the project, Tom had been a particular slave driver, personally dragging him out of bed before sunrise two days in a row, barking out orders, snapping when Jack failed to meet his standards.

Jack had skills, but none that dovetailed with house construction. It was unusual for him to feel so inept—he'd made a fortune that meant next to nothing to these Puddlingites. When there were only five shops on the five crooked streets, what good was money anyway?

Draped by a moth-eaten blanket, Jack was in his pajamas in his bedroom, cuffs rolled up to his knees. He was soaking his feet in a saltwater-filled roasting pan, willing the blisters to go away, or at least shrink in size. He'd been tempted to toss the borrowed work boots into the stove, but the odor would have been overwhelmingly offensive in his small cottage.

And Charley would want them back, even though they smelled atrocious enough without being burned.

Tomorrow was New Year's Eve, and the thought of staying up to celebrate seemed impossible. Jack had actually slept relatively soundly last night, after being worked right down to his fingertips as punishment for skipping work the day before. He had fallen into bed immediately after supper, too exhausted to complain about it.

Poor old Reverend Fitzmartin had been forced to come to Primrose Cottage for the daily morale boosting, shivering under Tom's watchful eye in the as yet unheated kitchen. It was unfair to torture the vicar, and Jack begged him to skip today's inspirational lecture. But, dutiful as ever, the man had not. He'd read a passage from the Bible that Jack half slept through, despite Tom's glare. If there were to be a test about its contents or meaning, Jack would surely fail.

He was failing the Puddling Program in general, and not succeeding with the British Manual Alphabet either. What had possessed him to think he could learn it in a matter of days? Especially when his work-worn hands were too sore to find the correct positions. He set the card down on a table, its images blurring together.

He gazed down at his hands and flexed his fingers. He'd always been adroit, able to manipulate the tiniest cog or spring or nut. Right now he was uncertain he could comb his own hair or hold a cup of tea without spilling it.

He'd reheated the thin soup Mrs. Feather had left for him, counting the floating slivers of beef. An infant could have enumerated them, so low in number as they were. The tea caddy had been nearly empty of leaves, so Jack had made do with Adam's ale, saving up for breakfast. At least the bread had been fresh, and would have been so much better with butter. Alas, no one had churned any.

It wasn't much past ten o'clock, and his bed looked very attractive across the room. If he slipped into it so early, would he awake at midnight, doomed to be conscious until Tom hollered him out of bed again? No, tomorrow was Sunday, a mercy. He could get up on his own—Mrs. Feather didn't come in until lunchtime—and go to church. If he was lucky, he'd get a glimpse of Nicola in a pew as she mouthed the words to the hymns. Try to catch her eye. Give her a reassuring smile that he'd forgiven her for forcing him to disrobe.

How would he entertain her tomorrow night? Keeping his clothes on, of course. There was nothing in his cottage to eat or drink, and he couldn't arouse Mrs. Feather's suspicions by requesting something out of the ordinary. Nicola would have to pack another basket for them from the riches in her pantry.

Once he was sprung from Puddling, he was going to write a strongly worded letter to the governors. It couldn't possibly be helpful to starve the Guests as they did, day after unsatisfactory day. Jack didn't care if their methods had been successful for almost eighty years; it was time for a change. In good conscience, he would never recommend the place—

Though it was not likely to come up in conversation. Jack could never admit to having checked himself in here to the world at large; his stay was confidential. The few people who knew—his mother, his secretary, two or three friends—would never say anything to besmirch Jack's reputation. One was never supposed to acknowledge weakness, especially if one was a male. To be branded peculiar would doom any prospects Jack had if he wanted to traverse society.

And he might. If he married, it wouldn't do to hide himself and his wife away. Any children they might have would carry the stain of his difficulties into the future as well. It was imperative that he somehow become normal again.

Which meant sleeping without hearing the cries for help.

When he'd met with the train's passengers, Jack had quizzed them on the details of the event. To a person they'd all stated that it was God's grace that the train had so few cars, that only a handful of people had traveled that miserable cold March day.

Following Mr. Fitzmartin's suggestion, Jack reminded himself regularly that it all could have been so much worse.

But it had been bad enough.

He picked up the card again, trying to focus his mind on something else. Something he had control over. Maybe that was at the core of it—the accident was a clear indication that Jack had lost control. Failed.

Ah, more failure to contemplate. As blue-deviled tonight as he'd ever been, he buried his face in his hands.

Something made him look up before he allowed the hot tears to spill. He opened his mouth, but had no words.

Nicola stood in the doorway like a slender bear, her scarlet coat reversed to its black fur lining. An incongruous tight-fitting workman's cap covered her golden hair, and she had smudged her face—smudged her face!—with soot.

"What are you doing here?"

She gave him a little smile, then whipped out her notebook from what should have been an inside pocket. She had already written in it.

I couldn't wait until New Year's Eve. I won't stay too long.

"Long? I'll say you won't! I can't believe you're here at all," he blustered. "The risk—I'm not worth it." Realizing how ludicrous he must appear, he hastily removed his feet from the pan, sloshing water on the carpet. That still left him in his paisley pajamas, but at least they were an improvement over what he'd been wearing—or hadn't been wearing—the other night. She appeared fascinated by his toes, and he dug them into the rug.

He continued to read her precise handwriting. *I wanted to see if I could qualify as a spy. If you see these words, I have succeeded!*

"And you can go straight back home. Damn it, Nicola, what if you get caught? There will be no New Year's Eve for you then. In fact, to be on the safe side, I am cancelling the whole thing. I don't know what I was thinking."

She snatched the notebook from him. *You don't have the power to hold back time.*

"But I do have the power to decide how to spend it. You must go home. Right now."

No. She waved her pencil with a flourish.

"Let me walk you back." Putting boots on over his poor damaged toes would be agony. But he could put trousers on over his pajama bottoms. Grab his overcoat. Drag her home. It was only two hundred and twenty-six steps.

You are being inhospitable. I wanted to see your cottage.

"Yours is much nicer, as you can see." If he stood up and moved around, the two of them would barely fit in the bedroom. The sloped ceiling was a daily reminder that he was too damned tall.

Show me the amenities. And then I'll go.

Amenities! As if the cottage had any. Really, she was being obtuse—she wasn't wanted. He was in a hideous mood. Didn't she notice?

Or had she been sent to lift him up out of his doldrums?

Interesting. If he believed in…if he believed.

He rose from his chair. "Don't mock my pajamas. I wouldn't have bought them in a hundred years. My mother gave them to me last Christmas." They were Italian silk, and expensive. The colors were rather florid, a surprising choice for his always elegantly attired parent. He'd left the packing for Puddling to his valet, which in the case of his nightwear had been a mistake.

But who was supposed to see him in the dark?

Nicola, whose bright blue eyes shimmered in the firelight.

"There is only one bedroom up here. You have two. The washroom does have running water, however. All the modern conveniences." Ha, for what he was paying he'd expect gold-plated fixtures. Jack picked up a candle, opened the door, and she poked her head in. He was grateful his shaving equipment and toiletries were lined up neatly. One might sport a beard, but one was fussy about its maintenance.

He'd let his guard down, so lost in thought he'd enabled her to sneak into the cottage and all the way up the stairs without detection. He should have locked the front door, but never in his wildest dreams did he think she'd come to visit tonight.

"Oh, hell. Come in. Hold still." He dampened a washcloth and wiped the dirt from her face. Quarters were tight in here too, and he could smell lily of the valley, watch the muscle of her jaw twitch with each stroke. Her skin was impossibly soft and warm, and it was obvious that he should kiss her.

She looked up at him, so trusting. There was still a trace of black across her nose, and he brushed his thumb across, noticing a small constellation of freckles for the first time. How had he missed them in daylight? They added piquancy to her elfin face, and he placed his mouth over the bridge of her nose.

She stood still, leaning into him, breathing lightly against his chest. Jack kissed her eyelids next, her eyelashes tickling his lips.

They should go downstairs, far from his bedchamber.

Should. Would. Could. Which one to choose?

Would. Bumping into the door, he backed away, closing his eyes to her startled expression.

"Let me show you the kitchen. We'll make a pot of tea and then you can leave. No, wait. I'm almost out of tea. There should be enough for a cup, though," he babbled. "I'll walk home with you, of course. Just slip my feet into some boots and throw on my coat." If they were noticed, perhaps his pajamas bottoms would somehow pass inspection as the latest style in gentlemen's evening trousers. Who here in this backwater would know the difference?

Chapter 27

Jack remained the most vexing man she'd ever met. That really wasn't saying much—as a gently reared Bath female, her male acquaintances had been limited. However, here she was in his lair, and he refused to take advantage. He didn't even know that beneath her coat she was wearing...

Nothing. Not a stitch. She was completely, utterly nude, except for her gloves, the thick woolen stockings squeezed into her sturdy boots, and the dark blue cap on her head—which she'd made all by herself today in a frenzy of haphazard knitting. Its lumps were giving her a headache, but that might also be attributed to Jack's reluctance to cooperate rather than the generous size of her head.

Nicola had tacked special fastenings all the way down the front so the coat didn't flap open and expose her legs. She'd been so nervous dashing here she hadn't even had a chance to get cold. She was cold now, however, awash with goose bumps after those lovely odd kisses. They were as stimulating as those he had placed on her lips, perhaps more so, being unexpected.

She was not much interested in tea at this hour, but found herself sitting in the poky kitchen, curtains drawn, as Jack messed about with the stove. Gingerly, she pulled at a ribbon near her ankles, wondering if Jack would notice.

He did not. The blasted man was measuring tea into a sad brown teapot, so different from her pretty flower-sprigged one. Slip, slip, slip went the knots up over her knees. The cool air stirred beneath the red wool, and she crossed her legs. They gleamed very white in the flickering lamplight. Surely he would notice *now*.

No. He was fetching a pitcher of milk from the oak ice chest, avoiding her with unnerving determination. She cleared her throat, but of course no noise resulted.

Look at me, she screamed, silently as usual. Nicola tried to kick a boot off but the jammed-in sock prevented it from flying through the kitchen.

She twisted the silver frog clasp at her throat, revealing pale skin until the next ribbon. She had never felt so ignored in her entire life, which was saying something. Modest young women were generally ignored, forced to fade into the background, and Nicola had been the definition of modest for twenty-six years.

Not any longer.

She stood and pulled all the added ribbons free. Her coat slid to the floor, and Jack dropped the ironstone sugar bowl. Lumps of sugar bounced and exploded on the tiled floor.

"Holy Mother of God! What are you *doing?*"

Nicola thought the answer to that was obvious. She shook her unbound hair free of the wretched cap and smiled, wobbling only the tiniest bit.

Jack covered his eyes, then thought the better of it. His dark eyes peeked between his fingers, his brows raised in question.

"Nicola. *Please.*"

Please what? Put the coat back on or climb on the table like Christmas night? Nicola actually had a better idea, had formulated it this afternoon while she was so furiously knitting. She picked up the notebook.

You are an excellent artist. I thought you might sketch me for posterity.

"Posterity? If you mean mine, you're going to kill me in about forty-three seconds. I won't have time to draw a fingernail. I beg you, cover yourself before we ignore our better angels."

At the moment, she'd prefer Jack to be a little devilish, but it was not to be from the stubborn jut of his bearded chin. Not quite as stubborn as he—or as brave as she had hoped—Nicola pulled up the puddled coat, draping it over her shoulders. It was not easy standing naked in Jack's cottage, no matter how much she had practiced in hers. It had taken no little time to look insouciant about pulling at those grosgrain ribbons, and Jack hadn't even paid attention.

Nonsense. I trust you not to touch me.

And she did, damn it.

You will have something to remember me by when you leave.

It wasn't as if she was propositioning him tonight, not really. Nicola hoped the drawing would be inspiration, that he would glance at it several times a day—all right, more than several—and eventually act upon the lust she hoped it would trigger. She only had ten days to snare him, and imagined some of them would be Jack-less for various reasons. This was her best chance of getting through to him, or so she had thought earlier.

Clearly, she had lost her mind as well as her power of speech.

"I won't ever forget you, ever, I promise. *Please* button that thing up." Jack bent and began to scrabble about on the floor, picking up pieces of the sugar bowl and clumps of sugar. Nicola hoped he wouldn't get them mixed up, swallow the wrong one, and kill himself.

A broom stood in a corner. With all the dignity she could muster, she stiffened her spine, fetched it, and began to sweep. The movement of her arms naturally resulted in her coat falling off one shoulder, giving Jack a very clear picture of what he was missing.

He ran his hand through already-wild hair. "Really, you might as well put a bullet to me. No, I will not sketch or paint any part of you. Sit down this instant." He grabbed the broom from her and a cloud of sugar sparkled into the air.

Nicola complied, allowing the coat to fall open again. Jack struck himself on the head and kept sweeping, muttering about deserved punishment and hell on earth. He was agitated, and it would have been almost amusing, if he hadn't been so thoroughly resistant to her advances.

Nicola did not know enough about men or seduction, and it appeared she wouldn't be learning anything new tonight. She decided not to take Jack's rejection of her too personally; she had, after all, interrupted his footbath and caught him in outlandish pajamas. No man liked to be seen at a disadvantage. The trouble was, no matter what Jack wore—his ill-fitting work clothes or his colorful paisley costume—she found him very attractive.

The feeling had appeared mutual. Which was why he, she supposed, in his quest to uphold his stupid honor, refused to look at any part of her except for her boots as he swept the sugar crystals off them. Nicola was slightly encouraged, but annoyed as well.

He did like her. But not enough.

Or was it too much? Was he putting her up on a pedestal she'd like to jump from and knock down?

Time was ticking away. With irritation, she began to fasten her coat. It had been easier to pull the ribbons loose than to tie them with gloves on, so she removed them. Her palms were damp, her fingers less than dexterous. But she managed to conceal her naked body, losing her one chance at love. Grim, she shoved her hair back in its cap and stood.

Jack needed a cap of his own—his hair was every which way. He still looked too good to her, clutching the broom with violence. She walked toward the kitchen door, ready to put this embarrassing display behind her.

"Wait! I'll go home with you!"

That was all she needed, having to dig deep and pretend nothing had happened for two-hundred twenty-six steps. Well, to be truthful, nothing *had* happened. Nicola shook her head and was out the door before he could find shoes to put on his long bare feet.

Puddling was silent. The night sky was lit by scores of bright stars, but she felt no astronomic temptation tonight—she needed to watch where she was going and not fall on her rump. She'd been foolish enough surprising Jack; she didn't need to be found *en deshabille* on the street by a Puddlingite out walking his dog.

Nicola counted each step as she hurried down the road. She'd left her cottage in darkness, so the neighbors wouldn't suspect what she was up to. Not that they were apt to. Never in their wildest dreams would they believe their wordless Guest was trying to woo another one. Nicola had been a model patient.

Until Jack arrived and aroused her womanhood.

Now that she knew what she'd been missing all this time, she was verging on anger. And the worst of it—she'd fallen in love with someone she could never have.

She kicked a chunk of ice in her path, and it skittered away to thunk up against a garden gate. A dog inside the cottage took exception and let out a volley of barks.

Where was she? In front of the Countess's temporary home, and Wellington had an excellent set of lungs. Nicola ran the last of the way, forgetting to count. She let herself into her cottage, tore upstairs, and threw off her coat. The result of what she'd thought had been ingenuity—reversing the bright-colored wool to the dark fur—had made her bottom itchy.

No good deed goes unpunished. Although what Nicola had been engaged in was not precisely a good deed.

Her nightgown lay pristine upon the coverlet. She pulled it over her head, then worked the boots off. There. She was ready for bed, if she could regulate her heartbeat. A cup of tea might have come in handy. A soothing book. Something with a happy ending and plenty of kisses.

She allowed her hand to tug up her nightgown. Nicola had no one to give her kisses, but she could touch herself, couldn't she? She was not in the habit of doing so, but she could see no clear reason not to, now that she knew what Jack had taught her.

She imagined a broader hand, one with some work-roughened skin. A hand that had more practice than hers did, that knew where to touch. The exact spot. *Yes, there.* A hand that could cause all the twists of anxiety to dissolve, push away the foggy, half-remembered past. A hand that would keep her safe, cradle her, cure her.

No one heard her cry out or saw the tears stream down her face.

Chapter 28

December 31, 1882

Jack had fought with himself all day and did not find a worthy opponent. Fought on his knees in church, immune to the vicar's sermon. Fought at the disappointing-as-usual luncheon table, Mrs. Feather measuring out a precise inch of butter for his bread. Fought on his brisk afternoon walk around the village, a perfect blue sky overhead which failed to cheer him. Even fought when he found himself back in the churchyard on "their" bench. There had been no message for him, nor had she appeared in church or anywhere he might have bumped into her.

He didn't deserve a message or a glimpse of her profile in the pew. How could he have treated Nicola so abominably last night? True, he hadn't expected to be disturbed, but her presence should have brought him joy. She'd offered—well, he couldn't get the sight of her bare body out of his mind, though he hadn't really tried hard. It was one of the reasons for the self-argument.

And another—he'd made her feel unwanted, possibly ashamed. Drove her out of his cottage like a fleeing Cinderella, though she'd left no glass slipper behind. He'd stood barefoot with his broom, his feet glued to the sugar-dusted floor, incapable of stopping her.

But Jack had done as she asked after all. From memory. He didn't need her in front of him, her soft white skin lit by candlelight. Those indelible brief seconds had burned into his brain. As soon as Mrs. Feather poked her head into the parlor to let him know his supper was in the ice box and wish him a "Happy New Year," he'd leaped from his chair to find one of his notebooks.

There were plenty of blank pages from the middle on—he'd not been inspired to create anything earth-shattering or world-changing since his first-week-Puddling boots. His previous notations resembled hieroglyphics to him, so disengaged was his mind from industry. He might never right himself, and the financial consequences of that meant nothing to him at the moment. He'd had more than his fair share of success—look where that had led.

To here in his old battered chair, he supposed, fingers smudged, a random thumbprint in the corner. Nicola gazed up at him from her page, hope in her eyes. Her wavy hair partly covered one small but exquisite breast, just as it had last night. The puddle of fluffy fur at her feet made her appear to be rising out of nature itself. She was slim but not thin, her delicate curves more beautiful than the fantasies he'd allowed himself.

He had held her and carried her, seen her sweet thighs and the mound of golden fuzz. Jack had had plenty of time to think about what she'd look like without clothing, but his imagination did not measure up to the reality.

And he'd turned her away!

For her sake, as well as his. Someone needed to protect her.

So his battle had been fought, and he'd both lost and won. It was New Year's Eve and had been dark outside for hours. He doubted Nicola would expect him to call for her, which gave him more time to get his drawings done. He posed a naked Nicola reclining on his sofa, her coat acting as a blanket. Jack drew her sleepy-eyed and half smiling, purely wanton. He'd never live long enough to see such a sight, but nothing could stop his hand from sketching it.

More pages followed. Naked Nicola in his kitchen sipping tea, with only Mrs. Feather's apron tied around her waist. Nicola reading in this chair, her legs crossed. Nicola on his bed, her hair spread across his pillows.

Enough. Jack slammed the book shut, wondering where he could hide it from Mrs. Feather. She'd never understand his mechanical formulations, but the nudes of Nicola were self-explanatory.

Feeling unusually superstitious, he couldn't bear to toss the drawings into the fire. He'd heard of primitive magic—spells cast, pins inserted in straw dolls. Burning Nicola's images would be unlucky, he was sure.

For a rational man, he was losing his wits.

He checked the mantel clock. It was close to midnight, when the supernatural didn't seem so impossible. The new year was almost upon him, and he recollected the country traditions. Suddenly knew what he must do.

He would be Nicola's first-footer, intercepting her on the lane if she was hare-brained enough to come to him tonight as previously planned.

It was bad luck for a blonde woman to be first to cross the threshold, and he needed all the good luck he could get.

He was still dressed, and shoved a handful of coal from the hod into his pocket. Gathered the few slices of remaining bread. It was the best he could do—in his greed, he'd eaten most of yesterday's fresh loaf. Filled a flask with water. Wrapped a pinch of salt in his handkerchief. He had no mistletoe, but a few coins in his pocket—a very few—would fulfill most of the myth. He'd just have to remember to exit by the kitchen door after he arranged his offerings.

And, he vowed, he would not stay long, echoing Nicola's words to him last night. There would be no lingering glances or tender touches or scorching kisses.

Then he remembered—he was supposed to gift her with something beyond the traditional items too. Well, why not his notebook? She could dispose of it as she wished, and he would not be driven mad by the images within.

His overcoat barely buttoned over the lumpy parcels tucked into his suit pockets, but Jack wasn't afraid of the cold. The bells on the church tower began to peal, and he devoutly hoped none of his neighbors would be out on the road to hear them more clearly.

It was a fine, clear night. The cottages between his and Nicola's were mostly dark, and no wild revelry was apparent. Puddlingites were practical people. They had to get up and go to work Monday morning, New Year's Day or not.

Would her door be unlocked? A spare key was kept under an empty flowerpot in his front garden in case of emergency, and Jack assumed the same would be true for Stonecrop Cottage. The governors required access at all times for surprise inspections—it was one of the rules stated in the Welcome Packet. Jack had been lucky so far that no one had barged in to catch him staring blankly at a wall, feeling sorry for himself. He was meant to be busy. Active. According to Dr. Oakley, too much time to brood was not helpful to his "condition."

He arrived at Nicola's in less than two-hundred twenty-six steps, only slightly out of breath. The cottage was in full darkness, and Jack wasn't sure whether he should be grateful or not. His scheme had been hasty, and the results might not be what he wished for.

The door handle turned but wouldn't budge. With a silent curse, Jack rooted around the bottom of the doorframe and nearly knocked over a clay urn. Beneath it was the key. After a few fumbles, the front door opened, emitting an eerie creak. Mrs. Grace had fallen down on her hinge-oiling duty.

He hoped Nicola would not wake up and be alarmed. He stood in the hallway, getting his bearings. Listening. The cottage was as quiet as the rest of Puddling.

Despite the lack of light, he'd been inside often enough to find his way into the kitchen, where embers in the fireplace still burned. He tossed the fresh coal over them, and lay the bread slices and water on the table. Carefully, he unfolded his handkerchief, stopping the salt from scattering. He placed a coin in next to the bread and stepped back to admire his handiwork by the revived fire.

Mrs. Grace mustn't be the first to find the New Year's bounty on the table. Jack didn't care if *she* had a lucky year ahead. He would go upstairs and wake Nicola, apologize for the lack of party. Apologize for everything.

He hoped she wouldn't bash him on the head with his notebook.

Jack lit a candle and crept up the stairs. He knew which room was Nicola's, would know even if he hadn't been upstairs before by the scent of lily of the valley. A sweet, delicate scent, perfect for her. He wished it was not winter so he could shower her with beribboned nosegays of the stuff.

The bedroom was chilly, yet she had thrown off the blankets. She lay in the center of the bed, curled into a ball, her nightgown riding up to her thighs. She wore an absurd nightcap over her glorious hair, and he longed to yank it off.

Jack had not made any particular effort to be quiet, and it was a bit unnerving to watch her sleep so soundly. He could be anyone, come to do her harm.

Of course, she had locked up the cottage for the night, and Puddling was as secure a place as any in Britain. It was literally walled off from access by the main road, and pretty much unknown to the outside world. The villagers knew which side of their bread was buttered and would never hurt a Guest.

"Nicola," he whispered.

There was no response. She slept on, her lashes flicking. Jack took a few steps closer, where the candlelight caught the gilt strands of her fringe.

He really could stand here for hours, watching the shadows dart, listening to her steady breathing. There was a blessed intimacy in his vigil, one that was unhampered by misunderstanding or past mistakes.

However, every minute he was here put them both in danger.

"Wake up. Happy New Year." He placed a hand on her shoulder.

She lurched up with a start, her eyes wide. When she saw that it was he, she hastily pulled down her nightgown and frowned.

"I'm here to bring you luck," Jack said, feeling like an idiot. He was no talisman of good fortune, certainly not to the travelers of that train to Bath. "Your first-footer, you know, a dark-haired gentleman. Come downstairs and see."

Nicola continued to stare at him with suspicion, and a touch of derision too. She must dislike him after last night, and who could blame her? But she pulled on her wrapper and followed him downstairs.

The kitchen fire was now ablaze, Jack's New Year's presents on the table obvious in the light. Nicola's eyebrow lifted.

"The coal's on the fire, as you can see. It's all the usual things, minus the mistletoe," Jack explained. "You can even keep my coin—I don't expect I need to buy a cinnamon bun or anything," he said with some regret. "But perhaps I'd better take back my handkerchief. Wouldn't want Mrs. Grace on our case."

Nicola nodded. She opened the salt cellar and shifted the grains into it. Instead of returning the handkerchief to him, she folded it into a tiny square and tucked it up her sleeve.

"Well, I'll go then. Sorry about the party, or lack thereof." Jack had decided his notebook was staying put in his coat. He turned to walk out the kitchen door.

Nicola got there before he did. She pushed him back into a chair, then grabbed a toasting fork from the hearth. Good Lord, did she plan on skewering him for his transgressions?

No. It seemed she wanted to toast the bread. A jar of apple butter was fetched from the pantry, and she poured the water from the flask into two small glasses.

So they were to have a party after all. Jack wouldn't even miss champagne if he could get her to look up at him with her wide blue eyes.

Chapter 29

This was the trouble with Jack—every time Nicola decided to wall off her heart from him, he did something to knock every brick down.

Clearly with much thoughtfulness, he'd brought the superstitious first footing legacy to life. He was indeed a tall, dark, and handsome man, equipped with his various New Year's presents. He'd tossed some coal on the fire for warmth and comfort. Brought water, salt, and bread for a healthy, long life, silver for future fortune. If he had brought mistletoe, she would kiss him under it, if he'd let her.

Maybe not. He'd been clear last night that she'd been much too forward. And when her head cleared from its sensual haze this morning, she was mortified at what she'd done. Turning up at a man's house in the state she'd been born in. What would her parents think if they ever found out? Nicola could picture her mother's horrified face and had shuddered in shame before she'd taken a step out of bed. She'd squandered every ounce of propriety she had—it was a wonder Jack was not thoroughly disgusted with her.

He had come tonight, however. Perhaps he still liked her a little. But he'd certainly proved he wasn't in as much of a rush to consummate their relationship as she was. In ten days—no, nine now, he'd be gone and she'd lose her chance with him.

He'd spoken of the future. When he was "better." Nicola knew there was no future. If he discovered why she couldn't speak…

No, definitely no future. She had only the present, and he'd come to make amends for his dismissiveness last night. She would restrain herself and her opinion, toasting bread, and toasting the new year with water. Nicola would be the perfect representation of a successful solicitor's daughter, even if she was still in a nightgown, a lacy nightcap on her head. She would accept what she was given and try not to complain.

She spread the apple butter on the browned bread and watched Jack wolf it down. Probably once he got back to civilization, he'd never leave his kitchen, making himself a nuisance to his cook. What was his country estate like? Was Ashburn very grand? Jack did not seem like a very grand sort of person, but then, he hadn't built the place.

From what little he'd said, he spent most of the time in London. There had been a Mayfair address in those letters she'd helped send, affirming the fact that Jack was well-to-do. Rich. Beyond her, really. Class lines were still very visible in Britain's fabric, and she had no ducal godfather or viscount uncle to elevate her to his rank.

She didn't think he was a duke or a marquess or an earl—he simply wasn't stuffy enough. He wasn't stuffy *at all*. But his signet ring bore a crest. She squinted at it across the kitchen table.

"What? Have I crumbs in my beard?"

She smiled and shook her head.

"Do you have your notebook with you?"

Another shake. It was upstairs on her bedside table. The sign language card was tucked into it, but she'd been too annoyed to make much progress with it. Why should she learn it, when Jack was going away?

"Good. For I want to talk to you with no interruptions."

Taking a sip of the warmish water, she waved him on.

"Look. About last night—no, don't glare at me. Let me finish. I admit I was stunned when you came to visit. I wasn't prepared for company. Any company, particularly not the woman I've grown so fond of. If I had expected a beautiful woman, I never would have been wearing those blo—um, those blasted pajamas."

Fond. Better than the word like, but not much. Beautiful was all right, but inaccurate.

"I—I treasure our friendship." Nicola rolled her eyes, but he continued. "I want everything to be right between us. I've never really been a stickler, but in this case, I fear I must be."

He raked a hand through his dark hair. "I'm a hypocrite, I know. There was Christmas, and every other time I took advantage of you. Oh, you'd tell me I'm being silly. You were delightfully complicit. Kissing you wherever and whenever has been the singular joy of my stay here. I shall never forget your generosity or your good heart. You almost make me believe—" He broke off, staring into the fire.

Good. He *should* believe. They both must look forward to better days, or what was the point of living? Nicola would learn to talk again somehow, and Jack would put the unhappy past behind him. She could nearly taste the assuring words on her tongue.

"Anyway, as flattered, no, *honored* as I am by your faith in me, I could never forgive myself if I dishonored you."

Honor. Bah. Nicola did not share his definition of dishonor, either. Her virginity was becoming increasingly inconvenient by the hour. She crunched into her bread without appetite, wondering when Jack would decide he'd apologized enough, open the kitchen door, and walk home.

Nicola was restless. And a little depressed. Jack was backing away from her, putting sufficient space between them, though he still sat at her kitchen table. The only thing that might calm her tonight was music, and she didn't dare to wake her neighbors.

She flexed her fingers, hearing random discordant notes in her head. Something cheerful to lift her spirits was required, if she could manage to find the right sheet music. She wished Tippy were here to curl at her feet. Nicola needed a focus to distract herself from her dismal attempt at seduction, and her piano would have to do.

The morning couldn't come soon enough. She'd never fall back asleep now. "You do understand?"

Nicola shrugged. What did it matter how she felt? Jack was obdurate.

"I don't want you to think I don't care." He reached into his suit jacket and drew out a slender folded notebook. "I wasn't going to give you this, but I don't dare to keep it. Too much temptation, I'm afraid. Do with it what you will." He placed it between them and rose from the table. "I'll say good night. And Happy New Year."

True to custom, he left by the back door. There was no kiss. No embrace, or even a friendly pat. Nicola shut her eyes briefly so the tears wouldn't spill. How useless to cry, when she was so very lucky in most ways.

Nicola opened the notebook to see a long column of figures and odd sketches in the margins. No temptation for *her* there. She cleaned up the kitchen, removing all traces of Jack's appearance. She'd have to hide and return the flask somehow. Mrs. Grace knew to the very last teaspoon what belonged in Stonecrop Cottage, and had discovered the missing plates and teacup under the sofa in one of her cleaning frenzies. Nicola had fibbed and written she'd forgotten all about putting them there for a reason she couldn't remember, and had weathered the housekeeper's gimlet eye.

She climbed upstairs, weary but enervated at the same time. Wrapping the water flask with a petticoat, she tucked it into a drawer, fairly confident that Mrs. Grace wouldn't snoop through her underthings. Then she tossed her hair out of the confines of the cap and set to brushing it all over again.

Her stroke was at regular intervals, rather like a metronome that counted beats. Her arm grew tired, yet she kept up the effort. Her hair would be shiny today.

For no one to see.

She threw the brush down on her dressing table, where it landed on the unfurled notebook. Had Jack written a secret message to her? If he expected her to tally up numbers or decipher a secret code at this hour, he was mistaken.

She flipped through the pages, having no comprehension of what was in front of her. From the squiggles and unfamiliar symbols, she judged Jack was some kind of mathematical wizard, certainly skilled far beyond her household accounts training. Nicola had no clue as to what the drawings represented, either. She stifled a yawn as she skimmed through the book; perhaps it would bore her to sleep.

And then—

Nicola sat up straight, her mouth agape. Goodness! Or Badness! That might be more appropriate.

Nicola barely recognized herself. This was not the woman she saw in the mirror every day when she bothered to look. She was somehow *more* seen through Jack's eyes.

The drawings were simple yet beautifully rendered. In a few deft lines, Jack had captured her every slight curve just from the few seconds she'd stood nude before him. He'd also imagined her in places other than his kitchen. There were a dozen pen and ink sketches that would have robbed Nicola of speech if she had any.

He drew her as a lover might, and she felt her face flush with heat. Jack admired her. If only she could convince him to act on that in the coming days.

Chapter 30

January 3, 1883

Primrose Cottage was finished at last, paint fresh, cabinets plumb, windows clean and shiny for the next Guest, and Jack felt like celebrating. There was only one person he wanted to see, the person he'd left his front *and* side door unlatched for in the hopes she'd make a repeat nocturnal visit.

She had not.

Was Nicola too shocked by his quick portraits of her? Had she balled them up and burnt them in the fire? It didn't matter—he'd made more. Now that his lust was unleashed, his hand could barely stop sketching in his spare moments. It had taxed his ingenuity to hide the images from Mrs. Feather, but he was fairly certain she wouldn't be inspecting the inside of his old boot.

Jack fished the rolled papers out and spread them across the kitchen table. Supper—if you could dignify it with the name—had been hours ago. Mrs. Feather had left him to his own devices, and he'd dutifully reheated the unappetizing mess. He was almost beyond caring about his stomach. The only thing that mattered was Nicola.

And he hadn't seen her since New Year's morning. She hadn't walked by Primrose Cottage on her daily swing about Puddling. He knew that because he'd looked out the window so often that Tom had cuffed him on the shoulder and told him to get back to work. He'd taken his own walks after dark, slowing down at Nicola's gate, peering up the walkway to catch her shadow behind a curtain, to listen for her piano. He'd been denied any visual or aural contact.

He should respect her wishes. Not try to go see her. But he was leaving in six days. Jack couldn't bear the thought of only seeing her in india ink on the papers he hid back in his spare boot.

There was nothing for it. He couldn't keep away. He dressed for warmth with a hat and scarf, as the night temperatures had dropped. The days and nights had been too cold for snow; the frozen stream showed no signs of breaking up. Jack should see about borrowing some skates from one of the Puddling residents. He might acquire some for Nicola too, if he could persuade her to come out with him before he left. Jack would like to see roses in her cheeks, her fair hair a bit flyaway, her coat furling out behind her. They might race all the way to Sheepscombe—

No. There was her ankle to contend with. She walked now with no trace of a limp, but it was best to be safe. They could skate arm-in-arm at a leisurely pace, his hand over hers. He could picture it in his mind like a Currier and Ives print or a Christmas postcard.

Jack always felt better with a plan, and now he had one. Letting himself out of his cottage, he took a deep breath of piercing cold air. Bracing, he tried to convince himself, as the shivers raced up his spine. The half moon gave just enough light for him to see.

It was nearly the witching hour, and all good Puddlingites were tucked safe in their beds. Two hundred twenty-six steps away, Nicola was in hers. If her door was locked against him, he'd palmed the key from the urn and carried it in his pocket. He was a thief.

And he wanted to steal Nicola's heart. Make her remember him in a positive way, not as the moody bastard he often was. Sometimes he felt as if he was on the brink of smashing through his melancholy, especially when he was with Nicola. When he was thinking about her. When he was drawing her.

He'd practiced the alphabet, and he made a few tentative signs as he walked up the lane. And then, alerted to a shuffled footstep, he stopped and ducked behind a bush.

Damnation! There was a moving shadow up ahead, unless his eyes and ears deceived him. No accompanying yipping dog, though, so it wasn't the Countess out for a midnight stroll. His scarf snagged on a branch as he tried to peer around it to see his adversary, and he was trapped.

Jack held his breath. Perhaps the villager would just go about his business and not notice the hulking man behind the very modest bush breaking his curfew. He steadied his breathing and pretended he was invisible.

The person approached across the road—scampered, really. He was moving swiftly, darting behind available bushes himself. A scruffy sort of person, with a too-big coat, baggy trousers, and a workman's cap.

And a hank of golden hair which had slipped out of it.

Jack stifled the rumble of laughter deep in his chest. He unwound the scarf and left it to sadly decorate the branch, much like his hideous potted Christmas bush. He was fairly sure he'd killed the thing by digging it up and replanting it in the frosty ground, but that didn't matter now.

Two could dodge behind bushes and trees. He ran a few steps, then hid behind a hedge. His fellow rule-breaker did the same. Had he been noticed? He thought not.

They were on opposite sides of the lane, inching their way toward each other. Soon his lovely nemesis would cross the cobblestones and be in his arms.

He was as still as a Buckingham Palace sentry. She looked both ways before she sprinted to his side, and he stepped out behind his hedge. There was no need to shush her; even if he'd surprised her, she couldn't scream.

"Don't be afraid. It's only I. I hope you were on your way to see me and not some other lucky fellow."

Nicola looked up at him, her mouth a perfect "o." Her checked cap was low over her eyes and on crooked—what on earth was she wearing?

"Let's go to your place. It's more comfortable," Jack said, steering her up the lane by an elbow. She didn't object, and in less than a minute they were in the front hall of Stonecrop Cottage.

She shook herself free and, after closing the curtains, lit a lamp in the kitchen, where the light was less apt to be noticed from the road. Her cheeks were flushed from the cold, and her hair had started to tumble down from the woolen cap.

Jack removed it, enjoying the rippling cascade of her unbound hair. "No one in his right mind would ever think you were a man, Nicola. What is this costume?"

Nicola pulled her notebook out of her jacket pocket.

I found a trunk in the attic today. In it were all sorts of odds and ends, probably left behind by other guests. They smell a bit smoky, though. I was so bored I tried everything on, even the men's clothes.

"You missed me."

Insufferable man. I missed having something worthwhile to do. It was too cold to go walking today.

"It's even colder tonight. But I gather those trousers kept you warm." It was a pity they were so large on her—her body was swamped by all the clothing. He would have liked to see her pert derriere encased in soft deerskin, made to measure.

I have never worn gentlemen's clothes before, of course. My mother would faint if she saw me now. But I find the trousers...

She paused, the tip of her pink tongue sticking out as she thought for the right word.

...freeing. I could climb over a fence without worry.

"No fence or wall-climbing tonight, my ragamuffin," Jack said firmly. "But you do look fetching. In a schoolboy sort of way. Why did you decide to come to see me?"

You didn't come to me. I wanted to show you how improved I am with the manual alphabet. Puddling was so stultifying the past three days without your company I decided to apply myself.

"I didn't think you'd want to see me."

Then why were you trying to come to my cottage?

"To apologize. Again. See how you were faring. Ask you to come ice-skating with me if I can procure some skates for us both." She put the notebook and pencil down. He watched as her fingers and hands moved. "Wait a minute. I wasn't ready. Start over."

I D O N T S. Her hands stilled, and then she shrugged.

"You don't s-something. Ah! Skate? I can teach you."

It was easier for them both when she wrote in her book. *I have skated. But not in years. I was never very good.*

"It's a bit like dancing. You dance, don't you?" He imagined Nicola in an off-the-shoulder ball gown, twirling about a parquet dance floor, much like the one at Ashburn. When she got overheated, he'd lead her through the French doors to the terrace for a breath of air. For a kiss in the garden. For more if he could get away with it.

I haven't danced in a long time either.

"We've got to remedy all that. Let me ask around the village tomorrow. What size is your foot?"

5

"I shall do my best to find something that fits. You'll be my Cinderella." At that moment, Jack's stomach betrayed him with an alarming gurgle.

You're hungry?

"I'm always hungry. I'm half the man I used to be."

Sit still.

"Yes, ma'am."

It was cozy sitting in the kitchen—Jack could have stayed here all night, if he wasn't already aware of the consequences of that sort of folly.

Spending tomorrow in the cellar held no appeal. The air between them was more companionable than sexually charged, and he was at peace with that. After staring a Nicola's nude portraits for three days, it was almost a relief to see her covered by wrinkled menswear, trouser cuffs rolled up exposing her ankles, which he steadfastly refused to stare at.

She was the soul of efficiency as she fixed him a sandwich and brewed a pot of tea. A tin of cake came out of the pantry too, and Jack felt a flare of domestic bliss.

He was, God help him, in love.

Chapter 31

January 6, 1883

What a showoff! But a glorious figure nonetheless. Nicola couldn't hope to keep up with him. Her ankle, while as good as new when she walked, felt somewhat weak as she skated at her turtle-like speed. She wished the frozen stream had an iron railing to clutch for support, or better yet, that she had a strong arm to cling to.

But she didn't want to hold Jack back anymore. He'd done his duty, squiring her back and forth at a snail's pace. It was obvious he needed more, and she'd released him with a smile.

He was pure masculine beauty, his face lifted to the watery sun, his hair tangling in the stiff breeze. He was hatless, as usual. Nicola suspected he knew exactly how attractive his disordered dark hair was. And the rest of him was not hard on the eye either.

For so large a man, he glided with athletic grace, his movements economical and sure. He had none of the wobbly spins or hesitations that plagued her—she felt as adept as an elephant in an omnibus, stomping on toes, squashing passengers, and being unable to come up with the correct amount for the fare.

Skating was like dancing? Ha! Nicola had fumbled and fallen too many times to count, but she'd finally waved Jack and his gentlemanly assistance off. There was no reason her clumsiness should infringe upon his enjoyment. He needed the exercise. He had too much energy to contain, his mind and body always busy. Puddling's limited five streets were insufficient to stimulate him.

In three days he'd be released upon the wider world. There were more than five fascinating streets in London—too many—enough to deplete the most excessively active person.

He'd declared the Puddling routine useless. But to her surprise, instead of London, he told her yesterday at tea he planned to spend the rest of the winter at his property in Oxfordshire, away from the hustle and bustle. He'd not seemed overly fond of his country property before, and she wondered why he'd changed his mind.

Jack promised to write. And she'd refuse his letters. Best to make a clean, very thorough break.

Would he continue to practice the British Manual Alphabet? It was unlikely he'd run into someone else who knew it. The idea of their having a secret language—which neither of them really understood—had been fun, but it wouldn't be practical for Nicola's future. Fingerspelling was tedious and slow, and she still required a pencil and paper to jot down the letters to make complete sense of Jack's words, especially when she didn't guess correctly. Her memory was not as good as it used to be.

She felt a pang. A serious pang, which poked right into her unprepossessing chest. No matter what Jack had said, the earnest looks he gave her, the tender touches, she wasn't going to tell him who she really was. She could say she didn't want to burden him with a lover who couldn't speak, which contained an element of truth.

She would tell him so in a letter once he was safely out of reach, making it clear that their affair—such as it was—was finished. In the meantime, she would eke out every second of pleasure with him before Puddling's gates opened to release him.

That meant the last of the peaches would come out of the pantry. Nicola was not going to let him leave without taking her to bed.

She had more confidence—and experience—in her potential as a lover now. The days since Christmas had brought her excessive wonder and a determination to bring things to their natural conclusion, no matter what heartbreak was ahead for her.

He must not ever find out *why* she couldn't speak. That would ruin everything that had happened between them, leaving a bitter aftertaste that no amount of peaches could overcome. She'd managed to keep her secret so far.

She would invite him to share her dinner tomorrow night. Most of the disapproval of their relationship had abated—Puddling believed Nicola was impervious to Jack's charm, that they were just convenient acquaintances, clubbing together out of neighborly propinquity. And anyway, he was going for good.

They didn't suspect that she'd crept out at night to Jack's cottage those two embarrassing times, and he had crept out to hers a few more. As he had suggested, she'd worked hard to convince Mrs. Grace that she didn't really care all that much about him, rolling her eyes when his name was mentioned, sighing in exasperation when he was at her door just in time for tea for the past two days, complaining in her journal about him to the poor old vicar. If she heard "Don't worry, he'll be gone soon" one more time, she was likely to burst out into giggles.

If she *could* giggle. It seemed she was capable of making some noises now, a very encouraging sign. If only they could be formed into words, she could be free of Puddling and all its well-meaning restrictions.

And then what would happen? A return to Bath sounded awfully flat. Nicola did not want to go back to her parents' house after experiencing considerable autonomy here. Why, she even knew her way around a kitchen now! She was a child no longer and didn't care to be smothered in her parents' concern for her marriageability.

A woman was meant to wed, or at least that's how Nicola had been raised. She'd never given the premise or its inevitability much thought before the accident, but now she wondered if she could manage on her own.

She rather thought she could.

Her mother's letters still bore news of Richard, as if it hadn't been *his* idea to break off their engagement. Would he want her back if she could talk again? It didn't matter—Nicola didn't want Richard. Anyone after Jack would seem too…tame. Anyone after Jack would be…not Jack. She blinked back a tear, telling herself her eyes were simply reacting to the cold air.

Straightening her shoulders, she tried to balance herself, holding fast to her fur muff. Maybe that was part of the issue; she was too stiff. Wooden. And scared. Jack was far ahead, moving his long arms up and down like a skating soldier. He looked like he was born to fly.

She hadn't been on ice in years, and then it had been a flooded cement rink made for the purpose. Puddling Stream was not as ideal. It had frozen in stages, and there were bumps and divots along the bank, undulating ripples destined to trip her up again if she wasn't careful. Soft spots to be avoided too. Jack was going so fast it was as if his blades weren't even touching the ground.

She envied his fearlessness. She'd never been much of a skater, should have told Jack she had no interest in freezing her posterior off, much preferring to sitting in her parlor with him. It was so frigid outdoors, the sofa by the fireplace and a hot cup of sweet tea would have been heaven. But then Mrs. Grace would have been hovering, and the chance to be truly alone with Jack for as long as she could would be gone.

She had him to herself for such a short time. While he might drop in to say good-bye on the last morning, there would be no opportunity for intimacy. No stolen kisses with Mrs. Grace planted in the room, no heated glances. They might joke with their fingers, if Nicola could remember the correct positions of the letters.

Two more full days left to accomplish what she needed. Her heart was breaking already.

But Nicola must appreciate and be grateful for her surroundings, heartbreak or not. Heavy ice-covered branches lined the banks and met overhead, giving her the feeling of being in a diamond-encrusted tunnel. The sky was silver, the sun a faded white disc. It was too cold for birdsong. The only sound was the cut of their skates into the ice and the resulting crackle.

They had this winter world all to themselves, not counting a few hardy sheep on the snowy hillside across the way. Years ago, the stream had powered a small mill, its brick building abandoned when the price of wool dropped. According to Mrs. Grace, nearly every cottage in the village still housed a loom in the attic, though the residents' current prosperity depended on the Puddling Rehabilitation Foundation.

Jack, for all his fearlessness on the skating front, was not going to be one of its successes. He still didn't sleep well and continued to be distracted and depressed. Nicola knew he made an effort to be cheerful around her, but sensed the darker undercurrents beneath his sunny smiles. Jack shouldn't have to live with false bravado. She was too aware of what that felt like.

Nicola was tired of being good. Being patient. Just once she wanted to break as many rules as she could in one fell swoop.

Tomorrow was the night. Or the day after, if her courage failed her.

And then…she would write to her father, asking him to find a modest cottage in a modest village for her. Not too far from Bath for the sake of her parents, but not too close for hers. She'd hire her own charwoman, someone who would *not* live in. Nicola valued her privacy and could prepare simple dishes to keep body and soul together after her apprenticeship with Mrs. Grace. She'd become an eccentric, if silent, spinster, free to develop an interesting reputation.

Nicola nearly looked forward to her future. But Jack wouldn't be in it. Her eyes filled again, and she was smart enough to know this time it wasn't from the cold.

He was so far ahead of her now, she'd never catch up. Nicola looked about for a place to rest her aching feet. The skating boots Jack had borrowed for her were too snug, and her toes were throbbing. There was a stitch in her side too. She was full of excuses for her poor performance and smiled at her cowardice.

What would happen if she pushed herself? Took long, low strides, her arms swinging by her sides? Raced as if the devil himself was after her?

She would fall on her arse again, that's what.

Nicola brushed the snow off a flat rock and sat, wondering how long it would take Jack to realize she was not right around the bend behind him. She didn't want to spoil his pleasure; he'd had so little of it.

Glancing around, she saw a neat farmstead on the Puddling side of the frozen water, its fields covered in white, its outbuildings square and sturdy. Not too far away was the school set within a stone wall, its bell ringing fitfully in the wind. It would be very hard to concentrate if school was in session, but it was Saturday.

They'd run into a group of village children unlacing their skates earlier. Jack had spoken to them, their faces crimson from the cold and exertion, their voices breathless. For a man with no children of his own, he'd had an easy way with them. He would make a good father, always keeping their interest with his creative inventions. Nicola let out a sigh.

And waited. There was no Jack on the horizon. How far down the stream did he intend to skate? All the way to Sheepscombe? She couldn't feel her fingers despite her warm fur muff and gloves.

If she were moving, perhaps she wouldn't feel so frigid. Her bottom was like a block of ice at this point.

Nicola stood, her feet awkwardly going in two different directions. She could do this. Just take it slow and steady. She aligned her toes and took a few steps, regaining her balance. Jack had likened skating to dancing, and she'd taken the requisite lessons with a French dancing master, even if her social life had not included many balls. Sober Richard thought such activities frivolous, though his political career could have benefitted from casual social conversation. She knew many deals were done over dinner tables and dance floors.

One glide in front of the next, nothing too ambitious. Her eyes were fixed on the whorls of ice beneath her to avoid the major bumps. It took all her concentration to get to the turn in the stream. Once she did, she looked up.

And saw a dark form sprawled a few feet off the ice, bright blood staining the snow. A leafless tree stood, a complicit witness to the accident.

It was her nightmare vision come to life. Nicola screamed.

Chapter 32

January 7, 1883

The room was so dark when he opened his eyes, Jack wondered if he'd gone blind. In any event, he had a blinding headache.

He'd been foolish, racing to get back to Nicola, convinced that something was wrong when she didn't turn up behind him. He pictured her falling again, immobile on the ice, unable to call for help.

There was something wrong all right. He couldn't move. It was he who was immobile.

He tried wiggling a toe. Whether he was successful or not, he couldn't tell. All of him felt stiff and sluggish, as if he were encased in wet sand. He closed his eyes, since there was no point in keeping them open, remembering the sudden slip and flip through the air, the obdurate black tree waiting to stop him.

Was he lying in his coffin? No, a bed, even though the mattress seemed to be made of stone.

Jack wrestled with the quilt to free an arm so he could touch his sore head. He was apparently turbaned like some sheikh. Where he could reach, he patted down the rest of his body and discovered he was strapped to a wooden board, thick lashings of leather cutting into his bare chest.

No wonder he was so uncomfortable.

Jack didn't think he was in Tulip Cottage. The whole place didn't smell right. Not that the odor was bad, just different. Odd spices and laundry soap and…dog. Damp dog.

"Hey!" he called out in the darkness. A muffled bark came from beyond the door, so his nose hadn't failed him.

The door burst open, a shaft of light falling into the room.

"Jack, you're awake!"

His ears weren't failing him either. The woman's voice was scratchy. Soft, barely above a whisper. Silhouetted by the lamplight behind her, he couldn't see her face, but he knew. It was Nicola.

And she had spoken.

Perhaps he was dead after all.

"Ham, please wake Dr. Oakley and tell him his patient is alert," she rasped.

Who was Ham? It didn't matter. Nicola was here, still in her skating costume, her fair hair loosely braided over one shoulder. She resembled an angel he didn't deserve.

"Come closer," Jack said. "Is it really you?"

Her shadowy form hovered over him. "It is really I." She clasped his hand and squeezed.

"Where are we?"

"Ham Ross's farm at the bottom of Honeywell Lane. He heard me when I found you."

"Heard you. You are talking," he said in wonder.

"And screaming, I'm afraid. My throat hurts, and Dr. Oakley has forbidden me to speak."

"And she's not paying a bit of attention to me," the old doctor said, coming into the room bearing an oil lamp. "Go finish your tea, Miss Nicola. The honey in it will do you good. Ham's own bees, you know."

"No, thank you. I'll stay."

Jack tried to sit up, forgetting that he was tethered. "What's wrong with me? Why am I tied up like this?"

"Just a precaution. You slammed into a tree, my son. Head first. We thought it best to keep you still until all your parts are back in working order."

Good God. Was he paralyzed? He tried wiggling his toes again and again couldn't tell.

"If you insist on staying, hold the light for me, will you, my dear?"

Nicola took the lamp and she was limned in gilt. Jack blinked against her beauty, then the glare. Dr. Oakley tutted, then held Jack's eyelids open with two fingers.

"Hm."

"Hm what?" Jack asked.

"Your pupils are enlarged, and don't quite match. Do you feel dizzy?"

Did he? Apart from being trussed up like a Christmas goose and the horrible headache, he was fairly jubilant. Nicola was talking! Well, whispering. It was a post-Christmas miracle.

"I'm not sure. Can one feel dizzy lying in bed?"

"I assure you, one can. Is the room spinning? Can you see more than one of me?"

Jack didn't want to look at the doctor when golden Nicola was right there. He focused on the doctor's nose. "No, sir. Just you."

"That's an excellent sign. I examined you while you were unconscious, and I don't think you've broken any bones. You have a hard head."

"So my mother always told me." An awful thought leaped into his hard head. "You haven't notified her, have you?"

"It's my understanding she's in the south of France. And it's the middle of the night, son. I thought it could wait until morning."

When Jack had signed himself into Puddling, he'd had to list next-of-kin. As tempting as it might have been to declare himself an orphan, he did not.

"I believe so, yes. For the winter. I don't think she needs to be disturbed. She wouldn't be of any use at all. Not good in the sickroom, my mother." Quite the understatement. "I'm sure I'll be tip-top in no time." He took another stab at the toe-wiggling.

Nothing.

"So we hope. But in the meantime, Ham has agreed to take you on as a boarder—you shouldn't be moved just yet."

"Can he cook?"

Dr. Oakley chuckled. "The man is a marvel in the kitchen. However, don't get any ideas about seven-course dinners. It will be nursery fare for you while you recover—simple, easily digestible foods suitable for the sickroom. Tea. Hot soup. Oatmeal."

Damn. The same old rubbish. Thwarted again.

"How soon can I get up?" Jack had half a mind that he needed to use the privy.

"Not for a day or two. We're stabilizing your spine after the trauma you experienced, you see. You took quite a jolt. We want to monitor you for a concussion too. It seems I'm forever stitching up foreheads," the doctor muttered. "In addition, you were lying in that snowbank for some time before Miss Nicola discovered you, and you probably caught a chill. All in all, complete bedrest is in order."

Was he going to lose toes to frostbite? Jack decided not to ask.

"I want to stay and help," Nicola said.

Jack's heart leapt. She must truly care about him. But he couldn't see how that would work out, especially if he was tied up and unable to kiss her.

Dr. Oakley shook his head. "I don't know if that's a good idea—you need your rest too. You've had an eventful day. We can have Mrs. Feather come down and assist Ham."

"I heard that, and don't like it much. Betty Feather is a featherhead."

Jack squinted at the doorway. A grizzled elderly gentleman in his nightshirt and nightcap squinted right back at him.

"Mr. Ross, I presume. Thank you for your hospitality." He tried to smile, but his tight skin didn't cooperate.

"Well, I was handy. Harnessed up old Ruby, put you on my sledge, and brought you back. Even gave you my bed. I don't mind—it was the most excitement I've seen since I brought Lady Sadie home by mistake."

Jack was glad to be good for something. "I'm sorry to put you out of your own room."

"Oh, think nothing of it. Moll and me are comfortable on the divan."

"I'm sure your wife can't be comfortable—"

Ham guffawed. "Wife! Never had one of those, and it's too late to start now. I'm seventy-eight, you know. Set in my ways. Moll's my border collie. She'll sleep anywhere."

And had recently been on Jack's bed from the whiff of it. He hoped it wasn't infested with fleas. "I don't want to inconvenience either one of you."

"It's all right. The Foundation will see I get taken care of. It's only for a few days anyhow before you can rest up properly up the hill."

Jack hoped that was true. Tulip Cottage wasn't much, but he was used to it. And now it seemed he wouldn't be leaving it after all.

"Do you have any idea when I can leave Puddling?" Though frankly a journey anywhere at the moment wasn't very tempting. Jack was as helpless as a new-born kitten. The straps felt heavy on his chest, as though they were made of iron and not leather. Horse harnesses probably.

Dr. Oakley patted his shoulder in a fatherly fashion. "Too soon to tell. You wouldn't want to make a liar out of me, would you? Just try to relax for a few days. If you won't have Betty here, Ham, I suppose I don't have too much objection to Miss Nicola coming during the day to spell you."

The doctor turned to Nicola, who gave him a bright smile. "Are you sure you don't want to go home to Bath? You're talking now, though it doesn't seem that Puddling was responsible for your recovery. It only took a hard-headed man for you to find your voice."

"Screamed like a banshee, she did. Woke me and Moll up out of a sound nap," Ham said, chuckling.

"Thank you for my rescue, the both of you," Jack said, looking only at Nicola.

She was cured, if hoarse. How soon before she would leave him and go off to live the rest of her life?

He might not be able to walk again—or have use of anything below his waist—and he'd never saddle her with a husband who couldn't *be* one.

He was anticipating disaster—he'd probably be fine. And then Jack sneezed, causing the dog to jump on the bed and bark at him. He was too weary to bark back.

Chapter 33

January 10, 1883

Jack never did anything by halves, going full tilt at whatever the world threw at him. Right now he was ending his embrace of a vicious bout of lung congestion with apparent great reluctance.

His chest had been filled with fluid, his breathing shallow, his fever ebbing, then raging for three days. Even though it had been established that he could walk a few hesitant steps, he was too weak to get out of bed.

Nicola wanted to kill him. Not because she minded wiping his sweat-stained brow or holding a bowl of hot broth to his lips or clipping his nails so he wouldn't scratch the site of his itchy stitches and scabs. No, it was because of every word he said when he was awake and relatively lucid.

The words when he wasn't were even worse.

"It is my reckoning."

Off his head again. Off *with* his head! He was back to the guilt over the train accident. If Nicola didn't hold him responsible for what had happened to her, why did he? *She* could have died. Instead, the voice within her died—temporarily, thank goodness. But these past ten months had taught her something about herself she might never have known, and saved her from what was sure to have been a loveless marriage.

"Sh. You'll tire yourself out." What she really meant was that she was tired of hearing him talk such nonsense. She wanted to smack him and tell him to snap out of his doldrums. She'd had to ball her fist countless times to prevent her from doing it, grinding her fingernails into the flesh of her palm so that the half moons might be permanent.

He made her angry. Dr. Oakley had advised her to be patient and let him ramble on, but she was getting increasingly annoyed. She didn't know how poor old Reverent Fitzmartin had put up with Jack for over three weeks. She was going half-crazy after three days with his feverish pronouncements.

"I deserve to suffer. Maybe even die."

Nicola put the broth down, slopping the liquid onto the bedside table. "Oh, for God's sake, Jack! Enough! You are sick, but you're going to get better! Your temperature went down last night, and Dr. Oakley says it's only a matter of a day or so before you can return to your own cottage to further recuperate." It had spiked again this morning, however, meaning that Jack was not yet out of the woods. She and Ham had sponged his brow with cool water for what seemed like forever. It was a wonder Jack's forehead hadn't wrinkled like a prune.

To give Ham Ross credit, the old fellow was as spry as a man half his age and had been an enormous help. He took care of Jack when activities became too embarrassing and masculine for Nicola to do so. Walking Jack to the privy, changing his nightclothes, shaving him—the old man was an excellent nurse. He'd been an absolute brick, and he made a very fine ginger biscuit to boot. Nicola had become quite fond of Moll too, who cheerfully shared her bed with Jack, snuggling up at his side, her muzzle on Jack's chest. Every time Jack spoke his stupid sentences, her tail thumped on the quilt.

"You are angry with me."

Yes, she was. Should she admit to it? Dr. Oakley had said part of the Puddling Rehabilitation Foundation's philosophy was to allow its Guests to receive a nonjudgmental hearing. One didn't have to agree, but one didn't have to argue. The object was to gentle the Guest to the truth of the matter on his or her own. True change came from the inside.

At the rate Jack was going, he really *would* be dead before he forgave himself.

"Sit up straighter."

"Must I? I'll disturb Moll."

"Doctor's orders. It's better for your lungs."

Jack wiggled a bit against the bank of pillows that had been arranged behind him, and the collie stretched and slithered down from the bed. "See? Look what you've done to the poor dog."

"She'll be fine. It's you I'm worried about."

"I thought you said *I'll* be fine."

"Maybe physically. It's your head I'm worried about."

Jack's hand went to the bandage, and she caught it before he could peel off the dressing.

"What's *in* your head, I should say," Nicola continued. "Did it ever occur to you that you are wasting the time you've been given?"

Jack frowned. "I can't get out of bed yet. You know that."

"I'm not talking about your recovery, but about—about—" Nicola wasn't in the mood to be diplomatic. "You feel so damned sorry for yourself. You have so many gifts, Jack. You're inventive and intelligent. There must be a reason you're here on earth. A plan. Who knows what you're capable of when you get well? What you'll invent. Maybe make some discovery that will change life for the better of millions."

She knew who he was now. Lord Jonathan Haskell Ryder, a baron whose ingenuity was famous throughout the British Isles. After Nicola's questions, in his latest letter her father had disclosed all he knew about the man who'd come to see them last year.

Jack gave her a skeptical look, but she was obliged to continue. "You *must* stop dwelling in the past. The accident—it's over, and there's nothing you can do about it now. There was nothing you could have done about it then—you're not super-human. You couldn't very well be everywhere at once, could you? You had lots of business interests, lots of factories. A mistake was made, a serious mistake, but *it was not your fault!*" Her voice had risen with each syllable, and she was shouting. She was just shy of stamping her foot, for all the good it would do. Moll gave her a reproachful look and crawled under the bed.

Jack raised an eyebrow. Even that looked like it took effort on his part. "You really *are* angry with me."

"I'm not angry. Frustrated is more like it. You have a chance to…channel your guilt into doing something *great*. It should be easy for you—you're the smartest man I've ever met. I've seen your notebook. I can't understand an eighth of what's in it. All those figures and symbols. They're like a foreign language." She made no mention of the nudes—they were as explicit as can be.

"More like a sixteenth."

Good. His mood was lifting. There was a flash of something in his eyes that hadn't been there before her tirade.

"Exactly. You have a superiority of understanding few people have. Stop beating yourself up before I do it for you!" Punching Jack would be cathartic, if ill-advised.

"You are terrifying me."

"Good."

"Have I really been such a bore?"

Nicola nodded. "Yes. I don't want to diminish what happened with that train—it m-must have been awful for the people on it. No wonder the thought of it upsets you."

She could remember so little about it, which was a mercy. Sometimes she caught a whiff of something bad. Saw a thin river of red. Felt herself tumbling through the air. Most of the day was a vast gray blank until she woke up in hospital.

What was fully in her mind were the months of poking and prodding as she recovered afterward. All the times her tongue was pricked with needles to encourage her to speak. The end results had been a mouthful of blood and misery.

"So you think I'm squandering my life."

"Not all of it," Nicola hastened to say. "Were you always...prone to black moods? I mean, before the accident."

He shook his head, slowly as to not jar the dressing. "You know, I never thought about that before. I'd have to say no, for the most part. Not that I was always happy-go-lucky, but I was mostly too busy with projects to borrow trouble. Even when they were failures, I wasn't discouraged. I paid no attention to my parents' criticisms when I could have let them bring me down. They were not always supportive, you see. Thought me a bit of a freak, if you must know. My father once actually told me I thought too much. Thought too much! How is that a bad thing?"

Nicola might tell him but she held her tongue.

"My mother just wants me to get married to a suitable girl." He gave her a pointed look, then winked.

Nicola's heart fluttered. Jack had talked of courting her. Had nearly asked her to marry him in a very roundabout way on any number of occasions. He had not gotten down on one knee, however, and wasn't likely to at this moment, mummified in bed.

"Some people cannot help feeling unhappy, even when there's no particular reason." Nicola knew melancholia was prevalent throughout society. People drugged themselves and drank, sometimes to death. Puddling had been created to deal in part with such circumstances.

"You have to admit, I've had a reason."

"Yes. No one is making light of what happened." Least of all her. She'd made quite a long journey to recover from it, which Jack didn't need to know about.

"I'll think about what you said. Try to concentrate on the positive." He didn't sound totally convinced.

"It's important that you stay busy when you are well. Speaking of which, your secretary Mr. Clarke is coming to see you tomorrow."

Jack's eyes widened. "Ezra's coming here? Did I send for him?"

"You did. Don't you remember? You wrote him a long letter after you walked to the…" She felt herself blush. "To the privy on Ham's arm the first time. You were quite determined. You wouldn't even let me help you compose it, even though you had a dreadfully high fever."

"I can't say as I remember any of it. I hope he could read it." Jack ran a hand over the dark bristles on his cheek. Nicola was still getting used to his face without his beard, but Dr. Oakley had been insistent about shaving him to deal with the cuts and bruising and guard against infection. Beneath the bandage, Jack was temporarily bald too.

All that lovely black curling hair had been swept away and burned. They had done to Jack what her father had forbidden to be done to her, and she gratefully tucked an errant curl behind her ear.

His hair was growing back in fast, though, a dark shadow against the white of his scalp. Dr. Oakley had left a neat row of stitches bisecting his crown which were currently covered with a cotton bandage. Jack looked a little like a swami, exotic and a bit dangerous.

Dangerous to her good sense, at any rate. Mr. Clarke was probably coming to make arrangements for Jack's return to civilization. It was almost time that she did the same. She'd notified her parents of the restoration of her voice, discouraging them from coming for her just yet despite their obvious excitement in their letters. Nicola was performing her Service, nursing a fellow Guest. In a week or two, she might be ready to go home.

The prospect did not cheer her. Once Jack recovered, there was no reason for her to stay. Her old life would beckon.

And it simply wasn't good enough anymore.

Chapter 34

January 11, 1883

"You've brought *what*?"

Moll jumped, turned around in a circle, and lay back down on the bed at the outburst.

There might be something wrong with his hearing, some unanticipated side effect from his injuries or the drugs he'd swallowed like a good boy. Jack was grateful Hamilton Ross had given them privacy and the bedroom door was shut.

Ezra Clarke tapped the leather folio. "It's right here. As you instructed."

"I instructed you to procure a special license. To marry." He didn't even know Nicola's last name. Presumably that was whom he wanted to wed, unless something had happened during the brief hours he'd been unconscious that he was unaware of.

"I confess it was tricky to get them to leave the bride's particulars blank on such short notice. But that's what you pay me so handsomely for." His secretary grinned, deservedly proud. Ezra was a fine young fellow, enterprising when need be. Jack overpaid him for just such achievements as this.

"Have I met the young lady, sir?"

Nicola had not come this morning. Jack had had to shovel his breakfast porridge in by himself.

"No. What exactly did I say?"

Clarke pulled a letter out of his pocket and handed it over to Jack. Most of it was illegible, even to him—his penmanship had never won any prizes. But a few choice words leaped out.

"I'll be damned. I must have been more out of my mind than I thought."

Clarke frowned. "You mean you don't want to get married after all?"

"No, no. I do. I'm almost certain of it. The problem is, I haven't asked yet. Not formally. I have been beating about the bush like a rabid beaver, but the circumstances were never propitious. And then I hit my head and wound up here. The doctor tells me I can go back to my own cottage tomorrow."

"Won't you be more comfortable at Ashburn? I thought that's where you were headed once you left the confines of Puddling."

"Yes, that was the original plan." So he could be close to Nicola, and somehow contact her avoiding Puddling's regular rules. But she was leaving now that she was cured, wasn't she? The only thing holding her back was Jack.

Should he pretend to be sicker to keep her here to continue her nursing? Dr. Oakley was an observant old fellow, and that plan would come to nothing. Besides, Jack was feeling ever so much better, especially now that he knew he was getting married.

Perhaps he should tell Nicola.

Not tell. Ask. The getting down on one knee business was still out of the question—he might not be able to get up.

"And there's this too. I got it out of the safe as instructed." Clarke presented him with a familiar velvet bag. Inside it was the Ryder betrothal ring, an aquamarine surrounded by diamonds. Jack's mother had given up wearing it long ago, as it reminded her of the philandering husband she had wished to the devil for decades.

Moll, who had been lolling on his bed pillow after the earlier disturbance, far more comfortable than Jack, gave a happy bark and raced to the closed bedroom door. She scrabbled against the wood, and Ham barked out, "Down, girl!" He poked his head around the doorframe.

"You have a visitor, Jack. Do you want me to tell her to go home?"

"It's not Mrs. Feather, is it? Or Mrs. Stanchfield?" The latter had brought him a jar of pickles from the store, which he was totally uninterested in consuming. Since the accident, he'd had quite the parade of Puddlingites making the trek down Honeywell Lane to Ham's modest farmstead. Checking in on their investment, he reckoned.

"Someone you like much better." Ham winked. "Shall I tell her to wait until you've finished your business?"

"No, send her in. This is the one," he whispered to Clarke. He tucked the ring and its bag under the covers and tried to sit up straighter. Out of habit, he brushed his hair down. It always came as a surprise when there wasn't any to be found. Well, there were bristly bits—Jack probably resembled a prisoner, though no one had handed him a mirror. His bandage had been reduced to a smaller sticking plaster by Dr. Oakley this morning, so he was no longer turbaned. "How do I look?"

Clarke blinked. "Do you want me to tell the truth or lie, my lord?"

"That bad, is it?"

"Well, your face looks like someone messed about with a paint set."

That's what happened when one hit a tree with one's face, Jack supposed. So, he wasn't at his handsomest—he was lucky to have all his teeth intact. His appearance hadn't seemed to bother Nicola as she'd tended to him the past few days. Apart from yesterday's dressing-down, she'd shown the patience of a saint.

She was right—it was time for him to start a new chapter. Acquiring a wife was just the way to begin.

Nicola entered, bearing a battered tin. Clarke leaped out of the chair like a jack-in-the-box.

"Plum cake. I made it myself this morning from Mrs. Grace's bottled plums. Don't forget to share it with Ham. This must be Mr. Clarke?" She gave him a friendly smile, and all the clouds of winter gloom disappeared.

Jack was amused to see Ezra blush to the tips of his ears. He was not the only one affected by Nicola's adorable presence. Today she wore a bustled tartan rough-silk skirt and white shirtwaist, her hair twisted up with a few loose tendrils escaping the tortoise-shell combs. An amethyst thistle brooch was at her throat, and he remembered her family had spent Christmas in Edinburgh.

"May I present my secretary and all-around assistant, Ezra Clarke? Ezra, this is Miss—good gracious, Nicola, I still don't know your last name." He gave Clarke a wink.

"Nicola will do—we're informal here in Puddling," she said breezily, shaking Clarke's hand. "How are you today, Jack?"

"Much better now that you're here. Clarke, you won't mind giving up the chair?" There was no place else to sit in the crowded little room besides the bed, and Jack didn't trust himself.

"Oh, I cannot stay. I have letters to write and want to practice the new sheet music my mama has sent. I got a lovely box from my family yesterday. Presents from Scotland. It was like having Christmas all over again."

Without the cunnilingus, Jack hoped. He would never, ever forget that day.

"I will walk you home, Miss Nicola," Clarke said, surprising Jack. He wasn't sure if he cared for those two plotting without him, but his night shirt was insufficient against the cold, and his balance still questionable.

When he was left alone with Moll, he drew out the ring he'd shoved under the bedclothes. How convenient that the stone matched Nicola's eyes—it was almost as if the original Baron Ryder had anticipated her advent a hundred and fifty years ago.

Jack's ancestor had been an inventor of sorts too, developing an improved gunpowder for the king. He'd been rewarded with a barony, though Jack didn't care to think about how many lives had been lost through his relative's discovery. Jack felt bad enough about the two men on the train.

He might always carry that with him—he was coming to terms with the fact that he couldn't put it out of his mind completely. But perhaps Nicola was right; he couldn't dwell on it and continue to travel the desolate path he'd been on. He was no use to anyone, least of all himself. He needed to forgive, if not forget.

Nicola would help him. Jack thought he could handle most any challenge if she was by his side.

Or beneath him. Above him. He'd spent too much time in bed and lasciviousness was overtaking him.

He would ask her to marry him tomorrow. One last night of sneaking into her cottage before he told the world that he'd found the woman he loved, even if he didn't know her name.

Chapter 35

January 12, 1883

Nicola had practiced her new music until her fingers were numb, trying to distract herself from the events of the day. Another letter from Bath had come, begging her to return as soon as possible. It had been three months minus one day exactly since she arrived, and she was "cured," wasn't she?

Nicola wasn't so sure. Not until she could see Jack.

She knew he was now safely ensconced in Tulip Cottage, for no less than Ham Ross, Dr. Oakley, the Reverend Fitzmartin, *and* the Countess had stopped by this afternoon to tell her. He'd been ferried up in Ham's wagon, for he still was not as steady on his feet as he could be, put to bed with an ice pack on his aching head, and fed a nutritious bowl of Mrs. Feather's broth that Nicola expected he'd wanted to tip over into a plant stand.

His prognosis was good—in the doctor's opinion, he could leave Puddling as early as the beginning of next week. As it was Friday, it left her only a handful of days to set her plan in action.

Nicola would give him a day to get settled. Then she would dress in her gentlemen's garb again in the dark of night, and, equipped with that last jar of peaches, seduce the man.

This seduction business had been stop-and-go from the outset—it was far more difficult than she ever anticipated to get Jack out of his trousers. She'd been trying since Christmas Day. He'd rebuffed her again and again out of his misplaced sense of honor, and quite frankly, she was tired of it. She wasn't getting any younger; there were no swains waiting for her in Bath. She was far too old for a Season in London, and anyway, she didn't want to meet anyone new.

She wanted Jack. Even just for a little while.

Nicola had every confidence that he would go back to Ashburn and do something meaningful with his life. Since her intemperate lecture, he'd been…better. More positive. She refused to let herself think about him marrying or having children, because it simply hurt too much.

She'd withheld the truth too long to confess now. And if she did, everything would change between them. So she would take what she could get.

It was nearly ten o'clock, time for her to extinguish the lamps, say her prayers, and go to bed. She hoped God would understand her Jack-prayer, even if it went against everything she'd been brought up to believe. She was entirely unable to convince herself that what she'd already done and what she wanted to do with Jack was a sin.

First of all, no matter where he placed them, his kisses felt too good to be bad. Nicola was sure they had contributed to her regaining her speech, from her first muffled moan to her final shriek upon seeing Jack's inert body in the blood-stained snow. If Jack hadn't come to Puddling, who knew how long it would have taken Nicola to be "normal" once again?

Not that she felt normal now—her heart beat rapidly as she thought of Jack's mostly naked form in her bedroom. Even his smallclothes and socks had their appeal. She smiled, remembering how embarrassed he'd been to reveal just so much of himself.

Tomorrow night, she'd see more. One couldn't copulate without removing one's smalls, could one? He had seemed far more well-endowed than the classic statuary she'd visited in museums, even if his hands had hidden what she was most interested in.

Prurient. It described her current state of curiosity. Nicola had no idea how she'd allowed herself to be in darkest ignorance for so long. In all the years she'd known him, she'd never been provoked into asking Richard to remove any clothes. That whole aspect of their future marriage had been clouded in obfuscation.

She took off her own clothes, not glancing at her reflection, and slipped into a pink woolen nightgown that her mother had purchased in Scotland. It was itchy, but one could not deny it was still very cold across the British Isles. Thick pink socks had been included in the package, and Nicola put them on too. How silly she must look, baby-blush from throat to toe, but no one was going to see her.

After poking at the coals in the fireplace, she brushed her hair and braided it, then got down on her knees. She really didn't want to think about Richard, although she included him in her prayer ritual anyway, just to ask that he find a proper mate. Some nice woman who was conventional both in looks and temperament—Richard didn't care for fuss or drama.

Nicola was not that woman anymore.

Prayers done, she climbed into bed, extinguished the lamp, and stared at the ceiling. Not that she could see it despite the flickering fire. If there were any spiders left after Mrs. Grace's thorough housekeeping, they were safe in their intricate webs, waiting for spring.

This was definitely a night for counting sheep or flying pigs, because when she went to seduce Jack, she didn't want to look like a raccoon, all shadowed eyes. She rolled around trying to get comfortable, tangling herself up in the voluminous nightgown. Nicola talked to herself with her hands, running through the British Manual Alphabet, skipping nearly a third of the letters. Once, she'd been a model student, but her glory days were over. Jack had meant well, but the adage about old dogs and new tricks seemed to be applicable. The alphabet was ultimately not helpful.

Nicola sat up and pulled the socks off—her feet were too warm. Her toes wiggled in freedom and she stretched her whole body, trying to relax. Even her braids pulled too tight against her scalp, so she untied their ribbons and loosened the waves. She dipped her chin to her chest and swung her head side to side. An alarming crackling sound came from her neck.

It was no use—sleep was not forthcoming. She was simply too tight everywhere, as if she was wearing an iron corset that couldn't be unfastened. If she were home in Bath, she would have resorted to a few drams of sherry, but alas, nothing of that nature was to be found in Puddling.

She couldn't go for a walk. Apart from being too cold, she was saving up her luck for tomorrow night. How horrible it would be if she were caught on an unauthorized post-curfew jaunt. Even though the Foundation was ready to release her, they'd probably stick Mrs. Grace across the hall overnight, serving as a kind of guard dog to save her from herself.

Some might think her judgment was impaired, and they would be right. Decent women didn't lust after gentlemen—or if they did, Nicola was unaware of it. Her sister, Frannie, had said nothing about Albert being irresistible when they were courting, and Frannie told her everything.

Maybe not. Albert was a perfectly nice man, but he might have some hidden attraction that Nicola was impervious to. Which was a good thing. It wouldn't do to pine after one's brother-in-law, would it? And those two little boys had come from somewhere.

Oh, her absurd turn of mind would never help her sleep. She relit the lamp, hoping her neighbors were asleep and wouldn't turn her in. She was in a sort of limbo, anyway, no longer a Guest who needed rehabilitation. The vicar had spoken to her gently today to ferret out when she intended to leave. Puddling cottages were in demand, even though the new one was finished and about to be inhabited.

The waiting list could wait. She didn't want to leave until Jack did, but couldn't very well admit that. It was a wonder they'd gotten away with the intimacies they had. Old Ham hadn't paid much attention to them as they'd signed misspelled words and grammatically challenged sentences to each other—he was not the strictest of chaperones.

Nicola wanted something more to remember Puddling by than nursing duties and thwarted desire. Tomorrow night couldn't come soon enough.

Punching up the pillows, she took a book from her bedside table and tried to read. The words wiggled about until she made herself focus, getting into the spirit of the thing. There was a castle and a governess and a brooding hero—that much she remembered from when she'd abandoned the book a week earlier. In her mind's eye, the brooding hero took on Jack's countenance, with his beard fully restored, and the heroine was a medium-tall, medium-figured young blonde woman a bit past her prime. There was no child to spoil the intrigue, though why a governess would be present was a dilemma she'd sort out later.

Maybe she should try her hand at writing once she was in a house of her own. She'd never thought of doing such a thing before, but why not? How hard could it be to get two attractive healthy people to fall into each other's arms? On paper, anyway. In Puddling, it had been the challenge of her life.

Nicola slapped the book shut and picked up the notebook Jack had given her, jotting possible scenarios. She was so engrossed in plotting, she didn't see Jack standing in the bedroom doorway, pale and windblown.

"I say, Nicola, would you mind very much if I joined you in bed?"

Chapter 36

He fell rather than joined. Perhaps he'd been premature coming out tonight, testing his recovery, but he couldn't help himself. The look on Nicola's face was worth every ragged step he'd taken as stumbled up Honeywell Lane.

Against doctor's orders. He was meant to stay in bed for the next twenty-four hours. That would have been fine if Nicola had been at his bedside to place a cool and calming hand upon his brow or order him about. He'd been deluged with people all day inquiring into his health, but none of them had been the one he wanted.

In vain, Jack had been hopeful Nicola might sneak out to him once it was dark, but she hadn't come. He simply couldn't wait any longer. He might have been wobbly from climbing the hill and up her stairs, but he was here, exactly where he wanted to be, a little overdressed. Jack would remedy that soon.

Nicola's pillowcases were heavily embroidered with white thread, with French knots and split stitches, satin and chain. Jack wasn't sure why he even knew their names—his mother was not a skilled needlewoman. Domesticity was not her forte. There must have been a maid or governess somewhere in his dim past who had calmed herself with sewing after his many antics in the nursery at Ashburn.

His rough finger caught at the threads. He couldn't bear to hurt her, to tear her.

But she had been very insistent about this, before his accident. Jack hoped she hadn't changed her mind in the interim—he wasn't as handsome as he used to be. Nicola had chosen him for this welcome task, however, and with any luck after this, she would agree to be his wife.

Yes, he was going to anticipate his marriage vows. Life was short, as he'd recently come to know. Jack had held off quite as long as he could. Nicola had worn him down until he couldn't with any honesty say why they should wait.

He *loved* her. And here she was for his delectation, her fair hair spread out on the pillow as it was in all his dreams. He'd drawn her in this position a dozen times—without the pink nightgown—had in fact done so today once he was finally left alone by all his well-meaning visitors.

"J-Jack!"

"Yes, it is I. I missed you today."

"You shouldn't be out of bed!"

"As you can see, I'm *in* bed. Just not my own." He gave her what he hoped was a saucy look. For all he knew, he resembled a hyena.

"But—but I was going to come to you! Tomorrow night." Her cheeks flushed in the lamplight.

That was especially good news. "Don't make me go home. I don't think I could anyhow." He'd thought Dr. Oakley was too conservative, but perhaps the man had had a point. Bedrest might be boring, but the trek from Tulip Cottage had been exhausting. Jack only hoped he could perform later in a satisfactory manner. He would hate to disappoint Nicola after all of her confidence in him.

"Why are you here?"

"I think you know. I give in. Capitulate. Surrender. If you find me a thesaurus, I'm sure I could come up with more words."

Her eyebrows knit. "I don't understand."

"Oh, I think you do. You've been trying to seduce me for ages. I'm going to let you."

For a second he thought Nicola would whack him with one of those pretty pillows. Instead, she rolled off the bed.

"Wait here."

As if he could move. He lay back while she disappeared in a pink blur from the room, watching the shadows undulate on the ceiling. Perhaps he should let her mount *him*—he understood that position was beneficial to a lady's satisfaction. To tell the truth, he was not feeling in optimal condition.

But he was here, and wouldn't waste his chance. Jack summoned some energy and began to take his clothes off with trembling fingers. Good lord, he was as nervous as a schoolboy.

Before he'd made much progress with his buttons, she returned, bearing a bowl and spoon.

"What's that?"

Nicola grinned. "My secret weapon. Unless you are really tired of them. I had planned to come to you tomorrow with peaches." Her smile faltered. "Maybe it's a silly idea."

"Oh, I don't think so. Even if they are not as sweet as you are. Where are we putting them?"

"Putting them?"

"Yes. Am I to eat them out of the bowl, or some other spot?" He waggled an eyebrow.

"Jack! I cannot—do people actually—I don't think—"

"Calm down, love. The bowl will be fine tonight. In the future, who knows where those peaches will find themselves?" He wasn't at all hungry, but dutifully downed a few slices as Nicola watched him with an anxious expression on her face. He held out the spoon, and she took a bite of her own.

"I warn you, I may not be at my absolute best. But I hope I have time to improve. A future, with or without peaches. Nicola, would you do me the honor of marrying me?"

"What?"

Her shock was evident—he caught the spoon before it stained the bedcovers. "I've been thinking. *You've* made me think. It's time I looked ahead, and I want you to be there with me."

It was also time for him to kiss the confusion from her face. She tasted of peaches and smelled of lily of the valley. Jack was transported to high summer, far from Puddling's frost. He would bask in her delicious warmth for the rest of his days.

Nicola would keep him steady. Steer him in the right direction. In turn, he'd never let any harm befall her if he could help it. Love her, because she was so very lovable. Diamond-bright in his firmament, the only star. He'd forgotten to give her the ring, but it was now in his jacket pocket on the floor, along with the other items of clothing that Nicola was so efficiently helping him to remove.

Her nightgown fluttered through the air, and Jack's breathing stilled. My God, she was lovely. And his.

He proceeded to kiss every smooth surface available—her shoulders, her breasts, her throat, even her chin. She still looked adorably dazed, her blue eyes half-shut. But she was touching him too, almost as if he would break. Each fingertip seared his soul and stiffened his already rampant cock.

He wanted more, but he reined himself in. Nicola was a virgin—for all her charming recent forwardness, she was an innocent. True, a little less innocent since he'd met her. He kissed her mouth deeply, moving his hand to the juncture of her thighs. His finger slid between her folds, and a slow swipe told him she was wet already.

But not enough. His mouth followed the path of his hand, licking her skin. She didn't skitter away, but thrust up toward him, offering herself for his delight. She was pure woman, and Jack felt as if he was discovering her body—and his own—for the first time. Blood spiked and swirled inside him, his heart racing, her taste on his tongue. All symptoms of his illness vanished, and he'd never been surer of anything.

He *loved*. He loved Nicola. There were no doubts. Why was he hesitating to make her his in the most elemental way? Time-honored. Traditional. He was more than ready, but he had to hear her assent from her own lips.

"You're certain?" he asked, his voice rough. "There's no going back on this seduction business once we get started."

She nodded, her eyes filled with tears. Happy ones, he hoped.

"You must do better than nodding. I want you to tell me."

"Yes, yes, yes. So many yesses."

"I love you." Jack centered his body and guided himself a fraction inside her. Her hiss made him pause, but she shook her head and squeezed his forearms.

"Don't stop now."

He probably could have, but was glad he didn't have to test his discipline. In seconds he was seated within her, her exquisite heat and moisture surrounding him. Jack took a moment to release the breath he'd been holding in. Nicola gazed up at him, her expression unreadable.

"Are you...all right?"

"Be quiet, Jack. No more talking. I just want to feel." Her eyes fluttered shut.

Her permission was all he needed. It had been such a long time since his last sexual encounter, he'd wondered to himself if he still knew how it was done.

It appeared he did.

He remembered to kiss lips and earlobes and eyelids. Cup her soft cheek. Nibble on her neck. Slip his hand between them. Press down so successfully upon her womanhood, she cried out and lifted off the bed. Flush with success, he rubbed her again and again until she was forced to speak, though he couldn't understand a thing she said. Lose himself so far inside her it was only sheer luck he was able to withdraw in time and spend against her.

Jack drew Nicola to him, their hearts hammering in a staccato duet.

"Words truly fail."

She nodded, but said nothing.

"You don't mind if I talk now, do you? I love you, Nicola. You've made me happy for the first time in months." He brushed a strand of her taffy hair behind her ear. "I have a confession—I'm a baron. Lord Jonathan Haskell Ryder. Isn't it absurd to do what we just did and not even know each other's surnames? You're going to be a baroness. I hope you don't mind."

Nicola pulled away and sat up. To Jack's disappointment, she held an embroidered pillow over most of her body.

"I—I can't marry you, Jack."

Her words clubbed him in the gut. "Why not?"

"You don't know who I am, and when you find out—I'm so sorry. It just won't work."

He elbowed his way up the bed. Nicola looked miserable. Not like a woman who'd been in the throes of ecstasy not five minutes before. "What in hell do you mean?"

"I didn't expect you to propose. I only wanted to...to have carnal relations with you."

Nicola might as well have been using fractured sign language—he couldn't understand a bloody thing.

She had been a virgin, he would swear by it. Why would she gift him with her body and then toss him away? "What do you have against marriage?"

"Nothing, per se. I cannot marry *you.*"

"Well, that's clear as mud. Is it because of my black moods? Because since I met you, I'm better—I know I am! I said I loved you, Nicola, and I meant it—I've never said those words to another woman in my life. You'd never want for anything!" Jack broke off in disgust. He was not going to *beg.*

She blinked back tears, which Jack was sure he'd had no part in. "You've told me your name, so I will tell you mine. It's Mary Nicola Mayfield. *Now* do you see?"

Chapter 37

January 13, 1883

After a troubled night, she had the dream again. Heard the screams. And she *knew*.

The revelation was sudden and startling. It told her everything she'd blocked away for all these months. Now, if only she could explain to Jack. Make him understand.

Nicola dressed in haste, unmindful of the crimp of her fringe or lack of jewelry. Ignoring the sore sensation between her legs. She bolted down breakfast only because Mrs. Grace was not to be trifled with.

"I am going to Tulip Cottage to check on Jack's progress," she announced, her voice wavering only a little. If he would let her in. She'd never seen a human being dress so quickly as Jack had last night. The look he'd given her froze her to her toes, and his words were like arrows to her heart.

"Do you think that's wise, Miss Nicola? You've spent too much time with the man as it is. I'll never understand why the governors allowed it."

"I was *helping*."

"That is Betty Feather's job," Mrs. Grace sniffed.

"But Mr. Ross doesn't like her now, does he? It was only for a few days, and I really had nothing better to do."

"There is your knitting," the housekeeper reminded her.

"No one will miss wearing one of my creations," Nicola said ruefully. "Even a helpless baby would reject my caps if it knew what was good for it."

Mrs. Grace almost smiled. "I suppose a brief visit would be all right. Betty will be there to chaperone."

Nicola threw on her coat and made her way down the hill to Jack's cottage. The sky was a piercing blue, as if there were no troubles in the world. As if there had been no horrific confession a few hours ago. No recanting of a proposal. No hate.

She stood at the door, working up her courage. Her hand raised to ring the bell, she heard a bellow inside, and a crash.

"I'm done with all your damned rules. With this goddamned slop. All of you in this nest of vipers. I don't care what Oakley says—I'm going home!"

Nicola opened the door. At the end of the hall, Mrs. Feather was cowering, dabbing her eyes with her apron. A disheveled Jack was shaking a bowl at her, its contents spattering the wall. A tray with broken crockery was at his feet.

"Jack! What are you doing?" Nicola asked, aghast.

"You! What the hell are you doing here? Come to tell me more lies? Get out. You too, Mrs. Feather—I can't stand the sight of you."

The woman scurried into the kitchen, and the slam of the back door confirmed she'd not waited to be told to leave again.

"I mean it, Nicola. I'll not be responsible."

She stepped forward, undeterred. "You won't hurt me."

"Won't I? It seems I already have."

He didn't look well. It was obvious he'd passed as bad a night as she had. She worried he'd have a relapse, but had to get this settled.

"I need to talk to you."

"No, you don't. I'll never believe a word you say."

"That's unfair, Jack. I didn't lie. I just never told you the truth." It sounded idiotic to her own ears, so what must Jack be thinking?

His mouth curled in disdain. "What's the difference? You've made a complete fool out of me."

"I didn't mean to, truly." *Courage.* Her heart was mostly pure. She unhooked her coat.

"You are not staying. Go home."

"I'm not leaving until we can talk like civilized adults." She glanced at the oatmeal dripping down the wallpaper. "You should clean that up before it leaves a stain."

"I don't give a toss about stains!"

"Don't take your anger out on Mrs. Feather—you can't blame her for what happened between us. No one knew all about you, did they? Not even the doctor or the vicar. You were never honest about exactly why you were here. No one knew about the train accident but me."

He opened his mouth to say something cutting, but at just that moment the doorbell rang.

"My God, does it ever end? Go away!" Jack growled.

"I'll get it. Perhaps it's Reverend Fitzmartin. You should speak to him and calm down."

"I don't want to speak to any bloody vicar. Or any bloody doctor. I'm getting out of this hellhole as soon as I can make the arrangements."

But he didn't move from the hallway. Nicola opened the door.

The very last person she ever expected to see was Richard Crosby, dressed for town and not for country, holding his beaver hat in gloved hands. His ginger beard was neatly trimmed, his hair pomaded to within an inch of its life.

It took a moment for her to recognize him. He was so...unfamiliar. Slick. My word, she'd actually forgotten what he looked like! Her mouth opened, but no sound came out. It was as if she was stricken with mutism all over again.

"There you are, darling!" Richard smiled at her fondly but made no effort to embrace her. "I've had a devil of a time finding you. First they wouldn't let me through the village gates, although I had correspondence from your papa designating me as a family representative. Then I had to deal with that jumped-up Sykes fellow. Just because he's married a duke's daughter doesn't make him God. And you weren't in your own cottage—I'd just missed you, according to your housekeeper. I say, however did you stand that poky little place all those months? This one is even worse! Aren't you going to invite me in?"

Nicola looked back down the hall, where Jack rested against the ruined wall, every bit as angry now as he'd been before the bell jangled. More so. He glared, then headed up the twisty staircase without a word.

"It-it's not my cottage," she stuttered. She took a step backward and Richard interpreted it as an invitation to enter.

"Who is that grim fellow? A local laborer?"

"Another Guest. Jack. Lor—" She almost gave his full name and title now that she knew it, catching herself just in time.

"What's his problem? He looks dangerous. I don't think it's proper you being here alone with him. Something untoward could happen."

It already had. "His housekeeper just stepped out for a minute," Nicola said faintly, remembering Jack's blistering tirade at the poor woman. She'd probably never return.

She led him into Jack's chilly parlor. She should leave and take Richard with her, but she *had* to speak with Jack. Explain. Explain everything. Throw herself on his mercy.

If he had any.

"What a funny little village this is," Richard sniffed, glancing out the window of the plainly furnished room. "But I suppose one must give it credit. You're speaking again, and that is most welcome. Your father has sent me to escort you home. His gout is troubling him in this weather, poor man, or he would have come himself."

"What? No! I'm not ready!"

"Nonsense. Listen to yourself. Every word clear as a bell. Your mother misses you dreadfully. And, ah, I do as well."

Nicola watched in horror as Richard put his hat on a chair and got down on one knee on Jack's shabby Turkish carpet.

"You can't stay here forever avoiding me. I know I've been a fool, Nic. You have every right to hold me in aversion. All those years you supported me in my advancement up the political ranks, and what did I do when you had your trouble? I abandoned you. I've been miserable ever since. Haven't been able to sleep a wink. Please say you forgive me. Agree to marry me again and we can put all this unpleasantness behind us."

Unpleasantness? Was he *insane*?

And there were no circles underneath his hazel eyes, belying his confession. He looked as healthy and gleaming as a roan racehorse.

"Please get up, Richard. We can't talk about this here."

"I agree this cottage is not the most romantic of places, and I know you ladies like romance. Hearts and flowers, what?" He dug into his pocket and pulled out a small leather box. "I got you a ring this time. I know we said that engagement rings were unnecessary and frivolous before, when half the world is starving, but you've had an ordeal and deserve a special treat."

He'd said that rings were unnecessary and frivolous, not she. He opened the box with a flourish. Within was a cluster of tiny diamonds and garnets. At least Nicola assumed they were garnets—the Richard she knew would never spend money on rubies.

"Put it on, darling. And please say yes. I'm getting a bit stiff down here."

Two proposals in two days from two men—that must be some sort of record.

"Get up!" she snapped.

A look of hurt crossed his face. "I admit it's not much, not what you deserve. What is that scripture quote? Something about rubies and virtuous women? These are just carnelians, but someday I'll buy you rubies, Nic."

"I don't want rubies, Richard. I—I don't want to get married right now either." At least not to him. And if she couldn't marry Jack, she'd rather be an old maid with a whiskery chin and a houseful of cats.

He pushed himself up with the aid of a chair. "We've lost so much time. Ten months. Don't be capricious."

"Capricious?"

He ignored the ice in her voice. "Well, you decided not to speak, even though there was nothing medically wrong. That was very inconvenient for all of us."

"I didn't *decide*, Richard. I assure you it was not a conscious thing." The epiphany had come last night in her dream, after the argument with Jack. She had to tell him, if only Richard would go away.

"I can forgive and forget about it, now that you've come to your senses."

Involuntarily, Nicola's hands flew into the air. F—U—C—

That was as far as she could get, still not remembering the configuration of the letter K.

Richard lifted a rusty eyebrow. "What's the matter? Are you having fits now?"

Nicola nodded. "Yes. I believe I am. They've overtaken me quite suddenly. Perhaps you should go." She wanted to go cross-eyed and stick her tongue out in the worst way, but didn't want to overdo.

"Isn't there a doctor here? I was under the impression Puddling is a sort of health spa."

"That's what they want you to believe." She tapped her right temple, feeling deliciously evil. "This is what they care about—what's up here. I'm afraid my brain is very disordered. I may be speaking, but there are ever so many more things wrong with me. Please don't tell Mama and Papa. I wouldn't want them to be alarmed."

"B-but your father!" Richard sputtered, looking pale. "He told me to bring you home. The fees here are outrageous!"

"That may be, but with the accident settlement, I have more than enough to cover my expenses. I am perfectly able to take care of myself."

"But—but you're a woman!"

"How nice of you to notice after all this time." The words tumbled out without forethought. "Tell me, Richard—did you ever love me? Want to kiss me until you didn't know which tongue was whose? Unpin my hair, unbutton my dress, unroll my stockings?"

"I never wanted to un-anything, Nicola. It wouldn't have been proper until we were wed. What has happened to you in this godforsaken place? You are not yourself!"

Nicola grinned. "No, I'm not. I think I've improved a great deal. My horizons have…expanded."

He grabbed her elbow. "I'm removing you from this den of iniquity right this minute!"

She shook him off. "Oh, I don't think so. I'll get that grim fellow upstairs to come down and show you just how grim he can be." At least Nicola hoped Jack would come down to help her, even if he loathed her at the moment.

Richard looked satisfactorily appalled. "I do not know what's come over you."

"Jack has come over me, if you must know. Just last night."

She really thought Richard might faint—his face, from what she could see above his beard, was a very unhealthy color. If she had any smelling salts handy, she'd waft them under his nose, which was nowhere near as attractive as Jack's. Noses were such funny things, weren't they? Flaring nostrils and odd bumps, occasional mucous, pointy hairs—

Perhaps she really did have something wrong with her brain.

Chapter 38

The door slammed, shaking the whole cottage. After waiting what he considered to be a decent interval, Jack came out of the lavender-scented linen cupboard and walked downstairs, ducking his head at the turn. The last thing he expected to see was Nicola sitting on his lumpy sofa. Steam rose from two cups of tea in front of her.

She had fixed tea. As if that would help matters.

He attempted to sound disinterested. "You're still here?"

Of course she was. She would do the proper thing, apologize again for lying, explain that she was going to marry Richard, return to her old life, wish him good luck. It had been an amusing interlude for them both, if a near-death experience could be termed such. Last night was just an aberration, even if it was the best aberration of his life.

Jack had lost. But he knew that anyway.

She opened her mouth, then shut it. How hard could it be for her to say good-bye? She'd played her trick, and it was time to end this charade.

"Do you have something you want to tell me?"

He'd heard quite enough before he'd stuffed himself in the linen closet and plugged his ears with striped tea towels. Her old suitor Richard had come to his senses. Wanted her back. Could offer her a normal life, not one with the highest peaks and lowest valleys.

"Yes. I do. That's why I came over in the first place. To—to explain. About what happened. And, um, apologize for keeping my secret. And to tell you I finally remember things again."

Did she remember she was still engaged to Richard?

"What do you mean?"

"It's about the train accident."

Oh, hell. That was the very last thing he wanted to think or talk about. Before last night, he'd made some progress after her prodding. All that business about some *plan*. Maybe he *was* still here on earth for some all-important reason he wasn't quite privy to. It didn't change the fact that Nicola had gotten her revenge and made a fool out of him. Lied to him, even if by omission. As if he wasn't guilty enough, he'd now ruined one of his victims.

He'd never eat peaches again.

He sat down in a chair opposite her anyway. His legs didn't feel quite strong enough to support him, and his head was beginning to pound. But he was not going to resort to the draughts that Oakley had prescribed; his dreams after were worse than ever.

Jack examined his fingernails, which could have used a good buffing. He'd go see Mr. Trumper once he went back in Town. Get advice about growing his beard back. Change his cologne. Maybe drink it and end it all.

"Don't you keep telling me it's all in the past? That I should just buck up and put it all behind me? If I'd known you'd bully me so, I wouldn't have looked forward to you talking." He looked up to see the result of his harsh words.

Nicola flushed. Jack could watch that rose color stain her throat and cheeks all day, but that wasn't in his future.

"That's not very nice."

"I don't feel very nice. Not after last night. You lied to me. And your... personal business with whatshisname has disturbed my morning."

"Richard. Richard Crosby. He wants to be prime minister someday, so remember his name. *I* wouldn't vote for him, but then women don't have suffrage. And I didn't ask him to come here! I had no idea my father sent him—no one wrote to tell me. He's gone now, anyhow."

"And you may join him anytime you please. I've got a headache."

"Oh! I'm sorry. Do you want Mrs. Feather to fetch you some medicine if—when she comes back?"

"No," Jack said curtly. "I'm used to your lectures by now. Say your piece if you must, and then go."

She clutched her hands together. "I know you feel betrayed that I didn't tell you who I was, and you've revoked your proposal. But I didn't know you were, well, *you* before Christmas Day. We were meant to be anonymous here, and when you told me everything, I couldn't quite deal with it. Or believe it. It seemed absurd, the two of us in the same place. I—I liked you. I was afraid if you knew I was one of the injured people on the train, you wouldn't like me in the same way. I wouldn't be...*me* to you. Just a victim you needed to take care of."

"Admit to more than *liking*, Nicola. You shared my bed. Or rather, I shared yours."

She looked directly into his eyes. "Yes, I did, and I don't go doing that with just anyone, as you must know. I was a virgin. I did my best to seduce you, Jack, because you wouldn't seduce me. If you had known my name, it would have changed everything between us. You would have felt sorry for me. Treated me with kid gloves. Been even guiltier than you are already, and Lord knows, you're guilty enough."

Everything she was saying described his feelings perfectly. How damned aggravating for her to be so accurate. "So much so that I seem to remember that I annoy you," Jack said, trying to distance himself.

"Yes, you do. I'm sick of it. I've tried to be understanding. Look— I've forgiven *you*, even though I don't believe for one minute you were responsible for my accident. I didn't speak for ten long months. What I went through was no picnic. My parents tried everything and every remedy with no result. It wasn't until I met you that I felt hope."

"There's irony for you."

He watched one hand become a fist. He could duck if he had to, though his reflexes were not up to par.

"You brought me back, Jack. Your...your attentions. From the moment you kissed me in the churchyard, I started to unravel. And then when you went and banged yourself on the head, I had no choice but to get help for you. To scream. I didn't even think about it—the noise just flowed. I'm surprised they didn't hear me in Stroud."

"You think *I* cured you?" The idea was preposterous.

She nodded. "Knowing you was the beginning. What if you hadn't come here? I don't want to think of more months of silence. I might never have spoken again. My whole life constricted by silence. You cannot know how miserable it made me and everyone around me."

"I have a fair idea." He'd only know her a few days before he had come up with his manual alphabet scheme. He'd wanted to reach her in a special way, give her one more tool to communicate.

"The puzzle pieces fell together for me. I haven't told you, but I've had a few bad dreams too. I kept seeing you—or someone I thought was you. You were injured. Just...just lying there. When I found you in the snow, it was as if that dream came to life.

"But I don't believe in portents or the occult. It wasn't you in my dreams for all these months after all."

His curiosity got the better of him. "So, who was it?"

"A man on the train. A nice man, for I'd spoken to him coming back from the dining car. He had a dark beard, like yours. He was next to me on the floor of the carriage after it fell, and he…died. But not at first. He groaned. Tried to speak. Looked at me with such need. There was blood on his face, but then it stopped flowing and I *knew*.

"I—had to push him away, but he just kept sliding up against me. Again and again until I had no strength left. I crawled into the corner of the car and thought he'd follow me. His eyes were open as if he could see me hiding." She took a breath. "No one came. Not for hours. I thought I was dreaming, but it was I. I was the one screaming and screaming until I couldn't catch my breath anymore."

Jack could see it all too clearly now. Did she think *this* was helping him? Her nightmare was now his. Could he feel any worse?

Yes. The woman he loved was going to marry someone else.

Chapter 39

"He—you know what happens to people when they die, don't you?"
Jack's eyes widened and he nodded.

"For months I couldn't get the smell out of my nose, but couldn't remember exactly what it was. I knew it wasn't truly there all around me, but I could conjure it up just the same. I hate myself for the ungrateful coward I was that day, alive but so useless. Afraid. I couldn't help that man, no matter how much I shrieked."

Nicola shuddered, the memory as fresh now as the day it happened. When she had stopped making noise, the man himself had...vanished. So had a part of her.

Jack leaned over and squeezed her hand. "Don't speak of yourself so. You were—are—brave."

"Am I? I retreated into my safe little silent world, making all those around me unhappy. I didn't—couldn't speak, for that way when no one came to help, it wouldn't be a disappointment. I hadn't asked and been denied."

"I don't think I understand."

"I don't think I do either. I'd just...given up, exactly as I accused you of doing. No one came to save me, no matter how much noise I made. No one came to save that poor man. There was no point in talking anymore." She plucked at her skirt, chosen so carefully today to make one last lasting impression on Jack. "I don't even know his name."

"Harry Prentiss. He was a jeweler. His son has taken over the business, and is doing well."

"I suppose you gave the family a fortune."

Jack left his chair and went to the window, the weak sunlight limning his profile. "Not enough. How can money replace a life? Do you see, Nicola? Nothing I ever do will be enough." He traced a frosted pane with a fingertip.

The exasperation rose within her. Did the man not listen? "Maybe it was his time, Jack. Written in some book somewhere: Harry Prentiss dies on the train to Bath, The End. You must stop blaming yourself, or you'll never get out of Puddling. Get on with your life."

"I'm not sure I want to now. Look at all that damn snow out there. I might get frostbite. Much better to stay in and have Mrs. Feather poison me. If she ever comes back." He attempted a joke, but wasn't smiling.

"Forget the snow. They need your cottage for some other unfortunate soul, and you are malingering. So am I, when it comes to it. I need to find a place to live."

He turned to her, his expression uncertain. "You'll not go back to your parents' house?"

Nicola shook her head. "I can't. I'm not their dutiful daughter anymore. The thought of running into Richard at every turn is another strike against Bath as well."

"He wants to marry you. I heard him. Until I put my fingers in my ears."

"I don't care. I don't want to marry *him*. Not if he was the very last man on earth," she said with vehemence.

A crooked grin appeared. "Good. Then you can marry me. I'll reinstate my original offer."

Nicola stared into his eyes. They seemed free of the drugs, but he was still ill. "I can't marry you, Jack. I'd never know if you offered because you love me, or if you were sorry for me now that you know who I am. And you don't trust me."

"I asked you yesterday when I didn't know," Jack reminded her. "And I can learn to trust you again."

She hadn't said yes when he'd asked, and had been surprised at the piercing sting she felt when he'd withdrawn his offer in his anger last night. She'd manipulated her way right into his arms and had been awfully proud of herself—who knew she had wanted more?

"Who was the one who hit his head on a tree here?" he continued. "Of course, I love you, Nicola! Haven't I shown you again and again? Right since Christmas, I've done everything to convince you my intentions were honorable.

"I proposed last night, I've proposed today, and I suppose if I have to I can propose tomorrow until you say yes. Look, remember all those times when you threw yourself at me and I pretended I couldn't catch you? I didn't want to saddle you with my problems, but then I saw a ray of light. Of hope. You made me see it, Nicola. All your nagging—the Puddling Rehabilitation Foundation should hire you.

"But then—to find out who you were—that you lied—it seemed pretty impossible. I was furious. With you and with myself. *I* caused your affliction. Your unhappiness. I can't cause you more, I swear it. I won't. I was even resolved to stand aside and let that wretch Richard take you away from here this morning."

"Never. Ever."

"That is excellent news. I don't know why you didn't say so sooner in this conversation."

"I didn't think it mattered."

He blinked. "I shall never understand women."

"For a rake, you are somewhat obtuse, it's true. It was only through my devious methods that I lost my virginity." And the peaches.

"Who said I was a rake?"

"Your secretary, Mr. Clarke. When he walked me home, he was most informative."

"The blighter. I'll fire him."

"Oh, don't do that. He was your champion, admonishing me not to believe the worst of you. He seems to be a capable young man. And you need someone to organize you."

"A wife could do that." He slipped ungracefully to one knee and took her hand. "Marry me."

"This is a really dreadful proposal, Jack. Worse than Richard's, and on the same rug. One doesn't want to be asked to *organize*."

"There are no flowers available—it's the dead of winter, you know. Come with me to Ashburn. I have a glasshouse there. I'm sure someone is keeping it stocked with roses or some such." He was circling her palm again, causing her to shiver.

He was pure temptation. And impossible. "I can't go to Oxfordshire with you."

"Why not? It's only the next county over. Won't take any time at all, even with bad roads in all this weather. You can examine the house and see if you want to be mistress of it. Be *my* mistress until you decide." He sprang up like a child's spring-toy and sat next to her, practically in her lap.

Nicola knew her face was flaming. Two proposals in one day, three in as many days if you counted yesterday. "Worse and worse! First you ask me to marry you, then instead I'm to be your mistress! Despite the fact

I am a fallen woman, I have not fallen so far as to…as to…" Her newly acquired voice failed her.

A woman did not simply visit a gentleman's house without a chaperone. She saw herself being looked down upon by a wealthy baron's servants, who would be much more aware of their own consequence than her mother's small staff.

And a solicitor's daughter was not really proper baroness material. She reminded herself that she'd come here to explain and say *good-bye*.

He kissed her knuckles, one after the other, despite her trying to pull her hand away. "Stop being so silly! Of course, I want you to be my wife! Old Fitzmartin can marry us. When Ezra Clarke came, he brought me a special license."

"He *what*?"

"Apparently when I was off my head, I asked him to get a special license. And bring the family ring. I didn't get the chance to give it to you yesterday. We rakes are sure of ourselves, Nicola, even when we have spiked a fever. I won't take no for an answer. I never take no for an answer. Or at least I didn't until the train accident. You might say I was derailed myself these past ten months. But I know what I want now. I want you, and I'm pretty sure you want me even if you think you don't."

Jack was becoming harder and harder to resist. Nicola was forgetting why she felt she had to.

He had such an overdeveloped conscience, which in some ways was admirable. Look at what he'd done for the victims of the accident—she was set for life financially thanks to him. But did he really love her, or just feel obligated? She might never know for sure.

And there was the additional complication that she had given herself to him. Was he feeling duty-bound to offer her the protection of his name? Even if he had wanted to marry her before, it was different now. He was such a gentleman, after all.

Nicola didn't feel much like a lady. With him so close, she was swept away by the scent of his shaving soap and the starch in his collar. She could count his long eyelashes if she chose. Admire his teeth. Feel his breath against her forehead. Tip her head back so he could steal a kiss.

No, not steal. It would be freely given. Nicola needed someone to talk some sense into her, but Jack was an unlikely candidate.

"Don't overthink it. That's what you've accused me of doing, isn't it? Just say yes."

Was it that simple? Nicola had been an overthinking sort of person her whole life.

"I can't. We hardly know one another."

Jack chortled. "I'd say I know you very well. You are kind. And beautiful."

"Saying I'm beautiful—which I'm not, by the way—isn't knowing me."

"All right. You cannot draw. You are willing to give up peaches with abandon, so I suppose you like other fruit better—I'll find out which ones eventually when I watch you over the breakfast table. You can make raisin sauce. You miss your dog, whose name is Tiptoe. Uh, that's not right. Tiptop?"

"Tippy."

"Exactly. You cannot skate. You play the piano like a virtuoso. You have a keen sense of justice and sympathy for those less fortunate. You enjoy reading romantic novels, although you doubted their veracity until you met me." He leered at her, winking, and she had to laugh.

"We can get to know each other, Nicola. We have our whole lives ahead of us, as you keep telling me. Say yes."

So she did.

Chapter 40

January 15, 1883

The wedding this morning had been a hasty and quiet affair. Nicola hoped her parents would forgive her someday, but it had seemed best to get it over with and get out of Puddling as soon as possible.

Her parents should have no objection to Jack; after all, they had met him even before she did. Her father's letter had been very positive about the young lord who'd come to make amends. Jack had been so quick to agree to all his demands, and so generous, Mr. Mayfield had been impressed.

But Nicola didn't want to wait one more hour in case she lost her nerve. Unlike her mother, she'd never been one to dream of orange blossoms and lace in Bath Abbey, and had been perfectly satisfied to marry in her good wine-colored dress in St. Jude's on a Monday morning.

Lady Sarah Sykes and her husband had provided the wedding flowers from their hothouse, and had hosted a small breakfast. Nicola had been too nervous to taste anything, and had been slow to respond to "Lady Ryder" from the few well-meaning guests.

There had been Ham Ross, of course, and even Moll, with a ribbon on her collar. Mrs. Grace and Mrs. Feather, without their aprons. Dr. Oakley and the Fitzmartins. As acting head of the board of governors, Mr. Sykes had escorted her down the aisle, although Nicola barely knew the man, and his eyebrows still frightened her. The Countess had consented to serve as matron of honor, and, out of her deep mourning in pale lavender silk, looked far more bride-like than Nicola. Curious, Nicola had tried to read the Countess's scrawl in the register, but could only make out the letter J.

With less than two days' notice, efficient Ezra Clarke had sent Jack's carriage to bring the newlyweds to Ashburn, and according to her husband—her husband!—they were nearly there. The short journey across Gloucestershire to Oxfordshire had been lovely, with snow-covered hills and country roads that were not too badly rutted. Nicola didn't mind the occasional lurch, as it threw her into Jack's arms. Dusk was upon them, now, however, and it was more difficult to see.

The carriage slowed at a wooden signpost and turned down a hedgerowed lane.

"Is this your drive?" Nicola asked.

"Don't be so impatient. For the last half hour, all you've said is 'Are we there yet?'" Jack teased.

Nicola nestled into the crook of his arm. "What should I say?"

"How about, 'I love you, Jack. I couldn't live without you.'"

"I don't think you need any more compliments from me. They will go to your head." Jack had come to her late Sunday night for one last unmarried fling, and he had been incessantly complimented. It was a wonder they'd both been able to wake up in their own beds and walk to the church in time.

The hedgerows ended at a small gatehouse and an open iron gate. The carriage continued onto a wide tree-lined avenue, with a large Georgian brick house in the distance.

"Oh! It's beautiful!" Nicola cried. At least she thought it was. She couldn't wait to see it in blazing daylight.

"It's even better in the spring when the trees are in flower." Jack squeezed her hand. "You'll be here to see it. Unless we're in London for the Season. I've never asked what you'd like to do."

"I don't care. I'll go wherever *you* are." Oh, she was a ninny. But very happy.

"Good thing I've given up traveling to all those smoky cities in the north—I don't think you'd like them all that much. I say, there's a traveling coach parked outside the stables." Nicola heard him mutter a very rude word, the same one she'd been unable to complete in the British Manual Alphabet the other day.

"What is it?"

"If I'm not mistaken—and believe me, I hope I am—I think my mother's not in France anymore."

Jack had not said all that much about his mother, apart from the fact that she'd fought with his father and held Jack in some disdain for actually working. Nicola thought the woman sounded sort of horrid, but was prepared to be on her best behavior. Mothers-in-law were historically difficult.

"Christ, I'm sorry. Some honeymoon this will be."

"I'm sure it will be fine," Nicola said, sure of no such thing.

"Well, she *did* want me to get married," Jack said, raising his hand to scratch at his healing scalp.

Nicola grabbed it before he could do any damage to the black thread winding through the new bristle of his hair. Dr. Oakley had advised him to get the stitches removed in a day or two. It was amazing to think just eight days ago he'd been unconscious.

Would Jack's mother think Nicola had taken advantage of her son when he was too ill to be in his right mind? Nicola bit her lip.

The coachman stopped at the front door, and several servants scrambled down the steps to help them and their belongings out of the carriage, including Ezra Clarke.

"Welcome home, my lord, my lady," Ezra said, his ears tipped bright red. "I'm afraid I have some, um, bad news. Something unforeseen—"

"Not exactly unforeseen. I can see her in the doorway now, Clarke. When did she arrive?"

"Just fifteen minutes ago. The front hall is a jumble of trunks and cases, and Miss Pemington has already taken to her room with a sick headache."

"Have you told her?"

"I couldn't get a word in edgewise—ah, Lady Ryder. Here is Lord Ryder come home."

"Mr. Clarke, you are a veritable font of knowledge. I'm not so old that I cannot see with two perfectly good eyes. Good God, Jonathan, what have they done to you? You look like a convict."

Nicola swallowed. Jack's mother was a handsome woman, with her son's dark coloring and height. Apart from a few gray streaks in her hair, she seemed ageless, a porcelain beauty.

Jack rubbed his shorn head. "I had a slight accident."

"You've been hurt! And scarred! No one told me!"

"A mere trifle. The news probably didn't reach you in time, as you were traveling," Jack fibbed. "Mother, I'd like to introduce you to my wife, Mary Nicola Mayfield Ryder. Lady Ryder, Lady Ryder."

Lady Ryder's left eyelid twitched for a fraction of a second, the only sign that she might be at all flummoxed. "I beg your pardon?"

Nicola dropped into her deepest curtsey, grateful Jack still held her elbow, as her knees had turned to jelly. "I am so pleased to meet you."

"Get up, girl. You have married my son?"

Jack helped restore her to a standing position. "Yes, ma'am. This morning."

Lady Ryder turned to Jack, her brown eyes flashing. "And I suppose *that* news didn't reach me either. You've been a busy boy in Puddling. Are you sleeping?"

"Better. Nicola has been instrumental to my recovery. I don't know what would have happened if I hadn't met her."

"Well then, I suppose I should welcome you to the family, my dear. I thought he said your name was Mary."

"I'm known by my middle name, Lady Ryder. My sister is Mary Francesca and is called Francesca. Frannie," Nicola babbled.

"Nicola. I like the sound of it. Just interesting enough, although your parents should not have confused everyone with so many names. You needn't worry *I'll* interfere—I've only come home to get rid of Pemington. The woman has no backbone whatsoever. Falls apart at the slightest criticism. And France was simply filled with far too many French people for my liking. I shall go to London and my things can be transferred to the Dower House. Return this summer, perhaps, when you two are settled."

"You're moving out?" Jack sounded surprised.

"Why, certainly. Now that Nicola is here to take care of you, I am completely superfluous. I remember *my* mother-in-law, a ghastly woman. No wonder my husband was such a weasel. Even after we refurbished the Dower House for her, she held on here like the albatross in that dreadful poem—you know the one I mean. All very sad and dreary. She caused a great deal of friction with the servants, countermanding my orders—too many cooks in the kitchen, and all that.

"Speaking of which, I expect you will want to hire your own staff, Nicola. You won't mind if I pinch a few for the Dower House, will you? Just Mrs. Burrell, the cook. The housekeeper, Mrs. Hand. And I suppose Burrell as well, since he's married to Mrs. Burrell."

"That's the butler," Jack mumbled into her ear. "Don't worry—I won't have you scrubbing floors just yet."

"I don't mind at all," Nicola said, smiling. God help her if she did.

"Good, that's taken care of. Come in, come in. It's much too cold to be standing outdoors like a flock of sheep. I will give you a tour of the house tomorrow morning before I go—Burrell, you can arrange for me to be taken to the station for the one o'clock train."

The butler, who'd been hovering at the edge of the flock, nodded. "Certainly, Lady Ryder. Congratulations, my lord. The staff wishes you many years of happiness, my lady."

"Thank you." Nicola heard the kindness in his voice. What if he didn't want to be pinched?

The hallway bustled with servants and luggage. Nicola hoped Jack's mother wouldn't mistakenly wind up with Nicola's own trunk on the train tomorrow.

"You children will be tired. Burrell, tell Mrs. Burrell to prepare a tray for Lord and Lady Ryder in their rooms." She paused on the stairs. "See? This is a perfect example of being a bad mother-in-law. Perhaps you're not tired at all, and want a twelve-course dinner. To dance until dawn. Already I am attempting to run your lives. *I* am tired at any rate. A tray for me, please."

"And for us as well." Jack threw his arm around his mother. "Thank you, Mama. For everything, especially for your recommendation to spend a month in Puddling."

"Pooh. She looks like a sensible young woman. I trust she wasn't one of the inmates too."

Nicola's heart sank. "I'm afraid I was."

A dark eyebrow lifted. "Were you indeed? What was your trouble?"

"I—I couldn't speak."

"What my late husband wouldn't have given to strike me mute. I see you're over your affliction. Your brain is in good working order? There are no lunatics in your family?"

"No, ma'am. Yes, ma'am. That's no to the lunatics. Yes to the brain." Nicola made every effort to keep a straight face.

"Well, that's all right then. I will meet you after breakfast tomorrow to show you about. Shall we say nine o'clock? Let her out of bed in a timely fashion, Jonathan—I have to supervise my packing."

Nicola, her mouth slightly agape, watched Lady Ryder and her elaborate black bustle go up the stairs.

"Well, that could have been worse. Someone else is obviously inhabiting my mother's body. I shall not call for an exorcism." Jack squeezed her hand as they mounted the staircase themselves. "Are you all right, my love?"

"I think so." Nicola straightened her own backbone, and kissed her husband in front of the staff below, some of whom she was about to lose. They could be replaced, but no one would ever replace Jack in her heart.

If you enjoyed *Redeeming Lord Ryder*, be sure not to miss the first book in Maggie Robinson's Cotswold Confidential series

SCHOOLING THE VISCOUNT

"*Schooling the Viscount* is a charming, sexy romp through the English countryside. Readers will fall in love with the little town of Puddling-on-the-Wold. I did!"
—Vanessa Kelly, *USA Today* bestselling author

Welcome to Puddling-on-the-Wold, where the sons and daughters of Victorian nobility come for a little rest, recuperation, and "rehab," in this brand-new series of rebellious romance from Maggie Robinson.

After a harrowing tour of duty abroad, Captain Lord Henry Challoner fought to keep his memories at bay with two of his preferred vices: liquor and ladies. But the gin did more harm than good—as did Henry's romantic entanglements, since he was supposed to be finding a suitable bride. Next stop: The tiny village of Gloucestershire, where Henry can finally sober up without distraction or temptation. Or so he thinks…

A simple country schoolteacher, Rachel Everett was never meant to cross paths with a gentleman such as Henry. What could such a worldly man ever see in her? As it turns out, everything. Beautiful, fiercely intelligent Rachel is Henry's dream woman—and wife. Such a match would be scandalous for his family of course, and Rachel has no business meddling with a resident at the famed, rather draconian, Puddling Rehabilitation Foundation. All the better, for two lost souls with nothing to lose—and oh so very much to gain.

Keep reading for a special look!

A Lyrical e-book on sale now.

ABOUT THE AUTHOR

Photo by Jan DeLima

Maggie Robinson is a former teacher, library clerk, and mother of four who woke up in the middle of the night, absolutely compelled to create the perfect man and use as many adjectives and adverbs as possible doing so. A transplanted New Yorker, she lives with her not quite perfect husband in Maine. Her books have been translated into nine languages. Visit her on the web at maggierobinson.net.

No one at Puddling-on-the-Wold ever expected to see Sarah Marchmain enter through its doors. But after the legendary Lady's eleventh-hour rejection of the man she was slated to marry, she was sent here to restore her reputation . . . and change her mind. It amused Sadie that her father, a duke, would use the last of his funds to lock her up in this fancy facility—she couldn't be happier to be away from her loathsome family and have some time to herself. The last thing she needs is more romantic distraction...

As a local baronet's son, Tristan Sykes is all too familiar with the spoiled, socialite residents of the Puddling Rehabilitation Foundation—no matter how real their problems may be. But all that changes when he encounters Sadie, a brave and brazen beauty who wants nothing more than to escape the life that's been prescribed for her. If only Tristan could find a way to convince the Puddling powers-that-be that Sadie is unfit for release, he'd have a chance to explore the intense attraction that simmers between them—and prove himself fit to make her his bride . . .

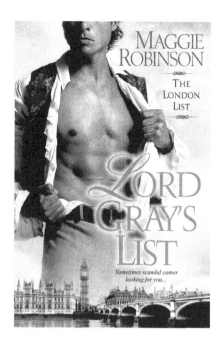

Sometimes scandal comes
looking for you...

From duchesses to chamber maids, everybody's reading it. Each Tuesday, The London List appears, filled with gossip and scandal, offering job postings and matches for the lovelorn—and most enticing of all, telling the tales and selling the wares a more modest publication wouldn't touch...

The creation of Evangeline Ramsey, The London List saved her and her ailing father from destitution. But the paper has given Evie more than financial relief. As its publisher, she lives as a man, dressed in masculine garb, free to pursue and report whatever she likes—especially the latest disgraces besmirching Lord Benton Gray. It's only fair that she hang his dirty laundry, given that it was his youthful ardor that put her off marriage for good...

Lord Gray—Ben—isn't about to stand by while all of London laughs at his peccadilloes week after week. But once he discovers that the publisher is none other than pretty Evie Ramsey with her curls lopped short, his worries turn to desires—and not a one of them fit to print...

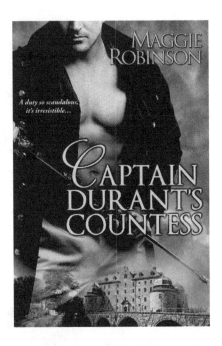

Tucked amid the pages of The London List, a newspaper that touts the city's scandals, is a vaguely-worded ad for an intriguing job—one that requires a most wickedly uncommon candidate…

Maris has always been grateful that her marriage to the aging Earl of Kelby saved her from spinsterhood. Though their union has been more peaceful than passionate, she and the earl have spent ten happy years together. But his health is quickly failing, and unless Maris produces an heir, Kelby's conniving nephew will inherit his estate. And if the earl can't get the job done himself, he'll find another man who can…

Captain Reynold Durant is known for both his loyalty to the Crown and an infamous record of ribaldry. Yet despite a financial worry of his own, even he is reluctant to accept Kelby's lascivious assignment—until he meets the beautiful, beguiling Maris. Incited by duty and desire, the captain may be just the man they are looking for. But while he skillfully takes Maris to the heights of ecstasy she has longed for, she teaches him something even more valuable and unexpected...

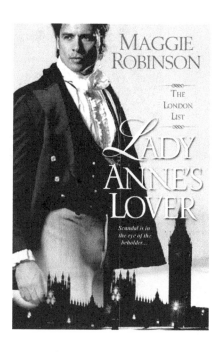

MAGGIE ROBINSON

THE LONDON LIST

LADY ANNE'S LOVER

Scandal is in the eye of the beholder...

Tucked amid the pages of The London List, a newspaper that touts the city's scandals, is a vaguely-worded ad for an intriguing job—one that requires a most wickedly uncommon candidate...

Maris has always been grateful that her marriage to the aging Earl of Kelby saved her from spinsterhood. Though their union has been more peaceful than passionate, she and the earl have spent ten happy years together. But his health is quickly failing, and unless Maris produces an heir, Kelby's conniving nephew will inherit his estate. And if the earl can't get the job done himself, he'll find another man who can...

Captain Reynold Durant is known for both his loyalty to the Crown and an infamous record of ribaldry. Yet despite a financial worry of his own, even he is reluctant to accept Kelby's lascivious assignment—until he meets the beautiful, beguiling Maris. Incited by duty and desire, the captain may be just the man they are looking for. But while he skillfully takes Maris to the heights of ecstasy she has longed for, she teaches him something even more valuable and unexpected...

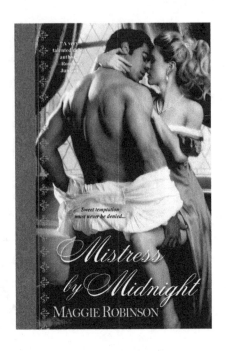

First comes seduction…

As children, Desmond Ryland, Marquess of Conover, and Laurette Vincent were inseparable. As young adults, their friendship blossomed into love. But then fate intervened, sending them down different paths. Years later, Con still can't forget his beautiful Laurette. Now he's determined to make her his forever. There's just one problem. Laurette keeps refusing his marriage proposals. Throwing honor to the wind, Con decides that the only way Laurette will wed him is if he thoroughly seduces her…

Then comes marriage…

Laurette's pulse still quickens every time she thinks of Con and the scorching passion they once shared. She aches to taste the pleasure Con offers her. But she knows she can't. For so much has happened since they were last lovers. But how long can she resist the consuming desire that demands to be obeyed…?

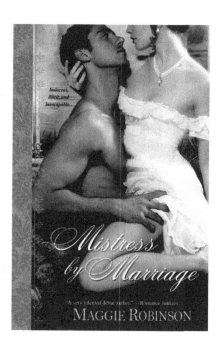

Too late for cold feet

Baron Edward Christie prided himself on his reputation for even temperament and reserve. That was before he met Caroline Parker. Wedding a scandalous beauty by special license days after they met did not inspire respect for his sangfroid. Moving her to a notorious lovebirds' nest as punishment for her flighty nature was perhaps also a blow. And of course talk has gotten out of his irresistible clandestine visits. Christie must put his wife aside—if only he can get her out of his blood first.

Too hot to refuse…

Caroline Parker was prepared to hear the worst: that her husband had determined to divorce her, spare them both the torture of passion they can neither tame nor escape. But his plan is wickeder than any she's ever heard. Life as his wife is suffocating. But she cannot resist becoming her own husband's mistress…

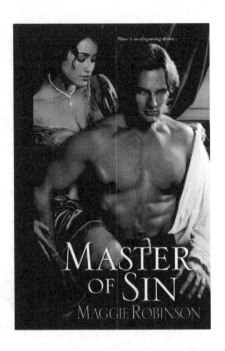

Flying from sin…

Andrew Rossiter has used his gorgeous body and angelic face for all they're worth—shocking the proper, seducing the willing, and pleasuring the wealthy. But with a tiny son depending on him for rescue, suddenly discretion is far more important than desire. He'll have to bury his past and quench his desires—fast. And he'll have to find somewhere his deliciously filthy reputation hasn't yet reached…

..into seduction

Miss Gemma Peartree seems like a plain, virginal governess. True, she has a sharp wit and a sharper tongue, but handsome Mr. Ross wouldn't notice Gemma herself. Or so she hopes. No matter how many sparks fly between them, she has too much to hide to catch his eye. But with the storms of a Scottish winter driving them together, it will be hard enough to keep her secrets. Keeping her hands to herself might prove entirely impossible…

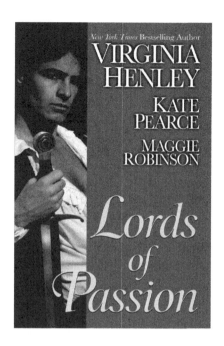

New York Times Bestselling Author

VIRGINIA
HENLEY
KATE
PEARCE
MAGGIE
ROBINSON

Lords
of
Passion

"Beauty and the Brute" by Virginia Henley
It's been three years since Lady Sarah Caversham set eyes on arrogant Charles Lennox—the husband her father chose for her to settle a gambling debt. Now Charles has returned, unaware that the innocent ingénue he wed is determined to turn their marriage of convenience into a passionate affair...

"How to Seduce a Wife" by Kate Pearce
Louisa March's new husband, Nicholas, is a perfect gentleman in bed— much to her disappointment. She longs for the kind of fevered passion found in romance novels. But when she dares him to seduce her properly, she discovers Nicholas is more than ready to meet her challenge...

"Not Quite a Courtesan" by Maggie Robinson

Sensible bluestocking Prudence Thorn has been too busy keeping her cousin Sophy out of trouble to experience any adventures of her own. But when Sophy begs Prudence's help in saving her marriage, Pru encounters handsome, worldly Darius Shaw. Under Darius's skilled tutelage, Pru learns just how delightful a little scandal can be...

Printed in the United States
by Baker & Taylor Publisher Services